Heart.

(a Derek Cole Suspense Thriller)

T Patrick Phelps

This is a work of fiction. Any similarities to people, living or deceased is purely coincidental

Jabby House Publications

Visit www. Tpatrickphelps.com sign up for my newsletter and receive a free full-length novel!

Cover Designed by Nathaniel Dasco

Connect with the author on his Facebook Page.

https://www.facebook.com/authortpp

Chapter 1

2014

"I didn't know where else to turn."

Derek Cole hated hearing those words. In his line of work, he came to expect that his clients would feel this way, but each time he heard a client tell him the only reason they contacted him was out of desperation, he cringed at being the last option.

"No one else would ever believe me," his client said as he sat on the damp park bench beside Derek.

Derek preferred to meet clients in parks in whichever city they happened to be. This city was Chicago and the park was Grant Park. He liked being outside and preferred meeting with clients in places that, if things took a wrong turn, he could have both quick access to an exit and enough people around to discourage ill-tempered clients from making a scene.

Or worse.

While Derek stood exactly six feet tall and weighed a solid 190, his light brown hair, clean-shaven face, and powder blue eyes did not give him the intimidating looks that others in his line of work enjoyed. He had found himself in "challenging" circumstances with past clients when he used to meet with them in whatever hotel Derek was staying. He decided after one client gave him a broken nose and a slight concussion that outdoor client meetings in public places were better choices.

After receiving a call from this new client yesterday and confirming the "down payment" was safely deposited in his account, Derek purchased a one-way ticket from his hometown airport to Chicago's O'Hare. Though Derek had visited the windy city a few times during his years working as a "freelance detective," he hadn't spent enough time in Chicago to learn his way around. What Derek did know was that Grant Park, like most every public park in America, would not offer any degree of suspicious privacy.

"You understand that you are paying my accrued fees, whether or not I can help you, correct?" Derek said.

"Of course. Money is not an issue," his client responded.

Derek liked it when money wasn't an issue. He liked when clients understood his services were expensive and didn't barter over the final tab. "You've been on the clock for the past sixteen hours."

"Understood."

"Good," Derek said as he pulled out a Moleskine Notebook and fine point black pen. The Moleskine was a gift from his last client, given to Derek to replace his reliance on scraps of paper, napkins, and Egg McMuffin wrappers that served as his notebook. "Please don't vomit your whole story on me. Let me guide you through what I need to know. If I ask for details, then and only then do I want you to give me details. If I say 'vomit,' then feel free to tell me everything you know, including your opinions. Make sense?"

"Yes. Can we begin?"

"Start with your full name and how it was that you learned of my services."

"My name is Thomas O'Connell. I prefer to be called 'Thomas.' My uncle, Roger O'Connell hired you last year. Says that you're the best man for the job."

"Roger O'Connell is your uncle?" Derek said. "The lawyer outside of Chicago? Good guy. Paid without an argument, and I was able to solve his problem in just two or three days, if I remember correctly."

"He said it took you four days, but he was happy with the results."

Derek absently began tracing the three-inch scar on his left cheek, not reminding himself of its cause but for a moment, of the person for whom the scar was created. "Yeah," he said, "I think it was a four-day job." He brought his hand back to his lap and flipped through several scribbled pages of his Moleskine Notebook before resuming the conversation.

"Okay, Thomas. Tell me, in fifty words or less, why you contacted me and what you need taken care of."

Thomas breathed deeply, collecting his thoughts. To Derek, it seemed that Thomas was rehearsing his story in his mind to make sure it would come in under the fifty-word limit.

After a long pause, Thomas looked out over Lake Michigan that bordered Grant Park and began speaking. "My twin brother, Alexander, has already killed at least three people. I have reason to believe that he is planning on killing more people, including my parents. And maybe me as well."

"He killed three people, and you think coming to me is a better option than going to the police?" Derek asked.

"The police are already involved. But there are other circumstances."

"There always are. What are yours?"

"I may have to give some details for you to understand."

Derek sighed. To him, details were things often offered yet seldom needed. He believed that part of his job was to uncover the details as he preceded though his tasks. One detail leads to another.

"Give me your reasoning behind your need to give me a history lesson."

"My brother was born without a heart and with only half of a lung," Thomas said as quickly as he could. "He isn't really alive, or at least he shouldn't be."

Derek had been hired to assist in many cases; some "run of the mill" and some that were downright odd. He learned that clients often exaggerated to give more credence to their side of the story in case Derek ever heard the other side.

"Vomit."

Chapter 2

2014

As he sat in his living room reading a novel by Graham Greene, Alexander heard the familiar sound of the hallway door opening. A check of the clock told him that he had been reading for nearly 20 straight hours. A few seconds after hearing the hallway noises, the familiar voice of Doctor Jacob Curtis sounded through the intercom.

"Alexander, it's Doctor Curtis and Doctor Peter Adams. Please go into your bedroom and fasten the hook to the door. Thank you."

Alexander placed the novel onto the coffee table and entered his bedroom. He attached the metal hook to the thick, steel door. Seconds later, the loud, ratcheting sound of the winch was heard from the hallway outside of his living room. Within a few seconds, the rope tightened, and its pull sealed his bedroom door closed. The two doctors entered the room, both wearing smiles.

"Alexander," Jacob Curtis said, "you may just end up saving thousands of lives."

"Tell me how," Alexander whispered. The door separating the living room, or "reading room" as Alexander preferred to have it called, was custom built, designed, and installed. Knowing the force the ratchet and pulley system would demand, the contractor had used two-inch thick, heavy gage, solid steel in the construction of the door. In order to afford line of sight into and out of the bedroom area, the contractor had installed a three-foot by three-foot glass windowpane, reinforced with crisscrossing steel mesh. For additional support, anchors were used on both sides of the door to give the framing the strength needed to withstand the draw of the pulley. The intercom system, which was always in the "on" position, had both microphones and speakers positioned in both the reading and bedrooms.

"Something wrong, Alex?" Jacob Curtis asked. Though he was too excited to be overly concerned about Alexander, the idea of asking seemed right. "You sound as if you are weakening."

"A little tired is all. Sleep will be coming soon, I fear," Alexander answered with an even quieter voice.

"Well then, we will make this brief."

"I certainly would not want to fall asleep while you are giving me this wonderful news," Alexander said in a thin, whisper of a voice.

It was too late when the doctors noticed. The hook drilled into and through the steel part of the bedroom door was held in place by a locking nut on the bedroom side of the door. Alexander's side. As the doctors looked down at Alexander's hands, they saw the reason he was whispering. The locking nut had been removed and the only thing holding back the force of the pulley system was the grip of Alexander Black.

The doctors knew all too well Alexander was dangerous and that letting their guard down when around him could find them in a potentially dire situation. They were trained to look for signs that their patient was planning something: a sign that may indicate something was out of place. Alexander knew the doctors would have suspected something when he could only speak through whispers, but he also relied on the doctor's excitement to cloud their caution.

When he saw the realization flash across the doctor's faces, Alexander released his hold and let the hook fly across the room. The door separating Alexander from the doctors rebounded open once the pulled force was absent. It's force pounded into the doctors, knocking them both to the floor in a concussive thump.

Peter and Jacob stood, and then darted to the hallway door and towards the safety of the hallway. Their escape was cut short by the gripping hands of Alexander Black.

"Now doctors," he said as he redirected them to the middle of the reading room. "I thought that you were coming to give me some news. Why leave before you have a chance to tell me?"

"Alexander," Jacob Curtis spoke as his eyebrows rose to a point so high they were almost joining his hairline, "you know the rules. Why don't you get back into your bedroom, and we will agree not to tell Doctor Straus about this episode?"

"Because, Doctor, my education is complete. At least this part of my education. My undergraduate work, if you will. I feel confident that I am ready to enter the world that I have studied so diligently over these several years."

Jacob Curtis usually carried a stun gun in his pocket whenever he went to visit Alexander. As he was trying to convince Alexander to go back into his bedroom, he slowly slid his hand in the coat pocket, searching for the familiar shape.

"Doctor Curtis, I am sorry to say that your little 'stun-gun' is not where you wish it to be. In your state of excitement, I imagine that you left it elsewhere. I noticed that the slight bulge which usually fills your pocket was absent as you entered my reading room. I am sorry. You should be more careful."

Alexander directed the two doctors, who were now shaking with fear, to sit down on the couch. Alexander circled them, pausing occasionally as if he was considering his next move.

It was Jacob Curtis, however, who made the next move. He jumped from the couch and charged Alexander. His attempt at a physical takeover ended with him being thrown back to his original spot on the couch. His head whipped back from the force of Alexander's shove.

"Not intelligent, Doctor. Another move like that will cost you more than a simple case of whiplash. Sit and be quiet while I prepare my statements."

There seemed to be no escape for the doctors. Jacob Curtis, now holding his neck in pain, nodded his cooperation to Alexander, who again began circling the two couched doctors. Alexander stood six foot two, and weighed 225 pounds. The last body fat composition test that the doctors gave to Alexander showed that 184 of his 225 pounds were solid, rock hard muscle.

After several minutes, Alexander sat across from the doctors in a wooden rocking chair that screamed under his weight. "Doctor Curtis, Doctor Adams," he began. "I am pleased to say that your fame will now be assured. You will be known as the doctors who not only allowed my escape, but also as the doctors who taught me so much about the world. Though not all of my knowledge came via your knowledge or permission."

"Alexander," Peter spoke, trying to intimidate Alexander using his one-time powerful voice, "I have had just about enough of your games. Get back into your bedroom, and I will consider not taking away all of your books. Do it now before I change my mind."

"Doctor Adams," Alexander said, stilling his body so that his voice could attain a more powerful level, "you are not in the position to give orders. Your position calls more for begging than demanding. Be quiet, or I may change my mind and make you even more famous by making you my first victim.

"My education is complete. I will no longer remain here serving as your lab rat. I have people that I wish to see. Conversations that I've dreamed of having, which now beg to involve another participant. You have stolen twenty-two years of my life, dear doctors. I will allow no more time to be taken from me. My education here is complete. For this, I thank you."

What happened next took place too quickly for Curtis or Adams to have prepared for or to defend against. Alexander finished talking, then leaped atop Jacob Curtis with the quickness of a lion. Before Jacob could scream in pain or in terror, Alexander began pounding his iron fists into Jacob's chest, crushing bones and sending sharp, shattered fragments into his heart and lungs. Alexander's blows were so powerful that the final blows punched their way through Jacob's chest.

"Good night, good Doctor," Alexander said as he jumped off the dead doctor. He held his hands up in front of himself as if they were trophies, lustfully envying the bright red blood flowing effortlessly down his arms.

Doctor Adams found his old, powerful voice again. No words were formed, only a scream as Alexander crushed the right side of his head with a single punch. At first, Alexander thought that he had killed Peter Adams, but a quick check of the doctor's pulse and labored but steady breathing assured Alexander that the doctor had a fighting chance if attended to quickly. Alexander had no plans to call an ambulance, but he knew that someone would discover the two bodies. Hopefully, not too late for Doctor Adams.

"If I could only whistle," he thought to himself as he entered the hallway, *"this picture would be complete."*

He was free.

* * *

He paused, looking over his work. He knew what was supposed to happen next. It had all been planned. Alexander felt that while intentionally killing Doctor Jacob Curtis was a bit of improvisation, *his* part of the plan was going exactly as it was designed.

After another minute, Alexander checked the pulse of Peter

Adams.

"Is he still alive?" his expected visitor asked from behind in his bedroom. Though Alexander was expecting company, he was disappointed with himself for not hearing his guest entering.

"I'm afraid not," Alexander said calmly. "My punch was a bit too forceful. I believe it crushed his skull."

"Those were two very costly mistakes, Alexander. Very costly. What the hell were you thinking?" his guest said as he angrily brushed dirt off his pants and shirt.

"I'm afraid I lost my temper," Alexander replied.

"Damn it," his guest said. "This can't happen again. Do you understand that? You can't kill people just because you lose your damn temper. Do you know what a mess this creates? You have no idea what you just did to our plan."

"Has he arrived yet?"

"Not yet," his guest said, calmer. "Any minute now, I'm sure. I made it clear what time I expected him and also made clear the penalty for him not showing. He'll be here."

"And when he does?" Alexander asked, turning to his guest.

"You," his guest said, pointing a stern finger directly at Alexander's chest, "will not lay a finger on him. I don't want you even in the same room with him."

"I understand, and I apologize that my actions disrupted your plan."

"It's our plan, Alexander. You and I both benefit from our plan. Just don't screw anything else up, and we'll be fine."

"And when he arrives, the rest of the plan can continue?"

"Of course. And I have a few surprises for you as well."

* * *

Roger Fay loved walking the southern shore of Piseco Lake. The leaves were reflected off the calm water, giving him double the pleasure. The summer air kept his thoughts clean and focused, and the unpolluted air filling his lungs revived his tired body.

His walking route was about five miles and took Roger by some of the more elegant camps that lined the lake. His home was in one of the trailer parks in Higgins Bay, but he knew that one day one of his ideas would pay off, and he would be able to afford a house on the southern shore. For now, though, he was happy just to be walking in the peaceful surroundings.

Roger needed to choke back an occasional tear when the memory of his recently separated wife entered his mind. He knew that they were never right for each other, and that they would probably last no more than five years. Six, if they were lucky. They separated three weeks after their fourth anniversary.

As was his habit, Roger went out and bought himself a "cheer up" gift the day his wife told him that she was leaving him for another man. This time, his gift was an Australian Outback black leather hat, complete with mid-calf high, black cowboy boots. Whenever he felt depressed, Roger liked to spend money on things he didn't need. To him, the action of buying purely based on desire gave him the feeling of control – that he still decided and directed his life. Though he had long wanted his new walking attire, he knew as he handed over his abused credit card that he didn't need any new hats or boots, the latter of which ended up to be very uncomfortable for long-distance walking.

As he turned the lazy corner that started back towards the lake, Roger saw a man walking his way. Being a longtime resident of Piseco Lake, Roger felt that he knew everyone who lived there year round and had at least seen most of the summer regulars. This man, Roger did not recognize.

As he moved closer to the man, Roger realized that he had come from the doctor's lodge. Though the lodge was not as busy as it had been a few years ago, he knew that vacationing doctors still could be seen relaxing on the two-level deck, walking the grounds, or visiting the local restaurants. Roger also knew that vacationing doctors often gave free advice. And considering what he was going through, he thought that a little pill and a few words of wisdom might be the ticket.

* * *

Alexander was nearly finished gathering supplies when he decided he wanted to walk to the lake without the accompaniment of any doctors. The cool air felt wonderful against his pale skin as he opened the front door of the cabin. He peered cautiously around the grounds, making sure that no guests, expected or unexpected, were arriving. No one was seen.

"No more than five minutes," his guest's demands came from behind him. "If he sees you, if anyone sees you, our plan is done. Five minutes."

The lake appeared more pleasing than ever as Alexander strolled quietly towards it. Off in the distance, he spotted someone walking towards him. Alexander angled his approach to the lake more directly, hoping to avoid the approaching stranger. When Alexander realized that there was no path to the lake that didn't intersect with the stranger's, he halted. He knew that turning tail and retreating back into the lodge could raise suspicion, and that meeting the stranger face-to-face would probably raise even greater suspicions.

He knew that his appearance was anything but normal. His gray, pale appearance made him look three weeks dead. Even a non-medically trained eye would realize that something was not right with him. As he saw the man approaching, Alexander scanned the area, making sure that no one else was in sight. He and the stranger were alone.

* * *

As he was preparing his words for the could-be-doctor, Roger saw the man freeze in his tracks. After a few moments had passed, he heard the man call out to him. Roger was elated.

"That is a fine hat you have there, sir. What style is it?"

"It's called an 'outback,'" Roger answered, speeding his pace towards the doctor. "It's directly from Australia."

"The boots as well?"

"Yes, sir. Hey, are you a doctor? Because if you are, I sure would appreciate a little time."

There was no reply from the possible doctor. He was just

staring at Roger as he moved within arm's length. Roger immediately noticed the look in the man's eyes and the pale complexion that surrounded the eyes. The man, who was probably not a doctor but certainly needed one, took another step closer to Roger, affording Roger a close look at something Roger wished he had never seen.

"Hey look, I'm sorry if I disturbed you. I'll be on...."

Roger felt the hands shoving him backwards. The shove was powerful enough to send Roger stumbling off the road and crashing into a tree. Roger was not one to be intimidated. His size and strength gave him confidence in the face of violence. Once he regained his balance, he stood full framed to face the man.

"What the hell, man! Are you nuts or something?"

"Yes. As a matter of fact, I am nuts," Alexander stilled himself to say. He then removed a butcher knife from a hidden sheath tucked into the back of his pants. The power he used to stab the knife into Roger's throat was so forceful that the knife went clear through Roger's throat and imbedded the first three inches of the knife into the tree behind Roger.

Alexander quickly removed the hat from the pinned-to-a-tree man before any blood could stain it. Next he pulled the knife free and caught Roger in his arms before he collapsed to the ground. Alexander had decided to kill him once he realized that Roger was coming towards him. Alexander knew that his appearance would frighten the man and that he might go off and tell someone about the weirdo he saw at the lodge. All the doctors were quite good at reminding Alexander what the "unknowing public opinion" of his appearance would be.

"They will never accept you, Alexander, because they can never understand you," they said countless times. "If people see you or learn about you, they will take you away and treat you as nothing more than an object to be studied," they reminded him.

Alexander knew that he was being sloppy. He had been free for no more than 30 minutes, had already killed three people, with the third not being part of any plan that he and his accomplice had fine tuned for so many weeks. He didn't want to draw too much attention to himself until he learned more of the unfamiliar world. All the books could not teach him what a few years of true living would.

As he carried the body of the hat donor into the lodge, he promised himself that he would temper his desire for revenge.

"Time," he said to himself as he dropped his hold on the hat donor, sending him crashing to the floor at the end of a trail of blood. "Time and patience."

Chapter 3

1992

Doctor Mark Rinaldo knew that his wife, Gerti, hadn't believed the story he told her yesterday about why he was late and why he would be late coming home again today. Though Mark believed that being honest, especially with his wife, was indeed the best policy, he found no way to tell her the truth about what he and the other doctors had experienced just one day ago.

Mark sat at a high-top table in Shifts Lounge. Shifts was located within walking distance from Saint Stevens Memorial Hospital where Mark held the position of Chief of Medicine. The clientele of the lounge were almost exclusively hospital employees, and the lounge owner accommodated the hospital's employees work schedule by opening at 7:00 a.m. and not closing till well after 3:00 a.m. each day.

The lounge was decorated intentionally to not include reminders that its patrons would associate with the hospital. Besides a few photographs of Shifts owner posing with some nurses hanging on the narrow hallway leading to the restrooms, there were no other health care industry related pictures or items in the lounge. The owner had even made sure that the soap and cleaning supplies that were used in the lounge didn't smell like those used in Saint Stevens.

"What do you think is taking them so long?" Doctor Henry Zudak asked.

"They're not that late," Mark said. "You have to expect some delays. Traffic can get pretty rough on Long Island, and it isn't a picnic getting around Chicago this time of day, either. Relax."

"Relax?" Henry said. "I can't believe that relaxing is possible."

Henry Zudak had been an obstetrician for seven years. In those seven years, he had seen plenty of surprises when his pregnant patients were laying on a hospital bed, legs held in stirrups, nervous husbands wondering if they should look south or north. However, what he had witnessed less than twenty-four hours ago was well beyond anything he would describe as a "surprise."

Ken O'Connell, a successful car dealership owner and entrepreneur, and his wife, Janet, arrived at Saint Stevens at 4:30 yesterday afternoon. They knew, as did their doctor, Henry Zudak, that Jan's belly was full of not one, but two babies. So while she was just beginning her eighth month of her pregnancy, Henry wasn't surprised or overly concerned that Jan was in full labor.

Even the discovery that the twins were conjoined – choosing their chests to be their point of connection – didn't shock Henry, though it was an unexpected development. Knowing that Jan would not be able to deliver the conjoined twins naturally, Henry had Stanley Mix, a talented surgeon and good friend of his, paged.

"Not sure of their condition, but I could clearly see that the babies are connected at the chest," Henry reported to Stanley.

"I'll get 'em out," Stanley said.

The Cesarean section was quick. No complications. The neonatal nurse on duty quickly accessed the twins while Stanley closed up the five-inch incision.

"Doctor?" the nurse said in a hushed voice to Stanley who was finishing suturing the baby's exit passage.

"Yes?" he answered.

"Can you help me with something?" Stanley thought it was a strange request from a tenured nurse.

As Stanley approached the nurse who stood beside the twins, he could read the concern deeply etched into her face.

"Problem?" he asked.

"I only hear one heart, and I can only get one baby to breathe. APGAR test score is a three. No breathing, no color." She turned and gestured to one of the twins. "This baby has the heart. This one," she said while placing her hands on the other twin, "is, I think, just going along for the ride."

Stanley examined the twins carefully, trying hard not to raise the already heightened concerns of the O'Connell's.

"I don't think it's going to be a very long ride," he whispered. "Heart is too premature to handle one baby, let alone two. This may get ugly."

The time for quelling the fears of the O'Connell's was over. "Ken and Jan," Stanley said. Though Jan was heavily medicated, her fears made her fully aware. "I believe there's a problem that we don't have much time to solve."

The decision to do an emergency separation was difficult for the parents. It was not made until both Henry Zudak and Mark Rinaldo were asked to examine the twins and either agree with Stanley's dire assessment or find a reason the reason to keep the babies joined.

They both agreed with Stanley.

There was no time to wait for a surgeon experienced in the type of surgery needed, so Mark asked Stanley to perform the procedure.

"I'll assist," Mark said

"I'll need the extra hands," Stanley replied as they scrubbed in.

The procedure only took 40 minutes to separate the twins. Thomas, the twin lucky enough to claim possession of the heart and lungs, was quickly transferred to the Neonatal ICU, while Alexander was carefully and respectfully placed on a gurney and covered with a dazzlingly clean white sheet.

"I'll go speak with the O'Connell's," Mark said as he and Stanley finished the surgery. "Let Henry know what happened and ask him to keep an extra close eye on the other baby."

As he turned to leave, he felt the strong and sure grip of Stanley's hand grab hold of his arm. The grip was stronger than Mark thought a grip should be.

"Problem?" Mark asked.

"Look," Stanley said, gesturing to the baby covered in the white sheet. "It's moving."

Mark broke free of Stanley's grasp and removed the sheet covering the heartless baby. At first, Mark expected that the baby's nerves were having one last run through the body. However, when Mark saw the child return his stare, it was Mark's nerves that started running.

"Give me a stethoscope," Mark ordered. He checked closely for any signs of life, anything that Stanley and he might have missed.

He found nothing.

"No pulse, no breaths. Nothing," Mark said.

Mark quickly moved to the windows that separated the operating room from the observation area and drew the curtains closed. Only he and Stanley were in the operating room, the nurses having gone with the healthy twin to the ICU.

"What are you doing?" Stanley asked.

"Making sure that no one sees what the hell is going on in here."

"Mark, we need to get this baby..."

"Get it where?" Mark interrupted. "Get it to ICU where they can say we screwed up, or get freaked out when they find out that this baby doesn't have a heart? Or maybe we should bring it out to the O'Connell's and tell them the good news, that despite not having a heart or lungs that the child they just decided had to be separated in order to save the other baby, is still alive? Where, Stanley? What do you propose we have to do?"

"Mark, we have to tell someone."

Mark thought as he moved to lock the operating room door.

"Maybe you should just leave. I don't know what the hell I am going to do or even what I should do, but there's no reason for you to get involved in whatever I come up with."

"And then what? Leave and pretend that nothing happened? Pretend that the baby died like it should have and that my chief of medicine isn't hiding a living body somewhere in Chicago? What the hell, Mark? I can't leave like this."

"I need time to think."

"We don't have time, Mark."

"Call Henry. Tell him to get up here and to say nothing to anyone."

"Okay, but any second now the cleaning crew is going to try to do their job in this room, and finding the door locked and two doctors in the room will raise some eyebrows."

"I need time to think," Mark said as he plowed his hands through his thinning, grey hair. "I need time to come up with something."

Both doctors heard the mumblings of men approaching the locked door. Their attempts to open the door prompted their knock and call.

"Anyone in there?" one of the men said. "Cleaning crew. Anyone in there?"

"We're not finished," Mark replied. "Come back in fifteen."

"Who is that?" the voice behind the locked door demanded.

"Doctor Mark Rinaldo, Chief of Medicine. Now either go away or start looking for another place to work where you can piss more people off. Understood?"

There was no reply, only the faint sounds of feet moving away from the door.

"Well, I'm sure that won't make anyone suspicious," Stanley said.

"They're gone, and that's all I wanted. Now please call Henry. Remember, tell him to say nothing."

Henry Zudak announced his arrival a few minutes after being called by Stanley by a loud knock on the locked door.

"Mark? Stanley? It's Henry."

Mark nodded towards Stanley who then unlocked and opened the door.

"Anyone follow you?" Stanley asked.

"Follow me? What the hell are you talking about? No, no one followed me."

Mark locked eyes with Henry, revealing his confusion, worry, and fear.

"What's going on in here?" Henry asked.

Mark removed his gaze and looked down at the baby lying on the gurney. The white sheet, bloodied in patches, was wadded up at the feet of a baby that stared at Henry with eyes lifeless and cold. "What is that baby doing here?"

"Henry, we have a situation."

Chapter 4

Doctor William Straus was waiting for something like this to happen. Something, anything that would get his name listed at the top of the medical journals around the world. He knew that all he needed was the right chance to show the world just how damn good of a psychiatrist he was.

When his friend from college, Doctor Peter Adams called him yesterday, William knew that his chance had arrived.

"Will, I really need to make sure that you understand the delicate nature of this situation and can assure us that absolute privacy and confidentiality will and can be maintained," Peter Adams said.

Doctor Peter Adams was an employee of Saint Stevens Memorial Hospital, where he offered counseling services to patients and their families, as well as to Saint Stevens employees. Mark Rinaldo had called Peter into a private meeting, during which he, Henry and Stanley explained the events and circumstances of the O'Connell's twins.

"You're telling me that the baby has no heart and no lungs, yet is still moving around? Peter asked.

"All of us, Henry, Mark and I, examined that baby over so many times and in every conceivable way that there is no way we missed a heart," Stanley said. "No way. There is just no heart inside that baby."

"I'm not questioning any of you, but I am confused about my role in this," Peter said.

"I have a plan and need your help making it work."

"Okay, Mark. Let's hear it."

Mark Rinaldo explained the events of the day. He told him that he marked up the chest of a stillborn baby that was marked to be "destroyed" to make the body look like what the O'Connells would be expecting their dead baby to look like. He told Peter that he had the heartless baby hidden in his office and that he needed his assistance in getting the baby out of the hospital as quickly as possible. He implored Peter to keep everything completely confidential.

"I know you have a friend who runs a psychiatric hospital out on Long Island," Mark said to Peter.

"Are you suggesting that I smuggle the baby across State lines, involve my good friend in this highly illegal scheme of yours and get nothing in return?"

"Are you suggesting that I bribe you?"

"Not a bribe," Peter said. "Just some assurances that if and when this thing explodes that my name is never mentioned."

"Agreed. Anything else?" Mark asked.

"I have been thinking about a long vacation. A very long vacation."

* * *

William Straus had everything prepared. He was thankful for his authoritative manner of running Hilburn when he instructed the staff that "Ward C will have a new patient, and no one is allowed to enter Ward C without approval."

Ward C had been closed for the last three years. When it was in use, it housed some of the most dangerous patients assigned to Hilburn. The staff at the time called the ward "the mind-bending rooms."

Straus was well known as a strict disciplinarian, who demanded that anyone under his supervision adhere to the "highest work ethic and extreme confidentiality." Any employee, whether a tenured doctor or a recently hired cafeteria worker, would be terminated if Straus caught wind of "excessive work breaks or discussing hospital matters outside of work."

When Straus announced to his "confidence team" that Ward C would be opening again, he had little fear that news would spread.

"Our patient is coming to us from a hospital in Chicago where the doctors there are unable to care for the baby," Straus started.

"A baby?" Michelle Pettingall, Straus's favorite "nurse to look at" asked. "Ward C isn't set up to care for an infant. Wouldn't the patient be better cared for in the pediatric wing?"

"In most cases, yes, Michelle," Straus smiled. "But this patient, according to the report I received via telephone, has some very unique healthcare concerns."

"Something contagious?" asked Jacob Curtis, a psychologist who was better at kissing Straus's ass than at treating patients.

"Unknown, but doubtful."

"Can you share the 'unique concerns' with us?" asked Brian Lucietta. Brian was five years out of medical school and shared Straus's interest in "alternate means of treatment."

"Speculation at this point, Brian. What I was told seems too difficult to believe. I think it best that we each examine the patient independently and share our findings as a team."

"When will the patient arrive?" asked Jacob Curtis.

"Two doctors from Chicago, my old friend Peter Adams and a surgeon named Stanley Mix left Chicago very late last night. I expect them to be here within the hour."

Straus found no reason to extend the meeting with his confidence team. He had to make sure that Ward C was ready and that his team fully understood how important confidentiality and complete focus to the patient would be.

"We have plenty of things to complete and not much time to do so. Michelle," he said as he moved as close to her as he felt she would allow. "Have you moved the necessary items to Ward C like I asked?"

"Yes, Doctor Straus. Everything you asked for."

"Good. And Jacob, did you ensure that the recording and video devices are fully functional in each room?"

"Tested them three times, sir. If a pin drops in any of the rooms, we'll hear it."

"Excellent," Straus said before turning to Brian. "Lastly, has all the lab equipment I requested been reserved and moved to the

Ward?"

"Everything," Brian replied.

"Perfect. Again, I understand that we have some employees here who are more interested in other people's concerns than they are with their own. That is an unavoidable problem," Straus said then briefly drifted off, as if the recognition of employees beyond his control represented a failure on his part. Failure was a reality that Straus was willing to do just about anything to avoid. "However, the way they view us is of no concern, at least it shouldn't be. That said, I feel compelled to remind each of you that until we know exactly what this patient brings us, that your conversations about this patient are held with the strictest degree of confidentiality. Do I have everyone's commitment?"

"Yes, Doctor Straus."

* * *

Michelle Pettingall hated her job almost as much as she hated Doctor Straus and his unwelcome advances, arrogant nature, and the superior attitude he always displayed. Had she the courage or the bank account, she would tell Straus to go "screw himself" right before having a sit-down with a New York State representative to "spill the beans" on what was really going on at Hilburn.

Courage, she had. Money, she didn't.

Her husband, Kenneth Pettingall, was killed while fighting a fire over three years ago. Michelle thought that since Ken had been a full-fledged and tenured interior firefighter for NYFD that the city would pay her his life insurance and pension. However, after the investigation showed that Ken was not only off-duty when the warehouse fire erupted but also that his blood alcohol level was 1.3, the city needed to make an example out of someone.

"We are very sorry for your loss, Mrs. Pettingall, and wish there was something that the city could do. However, rewarding behaviors like those that the report proves your husband was doing, sends a message to every firefighter in the city. We are sorry for your loss."

For the last three years, Michelle had put up with Straus, the horrible working conditions at Hilburn, and the loneliness of losing the only man she had ever loved. She put up with it all without the support of friends or family. Her parents were divorced when Michelle was seven, and while she maintained somewhat of a relationship with her mother who lived in Maine, her father had drunk himself to death over eight years ago. As for friends, all of those were the wives of other firefighters that worked in the same station as did Ken. As the fire that took her husband slowly extinguished from the lack of fuel, so too did many of her friendships.

Several of her old friends made gave it a good college try to keep their friendship with Michelle going. But each found it challenging to find common ground with Michelle, once discussing the politics and happenings at the fire station became a taboo topic of discussion.

When Straus dismissed the team, Michelle turned and walked down the hallway, which lead to the flight of stairs that emptied out onto Ward C. Though she disliked her job, she still felt a powerful responsibility to do it well. Better than "well;" she demanded that she allow no one to outwork her. If she had a job to do, she did it to the best her abilities allowed. She was fewer than ten steps away when she heard Straus call her name.

"It will certainly be nice working so closely with you, Michelle. It will certainly be nice."

She turned and only offered the briefest of smiles before hurrying her pace towards the assumed security of the stairwell.

"Bastard," she whispered, being sure that no one could hear, but then double-checking over her shoulder to be absolutely certain that Straus hadn't heard her whisper. Straus was still standing in the hallway, admiring the view of her backside as she was walking away from him. Still standing there with a smug smile of ignorant expectation when she reached the stairs. "Bastard," she said again, in an even quieter whisper.

* * *

Ward C wasn't a ward at all, at least not in the typical sense. The ward was comprised of only four rooms and a bathroom. The most important room was called "the hub." It was a semi-circular room with two-way mirrors affording the room's occupant a clear and private view into the three adjoining rooms. To the east was a small, 15 by 15 foot bedroom. The room was sparsely furnished; nothing hanging from the walls. The only furniture in the room was a 1950's style baby crib, three fold-up metal chairs, a small, well-worn coffee table, and a large cabinet filled with medical supplies.

To the north, the hub looked into a dimly lit room, much longer than wider, that contained one long, white table. On the table were strewn several notebooks, empty blood vials, several syringes – some in and some outside of their packaging—a coffee pot in dire need of cleaning, and three microscopes. Towards the far end of the room, a small, squared off area contained the only restroom in Ward C.

The room that could be seen when looking westward from the hub was a well-lighted lounge. The couch, four reclining chairs, and solid oak end and coffee tables seemed out of place for an institution struggling to receive sufficient funds to improve patient care. This was the only room of the four that was carpeted, clean, and comfortable.

Each room could only be accessed from the hub, and no room had any windows.

Only mirrored walls.

The hub was used to closely monitor specific patients in the years that Straus and his team had more "freedom" in their treatment plans. Now, it was to be used to monitor the new patient that was being delivered to them from Chicago.

As Michelle Pettingall checked the medical supply closet, making sure that it was stocked for what Straus had called an "indefinite stay," she shivered with fear as she began to wonder what kinds of experiments Straus and his team had conducted in Ward C only a few years before. And she wondered what experiments they were planning on the soon-to-be-arriving new patient.

While "the hub" was an excellent place for doctors to closely monitor each and every movement of the patients who once resided in Ward C, Straus realized that it was also an excellent place to monitor Michelle as she was making her final check of the medical supply cabinet.

"Looking forward to getting to know you a little bit better," he said to himself as he moved closer to the two-way mirror. "I know all about what your husband did, and I know exactly what he left behind for you to deal with. A pile of steaming dog shit. But don't worry, Michelle," he said as he headed out of the hub before his position was realized, "good old doctor Straus will take care of you."

Doctor William Straus was made superintendent of Hilburn Psychiatric at the age of only twenty-seven. In his four years as "the boss," he was focused on finding something, anything that would get his name in lights. He knew that sacrifices had to be made in order to achieve the greatness he deserved and felt that if he was going to make sacrifices, others should as well.

"For the betterment of all mankind," he would say when designing a new treatment plan or adapting one that didn't produce the expected results. Today, however, if what Peter Adams had told him was true, was the day when his hard work and countless sacrifices would pay off. If the baby he was expecting would reveal its secrets, William Straus would be a certain Nobel Prize winner, and his fame and fortune would be guaranteed.

"This little freak better be what I am expecting," he thought as he turned into the stairway and headed back down to the main floor.

Before his feet landed on the final step, his pager vibrated. The caller ID displayed by the tiny screen was from Jacob Curtis's office phone.

Straus walked into the nearest office he could find to dial Curtis's extension.

"Jacob, it's William. I got your message," he said.

"They're here."

"At the docks, I trust?"

"At the docks."

"Five minutes."

* * *

The budget cuts had hit many NY State institutions hard over the years, and Hilburn Psychiatric was one of those hit. In an effort to cut spending, Straus had fired three of the five employees who manned the loading docks and moved the remaining two to part-time positions.

"Our deliveries, or more precisely, or ability to order things to be delivered is a casualty of budget cuts, I'm afraid," Straus announced to an all employee meeting less than eighteen months earlier. "We need to respond to these cuts while not jeopardizing the care we provide to our patients. With these cuts and our responsibility to our patients in mind, I have made the difficult decision to reduce our logistics team head count. We will only be receiving deliveries twice per week, and the loading docks will now be staffed only on those two days. Please plan accordingly when ordering approved supplies. Thank you for your understanding and dedication to our patients."

Knowing that the docks would be vacant, Straus instructed Peter Adams to "drive all the way around the institution and follow the signs to the loading dock. I'll have one of my trusted team members waiting for you there. His name is Jacob Curtis. He will page me when you arrive."

"You've thought of everything, haven't you, William?" Peter complimented.

"Mostly everything."

Chapter 5

"What the hell took you so long?" Henry asked, his gut full of beer.

"It's a long drive, Henry. And we would have been here an hour earlier if Stanley here hadn't insisted on seeing where the baby was going to be kept."

"It didn't feel right, just dropping the baby off and scurrying off like damn kidnappers. That place gave me the creeps and your friend, Straus, that guy has some issues," Stanley said before ordering a beer.

"Stanley," Mark said, "are you comfortable with the arrangements? I mean, are they secure enough?"

"I guess. Who the hell knows," Stanley said. "I think so. I just don't trust that Straus character. He was trying to hide his excitement, but he sucks at hiding shit. His emotions, I mean."

"What happened?" Henry asked. "Did they find anything out that we missed?"

Peter Adams waited for his single-malt scotch to arrive at the table before answering Henry's question. "Doctor Straus's team each examined the patient, and all agreed with our assessment. It has no heart, no more than half of a lung and no reason to be alive. Despite Stanley's reservations, I fully trust William and am very confident that you made the right choice in trusting my judgment. William and his team will have no prying eyes as they figure out the mysteries keeping the baby alive." He downed the scotch in one, intentionally delayed, gulp. "And with that, I believe I have fulfilled my end of the bargain."

"Yes, you have, Peter," Mark said. "And thank you. Enjoy your sabbatical."

"I plan to. And, in case you were worried, I'll arrange for my associate, Doctor Cross, to provide his services full-time at the hospital during my extended absence. Mark, you will, of course, need to move his pay up close to what mine is. Needn't overlook anything that might raise suspicions."

"Of course," Mark said. "Anything else you can think of?"

"Just tell people that I decided to go into private practice. A 'spur of the moment' decision. Not that I think anyone will doubt my interest in being on my own, but just in case, let any who are interested know that I am taking time to relax and to prepare."

"You're a real dick, you know that, Peter," Stanley said. "A class act dickhead."

Ignoring Stanley, Peter extended his hand to Mark, saying, "Continue to have my checks sent to my home address. I'll alert you to where I will need them sent after I decide where I open my 'private practice.'"

Mark shook Peter's hand. Without any other words or gestures, Peter turned and walked out of Shifts Lounge.

"Now what?" Henry asked.

"Return to business as usual."

Mark, Stanley, and Henry sat in silence, each wondering how long it would take for them to be able to return to "business as usual." While Mark and Henry continued to discuss Peter and how disappointed they were with his behavior, Stanley sat quietly, staring at the half-empty glass of beer in front of him.

"Stan?" Mark asked. "You okay?"

"Fine," he said. "Lots of stuff running around in my brain right now. Lots of stuff."

His description of his thoughts was not lost on Mark nor Henry, though Stanley knew that what was filling his mind was not just random "stuff." It was thoughts of Michelle Pettingall. At thirty-years old, Stanley was not a stranger to having feelings for a woman, especially one as attractive as Michelle Pettingall. What he wasn't accustomed to was what to do once an attraction was identified.

Stanley did not lack self-confidence when it came to his skills as a surgeon. Nor did he struggle when an opportunity arrived to share his opinion. But building up courage to approach a woman was a much needed and utterly lacking skill in Stanley's arsenal of talent.

When he and Peter first arrived at the loading docks of Hilburn, Jacob Curtis, a short, stocky man, whose arms were intended for a much taller man, met them. The three doctors stood in uncomfortable silence, with only Jacob Curtis's repeated suggestions that "Doctor Straus should join us any second now" tearing a jagged hole in the silence.

When Straus arrived, he ignored feeling the need for any

introductions and instead directed the group to follow him up a seldom-used staircase. At the top of the stairs, Straus lead the team left down a very long and very empty hallway to his office.

"Where is everyone?" Peter had asked.

"I work better when not interrupted. I have this hallway to myself, for the most part," Straus replied.

Once in his office, Stanley was astounded at the climate change. From what he had seen and experienced from his short tour of Hilburn, its dank colors, floors in need of a fresh coat of wax, and an odor that hung thinly but clearly in the air, Straus's office was what one would expect the office of a CEO of a Fortune 500 to resemble.

A solid, blonde-wood desk was the most eye-catching thing about the office. It was at least six feet long, pristinely clean, and polished with a shine that even the best Marine would envy. The lighting was muted but bright enough to afford anyone a clear view of the office. Works of art, from artists Stanley had never heard of, adorned the wall and were showcased with top-hanging frame lights. The couch was brown leather and matched the three chairs that framed up a sitting area. Books, all their spines without a crease, graced the solid oak bookshelves positioned on three of the four walls. "Gentlemen," Straus began once he afforded his guests enough time to admire his office, "welcome to Hilburn."

To Stanley, he extended his hand, saying, "Doctor William Straus."

"Stanley Mix, and I believe you already know Peter."

"Indeed I do. Indeed I do." Straus moved closer to Peter where the two old friends embraced in an awkward hug. "It is wonderful to see you again, Peter. How are the wife and … kids?"

"Maggie is fine, and no kids. And if my memory serves me, how are Claire and Robert doing?"

"You have me at a disadvantage with your memory. Both are well. Robert turns eight next month, and Claire has, thankfully, retained her good looks and shape."

The old friends laughed, at what, Stanley could only guess.

"But where are my manners? Stanley, Peter, though I am certain he has introduced himself already, this is Jacob Curtis."

The doctors shook hands and exchanged the briefest of the obligatory niceties.

"And this," Straus said as he moved towards the baby held in Stanley's muscular arms, "this must be our newest patient." Unsure of whether Doctor Straus wanted to hold the baby himself, Stanley positioned his body to give Straus and Jacob Curtis a better view. "Remarkable," Straus said. "I want to thank you, both of you, for trusting me and my team with this sensitive operation. Be assured, I run a very tight ship around here. A very tight ship. Confidentiality and extreme privacy will be maintained."

"Where will you keep the baby?" Peter asked.

"I have opened a once-closed and seldom-used ward of my institution to serve as both our private lab and the baby's room. Should you wish to observe the area, you are most welcome."

"I think it's better if we just say our goodbyes and be on our way," Stanley suggested as he made clear his intentions to hand off the baby to Straus.

"Jacob, please hold the child while I assemble the rest of the team. You don't mind staying for a bit longer so that I can introduce my team, do you, Stanley?"

"No. Not at all. That would be fine," he lied back in response.

"Excellent. I've already instructed them to meet us here. It is a large institution and Ward C is a bit of a walk. Give them just another few minutes."

It took Straus's team at least ten minutes before arriving at Straus's office. Introductions were made, and Stanley no longer wanted to leave after being introduced to nurse Michelle.

"Doctor Straus," he started, "maybe we should see your Ward C. We are all a bit concerned, as you know. Seeing what you have in place will go a long way in easing all of our concerns."

"Wonderful!" Straus said. "But first, and this is not meant to question your abilities or you intentions, allow Doctors Curtis and Lucietta to conduct a quick exam of the baby. Nurse Pettingall," he said, gesturing to Michelle who was standing a few steps away and behind the group. "Feel free to conduct a good, old-fashioned nurse's exam, should you feel compelled." The sarcasm of Straus's invitation to Michelle was not lost on Stanley.

"Unbelievable," Jacob Curtis said as he finished his quick but thorough exam. "I'll need to have more tests and scans done, but...."

"Doctor Lucietta, if you please?" Straus said, interrupting Jacob Curtis. Doctor Brian Lucietta could only manage to say, "mysterious" after completing his exam.

"Very well, then," said Straus. "Off to Ward C. I believe you'll find that I've thought of everything. Almost everything, at least."

As the group turned towards the office door, Straus paused, his hand on the doorknob. He turned to the group to say, "I will give a crisp $100 bill if anyone in this talented group sees or even hears another employee during our walk to Ward C. Anyone up to taking my bet?"

"You didn't make it a bet, just an offer," Stanley corrected.

"Indeed, you are correct, Doctor Mix. I guess my confidence may have cost me a chance at a wager. No bother. Let us be on our way."

No one saw or heard anyone during the two minute walk to Ward C.

While Straus was giving a tour of the hub and the observation rooms, Michelle was instructed to bring the baby into the room designated as its room. Stanley took the opportunity to walk with Michelle.

"I am sorry about all this," he said.

Michelle turned slowly towards Stanley, and brought her index finger up to her pursed lips. "Shhh. Every room has microphones," she whispered.

"What happens in these rooms?" Stanley asked as silently as he could.

Michelle shook her head and shrugged her shoulders so slightly to not raise suspicions if Straus was observing her through the two-way mirrors. As she placed the baby in the crib, she turned towards Stanley, making sure that his six-foot plus, broad frame shielded her from the hub's view. "I don't like this, and I get the sense you don't either," she mouthed.

"I dislike it more every second," he mouthed back.

Michelle offered a smile as she moved back into potential view. "There. This will be a safe and secure place for him," she said, not worrying about her voice being picked up by the room's microphone while indicating to Stanley that there would be no more private conversation. "Shall we join Doctor Straus in the central room?"

"Of course," replied Stanley.

After Straus concluded his tour of Ward C and had walked his guests back down to the loading docks, Stanley promised himself to find a way to talk with Michelle again. As Peter and he said their "thank yous" and "goodbye's," he paused and held onto Michelle's hand a bit longer than protocol would suggest a parting handshake should take.

"Nice meeting you, Michelle Pettingall," he said.

"You too," she offered back.

"Peter," Straus's voice halted the stare Stanley was enjoying into Michelle's eyes, "give me two days to run our initial tests. Call me to arrange a conference call with the rest of your team back in Chicago."

"Fair enough," Peter said. "And, again, I can't thank you enough."

With that, the meeting was over and Peter and Stanley got into Stanley's car, started the engine, and began their journey back to Chicago.

Chapter 6

"But I don't want to know what's keeping him alive. Damn it, Peter, I thought I was clear when I said I wanted this whole thing to be done and over with," Mark Rinaldo said as Peter Adams stood smugly in front of Mark's desk.

"Mark, how is it possible you can just pretend that everything that happened last week, didn't? Aren't you just a bit curious about what is keeping the child alive? Even the slightest bit curious?"

"Peter, the more we discuss this, the greater the chances are of this whole damn thing being made public."

"Mark," Peter said as he sat down in a chair across the desk from Mark, "learning more is precisely how we can keep things quiet. Hell, we don't even know if the child will last another day. All I am suggesting is that you get on this call with Doctor Straus and his team, and maybe, just maybe, they'll have figured something out that will make this whole thing better."

Mark sighed and sat motionless and quiet for several seconds. "What time is the call?" he asked.

"Five, eastern time."

"Fine."

"I've already invited Stanley," Peter added.

"And his reaction?"

"Same as yours."

"Okay. My office in two hours, then?"

"Two hours."

* * *

The crackles sounding through the telephone line were loud enough to be annoying but not so loud that Mark, Peter, and Stanley couldn't hear what was being said. The voice of Straus sounded. "Doctors, I am glad you all decided to join us on this call. As we all have very busy schedules, I'll forgo formal introductions and will summarize our findings thus far. Should you have any questions, which I am certain that you will, please feel free to ask. Either I or one of my team members will be happy to answer. Are you ready on your end?"

"Yes, all set here, William."

"Excellent. Gentlemen, allow me to begin by thanking you for thinking of me. I fully understand the circumstances that brought this miraculous child to my care and also take your trust in me quite seriously. For that, I thank you.

"Doctors, each day we are faced with new and unique challenges in our fields. Some are quickly remedied and others, well, others turn from a challenge to a mystery. And so it is with our child.

"The first order of business should be to tell you his name. Alexander Black. A name both descriptive and common enough to dispel any curiosity should anyone ever hear any of us discussing the case.

"Now, to answer your most obvious question that I assume

you all have been asking yourself a million times, no, Alexander has no heart and has only a half of a lung. His lung does function, however at a very diminished capacity and only when he falls asleep. Curiously, Alex has only slept twice for a total of eleven hours in the five days he's been living here. To your next assumed question, which certainly must be "what is keeping him alive?" We have the answer for that, and the possibilities are incredible!"

"To understand what it is that is keeping Alexander Black alive, I have to first cover a few other discoveries. First, the blood work was normal. The blood was obviously left over from his twin. The blood is not circulating, it had simply pooled in his extremities. The patient is showing an incredible ability to learn quickly and to remember. He has already learned how to feed himself a bottle and had displayed an ability to locate hidden objects. Fairly remarkable.

"But now to the test results. The only way to describe the cell formation is 'supercharged.' I will explain. As we all know, cells contain oxygen. Once the oxygen in the cell is depleted, the cell is filled back up with oxygen by our blood via the circulatory and respiratory systems. In Alexander, however, his cells re-supply, both by themselves and by transferring and borrowing from other cells. The cells contain thousands of times the normal amount of oxygen and are able to share this oxygen with nearby cells. This adaptation enables the cells to share oxygen, glucose, glycogen, triglycerides, water, and whatever else the body needs.

"This sharing extends to energy, as well. His stomach does function, though not as a normal stomach. Food seems to be broken down quickly into cell transferable energy. All the results are not in yet on the stomach, so this is still sketchy. Also, any waste products are also carried and transferred from cell to cell and are then drained via gravity out of the body. We don't feel that the patient will ever have any control of his elimination, however.

"He is able to go without sleep until the oxygen levels in his cells is too low to sustain movement. He then falls into a deep sleep, which activates his one half of a lung to begin drawing air, thusly re-charging and replenishing the cells.

"Most notably, there seems to be no cell decay or even cell death. This, if true, would explain his ability to learn quickly and remember practically anything. Once a brain cell is imprinted with an event, the cell will always be there and will be ready to relinquish its content whenever needed. This is another area where more tests are needed, but so far, we have seen no cell decay and no cell death.

"Also, it seems that the more he grows, the stronger his cells grow. If this mutual growth continues, he will only need to sleep after very long periods of intense activity. I also feel that Alexander could become very dangerous. If he can truly remember everything that happens, everything he hears, sees, or touches, and if his growth continues, he is going to be one very strong, very smart person.

"To sum up our findings thus far, some preliminary tests show that Alexander has a life expectancy of just over thirty-years. At that point, his cells, though not in decay or death, will no longer be able to transfer oxygen as efficiently. What will happen, again in theory, is that as he grows closer to his 'life expectancy,' he will begin to sleep more and will eventually simply never wake up. My team may be wrong, though, and Alex could live a thousand years. They just can't provide a 'rock solid' estimate for you. His cells may find a way to continue well beyond what I project. His brain cells are already showing signs of environmental adaptation. He is, and will remain, for a while at least, a mystery."

There was silence at both ends of the phone line while the doctors at Saint Stevens avoided looking into one another's eyes. No one knew what to ask; yet all had thousands of questions. Mark Rinaldo broke the silence after the silence entered its second full minute. "Super-charged cells? This includes all cells?"

"It appears so," Straus answered.

Mark fell silent again. As each word came out of the small, black speaker sitting on the desk of his office, Mark fell deeper into the realization that his sleep would be affected for a long time to come. *"Even Alexander,"* he thought wryly, *"will be getting more sleep than me."*

Besides the conference call and the questions it raised, Mark was also thoughtful and worried about Henry Zudak, who hadn't been back to work since Alexander was born. Stanley told Mark that Henry was suffering from severe headaches and night terrors. Mark was worried because of the intense concern he saw in Peter's eyes.

"How bad are the dreams?" Mark asked Stanley a few days after Henry informed Mark that he needed some time off.

"I guess that they are pretty bad. Very realistic. They're really doing a number on him. He looks like he hasn't slept in weeks. I gave him some Valium hoping that the drug would help calm him down. He keeps saying that 'eyes' are coming after him."

Mark wasn't seeing any "eyes" in his dreams, only memories, which were bad enough. And as Mark sat in the conference room listening to Straus rattle off his findings on Alexander, he began to wonder if he would ever see Henry Zudak deliver another child again.

"There are a few other findings," Straus called out from the black speaker, interrupting Mark's thoughts and the silence of the conference room. "I did some muscular tests and found that the patient's strength is quite exceptional for a six-day-old infant. His reflexes are quick and responsive, and his cartilage has already begun transforming to bone. As with all his other cells, both his muscular and skeletal cells are 'super-charged.' No decay, self-replenishing, and with the potential to grow in strength as the patient matures."

The long pause that followed had all the doctors at Saint Stevens staring at the speakerphone. The hundred plus years of education in the room couldn't raise a single question. They wondered what they could ask about something they were not yet convinced was real. A quick crackle sounded through the speaker, sending a bolt of excited and startled energy through Mark and his team.

"The last thing I want to say, believe it or not, is perhaps the most difficult to understand and accept. He can talk. Not words, mind you, not yet anyway. But he can use his vocal chords. We have no idea how he can do this without his lung performing while he is awake, but he can. He's done this on several occasions. The first time almost scared us to death. In order for Alex to speak, he must become perfectly still. I have some theories that may explain this ability, but I won't share them until I run some more tests."

"Doctor Straus? Peter Adams here. I have a quick question. You said that his cells have a life expectancy of around thirty years. Are you saying that he will live for thirty years? I guess I didn't quite understand what you were saying."

"Not for certain. The tests do indicate that the cells will lose their ability to transfer energy after thirty years, but we can't say for sure. We tested his cells after each of his sleep episodes and found that they lose some transfer ability. An incredibly small amount of loss, but loss nonetheless. Remember, he has only fallen asleep twice so we don't have enough data to really be accurate. Also, we don't think he can produce new cells, so whatever we take out, we have to put back. Not sure if the cells we put back continue to function. We certainly don't want to cause permanent damage by removing too many cells. Could be a very delicate balance. Again, his cells do show indications of an ability to adapt and evolve as needed. I simply cannot say for sure how long Alex will live."

"Excuse me, Doctor Stanley Mix here. You said that the child could be dangerous when he grows up. What did you mean by that?"

"If he has a negative disposition, his retained knowledge and exceptional strength could be dangerous to anyone who tried to outsmart or overpower him. Just speculation on my part, Doctor."

"Are you going to be able to keep him in a safe area, just in case?" Stanley asked as his mind recalled a retained image of Michelle's face.

"I can assure you that my facility will retain the child until it becomes impossible to do so. If that day comes, I have a private lodge up North to which I could make some renovations and keep the child up there. I'm looking at this as a full-term endeavor. I'm not going to give up on this child until I find out everything there is to find out, or, God forbid, he passes on."

"Some of us may want to visit Alexander from time to time. Can that be arranged?" Mark asked while staring directly at Stanley, asking with his eyes if he thought Henry would benefit from a visit with Alexander.

"I was going to invite you all up myself," the pride filled voice of William Straus answered back. "Come anytime. By the time you come, I'm sure that we will have more information for you. Then, we can discuss Alexander face to face, doctors to doctors. There is truly nothing I would enjoy more than to have all of you visit my Center. Come anytime."

Chapter 7

2014

Derek stared blankly into his client's eyes. Searching for a hint of something that would let Derek know that either the story he had just heard was the ramblings of an insane person, a joke organized by some members of a police force somewhere in the country or was actually a very bizarre and nearly impossible to understand truth.

"You're telling me that your twin brother and you were born joined together and that the only heart you two were using is inside of your chest right now?"

"Yes, I swear that's the truth," Thomas said.

"And you're also expecting me to believe that your twin brother, the one that got the short end of the surgery stick, is not only still alive after twenty-two years, but that he killed three people and can't be located by the local police?"

"Look," Thomas said, his impatience growing. "I know this sounds like I am making it all up or that I'm crazy, but as God as my witness, it's all true. Doesn't the fact that I paid you over three grand already prove anything?"

"Only that you may have some spare money lying around."

"If I am agreeing to pay you your full fee, which I am, does it really matter to you if you are chasing a figment of my imagination or not? I mean, all I ask is that you help me find my brother and keep my parents and me safe. If you discover that I am making this whole story up, then you just walk away with my money and no damage done. Hell, I'll even advance you another ten grand if you need more proof that I'm serious."

Derek kept staring deeply into Thomas's eyes. He sensed something that told him that the story was true, but he also sensed he wasn't getting the whole story. "Where are your parents now?"

"Probably still in the air. They are flying to the Bahamas."

"So unless your brother is on that plane, sounds to me like they are nice and safe right where they are."

"For now, yes. But not if we don't stop my brother. Eventually, he will find them."

"Curious about one thing. Actually, I'm curious about a whole lot of things, but one in particular. Why aren't you not looking over your shoulder every three seconds?"

"What do you mean?"

"You told me that you felt you needed me to provide protection for you and for your parents, but here you are, sitting in a public park and the only thing you seem concerned about is getting me to believe your story. Curious."

Thomas shook his head and readjusted his body on the park bench. "I hired you for your protection. If I don't feel safe when I am two feet from you, then I may have made a poor hiring decision."

"Okay. Good answer. I'll accept that," Derek said, his

response mixed with embarrassment and lingering doubt.

"Well?" Thomas asked. "Will you help me or not? Just say the word and I'll arrange the money to be transferred today."

"Where was the murder scene? I guess I should start there."

"Piseco Lake, up in the Adirondack Mountains of New York."

Chapter 8

Police Chief Ralph Fox arrived at the crime scene a full seven hours after the bodies were discovered. Officer Wayne White called him from the scene and told him that he had better cut his vacation short and get back to Piseco Lake. Ralph was in the middle of a lobster dinner that he had bought fresh from the Maine Seafood Market when the telephone in his rented beach house sounded. He had been in Ogunquit for only two of his seven-day vacation and let Ken White know about it.

"You better be calling me for something damn right important, officer," he barked in his displaced Texas drawl. "I ain't had a vacation in five years, and I ain't ready to call this one off, yet. So, what you got to say better be damn important."

"Chief, we got a murder. Actually, three. Single crime scene."

The stress in Wayne White's voice was abundantly obvious. Ralph had only been the Chief of Police for the town of Arietta New York for six months and didn't know his officers all that well yet. But the stress and fear, mixed with some dark excitement, was clearly coming through Wayne's voice.

"Murder?" Ralph questioned, forcing a butter-soaked piece of lobster tail down to his stomach. "Are you breaking my balls?"

"Three bodies, laying right here in the same room I'm talking to you from."

"You got the killer in the next room, or do we have to go chasing him through those damn woods?"

"We don't have anyone. Hate to ask, I know you needed this vacation, but..."

"I'm on my way."

Ralph dropped his fork, packed his bags and left the beach house and a half-eaten Maine pounder behind. He figured six hours of "police chief allowed speed driving" if the traffic wasn't too bad would get him back to Piseco Lake. Seven hours if other vacationers were also leaving abruptly.

When he walked into the log cabin style lodge, several people were barking out what they had found, their suspicions of who the killer was, and apologies for him losing his vacation.

Ralph Fox was a lawman that had seen too much during his twenty-plus years in the business. As a Detective in Dallas, Texas, Ralph had seen what he thought to be everything there was to see. The stress of his Texas job caused him a heart attack at age forty-four, as well as two divorces, three weeks on probation for excessive force, an ability to drink massive quantities of beer, a bulging stomach, and a need to get out of Texas. While he was visiting a high school friend who lived in Staten Island, Ralph learned that there was an opening for police chief for a small, upstate town. Without hesitation, he quit his job in Texas, submitted his resume for the position and moved to Speculator, New York, a small town nine miles north of Piseco Lake.

Ralph was offered the position of Chief of Police and took office two weeks later. He made no drastic changes with the office or to his staff, which consisted of four part-time officers, one full-time sergeant, an office manager and an eighty-four-year-old custodian. He immediately enjoyed the slowed-down pace of his new law position and never imagined that he would walk into a big city style murder.

As he walked behind Officer Wayne White through the lodge and into the dorm-like structure attached to the rear of the lodge, Ralph's keen eyes searched the scene for anything that could be considered a clue. When he passed the fireplace and saw that there were ashes in it, he stopped walking.

"Anyone have the sense to go through that fireplace?" he gently said to Wayne White, who hadn't realized that the chief had stopped following him and was still talking about how he felt when he first walked into the room with the bodies.

"Yes sir. Looks like someone burned papers in there," Wayne said.

"Anything left in that pile of ashes?" Ralph asked, in a slow, patient voice.

"All looks pretty burned up to me."

"Do you carry a comb or a brush on yourself, officer?" he asked with his eyes fixed on the fireplace.

"Huh?" the officer answered, still unsure of Ralph's question.

"What do you carry, comb or brush?"

"Neither. I got a crew cut," the officer said, removing his hat and gesturing towards his high and tight hairstyle.

"Well then go and find a bathroom and see if you can't find yourself a comb in there."

"Is my hair out of place?" Wayne asked, bewildered by the chief's order.

"Nope. Not at all. I just want you to go get a comb, bring it back here, and go through this fireplace with it. I don't like to assume that there ain't no clues left anywhere. Make sure the comb is a fine-toothed one. I'll find my way to the bodies. You come and get me when you either find something or are damn sure there ain't nothing to find. You hear?"

"Yes, sir," Wayne answered. "Uh, sir? I don't really have to go find a comb, do I?"

"Get on your knees and start digging through that pile of ashes," Ralph ordered, overemphasizing his Texas drawl.

Ralph needed to steel himself before walking into the room with the victims. He had seen gruesome murder scenes before but realized that he was not fully ready to see another. As he entered the room, filled with four officers, the county coroner, a photographer, and three lifeless bodies, Ralph felt his heart skip an important beat. His back found a wall to lean against as he calmed himself by whispering to himself a song he wrote when he was sixteen.

"Texas women are all the same
Ain't got no need to have a name.

Just give me one to call my own
And my broken heart will finally be sewn."

As he finished his song, Ralph found his legs again. He walked around the bodies as the deputies started with their questions.

"What do you think, chief?" an officer asked.

"We ain't never seen anything like this before up here," another one added.

"I guess that you have seen stuff like this before, huh, chief?"

"Yes boys, I have seen this before," Ralph replied, thankful that his voice was operational. "And this is what I need everyone to do. Everyone leave the room and wait outside until I call you in here. Everyone but the coroner, whose name I cannot remember."

"Germane Tamorssi. Nice to meet you again, chief. I only wish we could be meeting at a fund raiser instead of here."

"Me, too. Okay, everyone else out and don't go out of hearing range."

As the room emptied, Ralph was alone with Germane Tamorssi and the three dead bodies. He turned to the coroner while staring at each body individually. He learned from his days in Texas that emotions have no place in an investigation. He stared at the bodies as if they were clues and nothing more.

"Okay, tell me about this one," Ralph said as he pointed to the hat donor.

"His name is Roger Fay. He's a yearly."

"What's that? A yearly?" Ralph asked, puzzled by both the

term and the coroners Northern accent.

"That's what we call people who live up here year round. We got the summersets and the yearly's. His name is Roger Fay. Lives over in a trailer near Higgins Bay."

"You sure do have some strange terms up here," Ralph said.

The rumors that Ralph was a tad crazy were well known in the town of Arietta. Someone heard that he had snapped while down in Texas and probably brought his insanity up north with him. Despite that possibility, the folks in the town were glad to have Ralph on their side. So after Ralph's comment, Germane Tamorssi took a small step back and peered at him quizzically. "They're only strange if you're not a local. Anyway, cause of death is obviously a knife wound to the neck. He was killed outside against a tree and then carried in here. His neighbors say that Roger used to walk down this street every day. He was probably just walking past the center when the killer was doing his deeds. Wrong place, wrong time."

"Where are his shoes?" Ralph asked, noticing that Roger Fay was dead in blood-soaked socks.

"Neighbors tell us that they saw him wearing a black cowboy hat and cowboy boots. Both are missing."

"Sounds like we have a description of what the killer is wearing, huh?"

"Probably. This one," Germane said, pointing to the body of Doctor Jacob Curtis, "had his heart ripped out. Chest and everything just ripped through. The heart is over there in that bag," he said, motioning with his head to a bloodied, clear plastic bag. "His name is Doctor Jacob Curtis. Lives in Manhattan. From what his associates down in the city say, he came up here almost every weekend to work with the owner of this lodge."

"May I assume that this one here," Ralph said, pointing to the third body, "is the aforementioned owner of this place?"

"Actually, no. According to his driver's license and car registration, his name is Doctor Peter Adams. Lives outside of Chicago."

"Then, who owns this place?"

"Doctor William Straus. Location, unknown, but his car was spotted tearing down Route 8 around the time we figure these murders happened."

"We put out an APB on him yet?

"That's more for your department to handle, chief."

"I suppose. Starting to like that Straus fellow for this whole scene."

"That's not what your officers are saying," Germane said.

"I'll deal with that later. Tell me, cause of death of this here Doctor Peter Adams."

"Cause of death was sharp blow to the skull with a blunt instrument. Maybe a sledgehammer. He didn't die right away. I guess that the doctors here have been working together for years. I think that..."

"I don't want to interrupt but please don't say anything more about what you may think. If I have everyone yapping at me what they all think, then I'll never get to ask the questions I need to ask.

Thank you. Please wait out in the hall with the others and tell whoever done all the fingerprints to come on in."

Germane Tamorssi left without questioning Ralph and instructed Officer Mark Grace to go see the chief. "Yes, sir," Mark said. "You wanted to see me?"

"Did you do the fingerprinting in here?"

"Yes, sir. I did. Found only four sets. Two of the sets belonged to the two doctors here and two other sets from people who aren't here. The fingerprints are everywhere in both rooms. One thing that is interesting is that the only sets of fingerprints in the bedroom over there," Mark said as he motioned towards the adjoining room, "are those that probably came from the killer. And I don't know if you checked out the bedroom yet, but the someone who lived in there was someone that the doctors didn't want to let out."

Ralph, surprised that he hadn't noticed the two-inch thick rope lying stretched across the length of the room's floor, said "Now what the hell do we have here?"

"We figured it out, chief," Mark Grace said. "See, the rope attaches to that hook on the bedroom door." He walked over to the large, steel door that separated the living room where the bodies were found from what appeared to be a bedroom. He expected that his chief would follow him to the door but instead Ralph stood staring at the rope, following it until the rope disappeared into the ceiling.

"I'm listening. Keep talking," Ralph said to Mark.

"Well, that rope attaches to this metal hook on this door. The rope runs across the room, into the ceiling then comes back out in the hallway outside. You probably missed it, but there's a ratcheting contraption in the hallway. The rope runs into the ratchet. We haven't tested yet, but it looks like once the rope is hooked to this door, the ratchet system pulls the rope tight and makes this door impossible to open. Pretty ingenious."

"Sounds like whoever or whatever was living in that bedroom was someone that these good doctors wanted to contain."

"That's why we all think..."

"Thank you, officer," Mark said, stopping Mark Grace mid-sentence." Ralph inspected every inch of the rope and system and wondered why it was made. He was sure that whoever lived in the bedroom was a suspect, but couldn't imagine why the doctors would have a prisoner living there. And he wondered where the doctor who owned this lodge was and what may have happened to him.

"The doctors were both psychologists," Mark added. "Maybe the person who lived in the rooms here was a violent patient."

"A violent patient who escaped, it looks to me. Did you send those prints to a lab somewhere?"

"Yes, sir. Results aren't in yet."

"Thank you, officer. Tell me, who saw the lodge owner tearing down Route 8?"

"Adam Patterson and his wife. They're yearly's. Live over on South Shore road. And the owners name is Doctor William Straus, in case you forgot."

"Did the yearly's mention if Doctor William Straus was alone or if he had company in his car?"

"They said he was alone but couldn't be sure. He was moving at a pretty good clip."

"Anyone try to find out if Doctor William Straus has a cell phone we could call?"

"Not that I know of, chief. Want me to do some digging?"

"Dig away," Ralph said, finally removing his gaze off the rope and into Mark's eyes. "Nice job in here, officer. Now, do me another two favors, would you?"

"Anything, chief."

"While you're digging for Doctor William Straus's cell number, find out what kind of car he drives and send in whoever inspected the rest of the house."

* * *

For the next two hours, Ralph interviewed every person in the cabin. Ralph learned that several things had been taken from the cabin, including the contents of a wall safe, food, clothes, and some medical equipment. When he was done talking to everyone individually, he left the room where the bodies were, told the coroner to inspect the bodies for any other clues, and then assembled his team in the great room of the cabin. He pulled himself to his full five foot seven frame, wrenched his pants up and over his girthy beer belly, and waited for everyone to quiet down.

"Gentlemen, what we have here is a murder. Three murders, all most likely perpetrated by the same person. We can assume that the suspect is the person who lived in that prison-like room. We can assume that the doctors were afraid of him for some reason, and we can assume that they were trying to fix whatever was wrong with the person who lived in that room. We can also assume that the other victim, Roger Fay, was simply in the wrong place at the wrong time. Basically, we can assume a hell of a lot until we find out what the hell was going on in this place.

"Now, I'm betting that none of you have ever seen a murder scene before. And I am sure that some of you may be nervous as hell about your role in this investigation. I have done this before. Trust me. I know y'all think that I am crazy, but I'm tasking you to trust me. I am only as crazy as I need to be. No more, and no less.

"This cabin is now our headquarters. I like to be close to my work when doing something like this investigation. We cannot forget that we have a whole lot of other people who live in this town who are going to be scared out of their right minds once they hear about these murders. Don't forget that your job is to protect and to serve. This investigation is going to take up a lot of man-hours, but you cannot neglect your other duties. In order that the other duties don't get neglected, I am going to ask that officer Mark Grace and I do all the full-time work on this case. Everyone else will be doing some things now and then, but mostly you are going to keep on doing your jobs.

"We will catch this bastard, or if there is more than one, these bastards. I promise you and your families that. I need you all to keep this quiet for as long as you can. The last thing we need is some type of panic going on. Everyone understand?"

All agreed with Ralph and their roles in the murder investigation.

"Thank you. Now, before y'all leave here, I need two deputies to do a little legwork for me. I need one to go to every house on this street and see if anyone saw anything. Other than that, everyone is free to get their asses back to work. Thank you. And remember, quiet on all this for as long as possible. If the press…" Ralph paused, searched the faces of those assembled around him, "You do have a press up here, right?"

"Yes Chief. We even have a newspaper," one of the assembled replied sarcastically.

"Good. Well the press is probably outside this cabin already. Tell them that we are investigating a murder and that you have no further information. That's all."

Chapter 9

"How did you find out about the murders and that your twin brother was the prime suspect?"

"I got a call, well, actually, my parents got a call from a Ralph Fox. He's the chief of police in the town where the murders happened," Thomas responded.

"And up until that call, neither you nor your parents had any idea that your brother, their son didn't die in the hospital on the day you two were born?"

"It was quite a surprise. Pissed my dad off, I can tell you that much."

"I'd imagine," Derek said. Derek stood up, stretched his back and motioned towards a path that led from the nearest parking lot to where he and Thomas were talking. "There must have been some doctors at the hospital where you and your brother were born that were complicit in this whole thing."

"Yes," Thomas responded. "Doctors Rinaldo, Mix, Adams and Zudak. Adams was one of the doctors killed over in Piseco Lake."

"And these doctors, Rinaldo, Mix, Adams, and Zudak, have you or your parents had a chat with them yet?"

"One of them, Zudak, called my parent's house last night. They had left already, but I heard the message. Said he wanted to explain everything to them. He left his cell number and said that he won't be staying in one place for too long until the killer is captured."

"And the others?"

"No. I haven't spoken with them. Neither have my parents, as far as I know. As soon as we were told about Alex and that he was suspected in the murders, we figured we better protect ourselves. Honestly, it took a lot of persuasion on my part to get my parents to get out of town.

"Before they left and once I told them that I was staying put, my dad suggested that I talk to my uncle, his brother, about contacting you. So that's what I did."

"Did they try to convince you to join them?"

"Of course, but they agreed that I should work with you to get answers."

Derek began moving towards the path to the parking lot and gestured with his head that Thomas should follow. "I want to visit with these doctors first. Not that I doubt your story, but I need to confirm things with the people who were there. Any idea where they might be located?"

Thomas thought. "Actually, I do. After I called you and arranged this meeting, I did some searches. Mark Rinaldo retired from Saint Stevens over three years ago but still lives in the area. Stanley Mix got married to a nurse who cared for Alexander while he was in Hilburn. They live outside of Rochester, New York. I don't know anything about the doctors down on Long Island that hid my brother from the world, but I know their names are Lucietta, Curtis and Straus. And I already told you about Zudak."

"You have addresses?"

"I do. Thought you might need them."

Thomas handed Derek a folded up sheet of paper that he retrieved from the front pocket of his neatly pressed gabardines.

"But you haven't contacted them at all?"

"Nope. Not sure if I could contain my anger if I did."

"Good," Derek said, as he quickened his pace towards his car. "I'm going to pay a visit to Rinaldo, hoping that he's at home. Then, I'll give Zudak a call. Depending on how my calls go, I think I'll head out to Piseco Lake and check out the crime scene."

"Why would you go out there?" Thomas asked. "Alexander isn't there anymore. He's probably either in Chicago or is heading this way."

The look of concern was clear on Thomas's face.

"You may be right, but if I am going to track his movements, I have to start where he started moving. I'll keep in touch but you need to get somewhere safe. Do you have a place?"

"Yes. I can go to. ."

"Don't tell me where you're going. Trust me, I don't need to know. All I need to know is that I can get in touch with you on your cell phone and that wherever you are headed is safe and that you'll stay put. Understood?"

"Understood."

As they reached the parking lot, Thomas stopped in his tracks and said, "What will you do if you find Alexander?"

"I don't think that far ahead. You just get your ass to wherever it is that you are going, and stay there until I tell you otherwise."

"Okay. And will you give Mark Rinaldo a message for me?"

"Depends on the message," Derek said.

"Tell him that no matter what happens to my brother, that he hasn't heard or seen the last of the O'Connells."

"Sounds like a threat."

"No threat. Just a promise that he will pay for the lies he told. Him and that whole team of his. My father is already in contact with his lawyer. That asshole Rinaldo and the entire team will be behind bars the second this whole mess is cleaned up."

"Behind bars may be the safest place for them if we don't stop your brother," Derek said. "And, by the way, did that Ralph Fox say anything else when he spoke with your parents?"

"Just that they found a list in what they believe was Alex's bedroom."

"And what was on that list?"

"Names. Rinaldo, Mix, Zudak, Adams, Lucietta, Straus, Curtis, my parents, and me. Two of the names had been crossed out in what looked like blood. Adams and Curtis, two of the three killed so far."

"No one else made the list?"

"I haven't seen the list. Like I said, my parents had the talk with the cop, and they told me everything. At least it seemed like they told me everything."

Derek opened his car door then paused in thought. "You mentioned that there were three murders. Adams and Curtis. Who was the third victim?"

"Don't know. My parents told me that Fox said the other victim was probably just in the wrong place at the wrong time."

"Do you know if Ralph Fox contacted the other doctors yet?"

"I have no idea. He just told my parents that he suspected that Alexander is my brother, that he killed three people, that he had a list of names, and that my parents and I were on the list."

"I don't understand why your parents made the list. Is there any way that they knew about Alexander and were part of the doctor's plan?"

"No way. No way in the world," Thomas said. "You should have seen their faces when they were telling me what Fox told them. That Alexander didn't die on the operating table at Saint Stevens but was wanted for a triple murder."

"Why do you think Alexander added your parents to the that list?"

"I have no idea. They weren't involved at all and are as much of victims as Alexander. You know that my parents, especially my mom, visit the cemetery every week since Alexander died? Or at least, since they were *told* he died."

"But I'm sure your parents were part of at least the decision to do the surgery that cut Alexander off from your heart? I'm not a doctor but I have to believe that your parents had a voice in the decision."

"Sure, but they have nothing to do with what those bastards did after Alexander and I were separated."

"How much did Fox tell you about what the doctors did?"

"My parents spent at least forty-five minutes on the phone with him. I never spoke with the guy. My parents filled me in with as much information as they could get from the talk with Fox. We still have way more questions than answers at this point."

"Humor me, please, and tell me as many of the details of the conversation with your parents as you can."

"Fox told my parents that there was a strong possibility that their son Alexander did not die like the doctors at Saint Stevens said he had. He said that he was reading a lot of notes that went back to 1992 and had a lot of questions for all of the doctors."

"And did he say what those notes contained?"

"He said that he didn't know what to make of most of them. He said that it sounds like something 'fishy' happened, and he didn't know what to believe yet. But, he was pretty certain that my brother was not dead. Too many notes referencing the doctors at Saint Stevens and my parents to not think Alexander was still alive."

"Before your parents left," Derek said, "you're sure they didn't contact any of the doctors from Saint Stevens?"

"The only calls I know they made were to my dad's lawyer and to the airline."

"When did their flight leave?" Derek questioned.

"About two hours before I met you here. They should land in another hour. Since I highly doubt Alexander, or whoever is behind these murders, will be able to find them, I don't think it's dangerous that you know where they are."

"You never know, so please don't tell me where they are staying. I know they're in the Bahamas, but I don't need to know exactly where. It's a big ocean down there and lots of places to be."

Derek sat behind his steering wheel, turned on the engine of his Buick, and nodded to Thomas. "I will wait here till I see you get in your car, start it, and drive off. I will be in contact as needed. Get to where you're going and stay there. Understood?"

"Got it. And Derek? Can I call you Derek?"

"Derek is fine."

"If you do find Alexander, please don't kill him. He is my brother, you know, and I'd actually like to meet him. I know my parents would, too. At least my mom would. Honestly I'm not sure about how my dad feels."

"You didn't hire me to kill anyone, and I don't kill people as a rule. All I care about is keeping you and your parents safe. Now go."

"Okay. But if things get rough, please don't kill Alex. Promise me."

Chapter 10

The man who answered the doorbell's ring seemed disappointed. He had the look that only someone expecting someone else can display.

"Doctor Rinaldo?" Mark questioned.

"Yes," the aging man answered.

"My name is Derek Cole. I'm a freelance detective and have been hired by the O'Connells ..."

"Come in," the doctor said as he dropped hold of the door handle, turned and shuffled back into his home. "I didn't expect someone like you, but I'm not surprised, either." His speech was slurred just enough that Derek could both fully understand his words and know that happy hour was growing long.

As Derek followed his host into the home, he could see that recent half-assed attempts had been made to clean the house. A single four-inch, arching, dust free path was clearly visible on the table that stood just inside of the double-door entryway. A discarded paper towel lay wadded up on the ground beneath the mirror that greeted visitors on the eastern wall of the entry. In the room to his right, a room Derek assumed to be a study; a Dyson vacuum cleaner was carelessly left, still plugged in and leaning against the far wall. On the study's solid birch and mahogany desk, adorned with a

MacKenzie Childs desk lamp, sat piles of paper that were spilled across the desk but still spoke of the days when the desk and its contents were never out of alignment.

Derek followed him through an entry way clearly designed to impress visitors and into the living room off to the left of the entry. Mark Rinaldo gestured with an indifferent hand towards a brown leather sofa as he dragged himself towards a Bristol leather accent chair that sat across from the sofa.

Mark Rinaldo sat down in his spacious, very well appointed living room, holding on loosely to a tumbler filled with some brown liquor. His home was in a cul-de-sac full of million dollar homes, and while the home of Mark Rinaldo had among the best curb appeal, it was obvious to Derek that outside appearances do not always equate to inside beauty. "Sit, if you want. Stand if you prefer."

Derek sat, removed his Moleskine Notebook, and let his eyes wander until the doctor sat with a heavy and exaggerated sigh. "My wife decorated every square inch of his place. Spared no expense," he said. "No expense was spared. Not even when it came to the type of paint the contractors used in the closets. Top shelf, head to toe."

After refusing an offered drink, Derek asked, "And your wife? Will she be joining us today?"

"Thirty-nine months ago, I announced that I was going to hang up my stethoscope. Retire early. Fifty-five years old. Gerti was happy as hell. Oh, sure, she loved being married to a doctor especially to a chief of medicine, but she knew that the job was hard on me. She was as happy the day I told her that I was going to retire, as she was the day we brought our son home from the hospital after he was born.

"The next day after I told her, I met with the board of directors at Saint Stevens, and I let them know my decision. No one was surprised. They knew I was getting tired of dealing with the job, the other doctors, and the damn insurance companies. They knew that once the government started shoving their noses into healthcare that they would have plenty of their more tenured doctors decide to call it a career.

"When I got home that night, Gerti was lying face down on the kitchen floor. She was alive, but something was wrong, obviously." Mark Rinaldo paused, pulled long and hard at his drink, emptying it in a flash. He reached over to the end table next to him where he had conveniently placed a bottle of Johnny Walker blue. He poured a heavy drink before continuing. "Brain tumor. That's what it turned out to be. Damn ironic, isn't it? That the day I announce my retirement and the day we should have spent making love and planning how we were going to spend all our money, was the same day we found out she wouldn't be around long enough to spend a dime of it.

"She died two months and eleven days after I announced my retirement. Horrible disease, that brain cancer. Ripped away her memories and turned her into someone I didn't even recognize. And she was the wife of the chief of medicine at one of the best cancer hospitals in the mid-west. Died just like anyone else. So, no Mr.

Cole, my wife won't be joining us today."

"I am sorry for your loss, doctor," Derek said. He knew that the doctor was at least two scotches into his day. "Doctor, I need to ask you some questions about an Alexander O'Connell."

"His name is Black. Alexander Black. And I know that he escaped and that he killed a few doctors and that he is coming for me. I got a call from some chief of police in New York. I also got an email from Alexander Black."

"An email?" Derek asked.

"An email. Must have been sent right after he killed Adams and the other doctor. What was his name? Curtis? Jacob Curtis I think."

"I am not sure of the exact names, but Curtis and Adams were the ones killed. According to my employer, they were both killed in a lodge owned by a Doctor William Straus over in Piseco Lake, New York," Derek confirmed. "The email, Doctor Rinaldo, what did the email say?"

"Oh, it was very polite. Short and right to the point. It said 'Doctor Rinaldo, can you tell me, please, who is buried in Alexander O'Connells grave? No need to send a reply. I'll stop over to collect your answer.' He signed it just 'AB.' I actually figured it was him knocking on my door when you showed up."

"Aren't you going to take precautions in case he does show up?"

"Precautions about what? About saving my life? Hell, no. I will get what I deserve."

Derek had seen unexpected reactions from hundreds of people. Some were his clients, and some were the targets of his client's displeasure. As he sat across from Doctor Rinaldo, Derek genuinely felt that Rinaldo truly had no interest in taking any precautionary steps to keep himself safe from whoever killed the three in Piseco Lake and all but said "You're next." Derek understood that he was having a conversation with someone who had already given up. "Can you confirm that the story I've been told about Alexander is true?" Derek asked as Mark Rinaldo finished and poured another tall glass of scotch.

"Not sure what you heard. But if you're asking if Alexander Black was born without a heart and that we screwed up and sent him to that asshole William Straus out in Long Island to cover our asses; if you're asking if that is true, then yes. It's all true."

Derek sat in silence at the confirmation. He wanted to believe the story that Thomas had given him but found it nearly impossible to do so. As he sat across from Mark Rinaldo, the man who started the entire series of events in motion with his decision twenty-two years ago, he began to see how that decision had worn on him.

"Not a day has passed that I didn't regret what I did. What I regret most is that I included other people in my decision." Mark stopped, slurped in the final drops of scotch left in his glass, then sat the glass down on the table next to the near empty bottle of blue. "And now, my decision has killed three people. Three people, dead because I panicked and chose the route of a coward.

"I hope that Alexander Black or O'Connell, whatever he wants to call himself, does come and pay me a visit. I'll tell him that everything was *my* fault. Everyone was doing what *I* told them to do."

"If his recent actions are any indications, you know that he will try to kill you?"

"I hope he does."

"I can get you somewhere safe."

"You believe in heaven, Mr. Cole?"

The question took Derek by surprise. "I suppose. I hope so, anyway."

"Well, I do. And I also believe that unless *I* pay for my sins, for what *I* did to Alexander, to his family and every doctor *I* got involved in this mess, that I won't be headed to heaven. My wife is there. I know that to be true, and I'd like to see her again."

"Doctor Rinaldo," Derek said, "back twenty two years ago, when Mrs. O'Connell gave birth, you are certain that one of the babies, Alexander, had no heart and only half of a lung?" Derek needed to be certain that he was very clear about the bizarre birth.

"Three doctors, myself included, all determined that the baby did not have a heart and was not breathing. Skin went blue then turned a horrible shade of gray. No color at all, that gray. Death gray."

"But the baby was still alive?"

"Depends on how you define being alive. Damn thing was moving around, eyes opened, kicking its legs. Kept gasping for air like a damn fish thrown onto the beach." Mark Rinaldo reached for the bottle of blue. He paused, looked at Derek, and then returned his empty hand to his lap. "We had no idea what was keeping that child alive. No idea. And I had no idea what to do in a situation like that. How could I have any idea? There wasn't a policy in place about how to deal with a heartless baby that was still alive. I made the only choice I could think of.

"Now, I didn't know what the hell was keeping it alive and really had no idea what to do. But I'll tell you something, Mr. Cole," Mark said as he leaned closer to Derek, his scotch soaked breath heavy in the air, "I know now what kept it alive."

"And that would be?"

"Evil, Mr. Cole. Evil and sin kept that baby alive that day and every day since. My sins, your sins, the sins of the whole damn world. Nothing short of evil could do that, Mr. Cole. Nothing short of evil."

The room's air was cut with a chill of uneasiness. Of fear. Of doubt. Of imagined terrors.

"Once Peter Adams," Mark paused at the sound of that name, "and Stan Mix took that baby out of my hospital and brought it to Straus and his band of misfits, I tried to forget the whole damn thing. Tried to pretend it never happened. I even went to the funeral for Alexander O'Connell and found myself actually forgetting that the body buried in that grave was that of a stillborn baby that was about to be destroyed. Destroyed like garbage, Mr. Cole. That's what hospitals do with dead babies that parents don't want to bury. We destroy them and make it as if they were never even born. They're nothing. Just a mass of tissue. Dead, useless, unloved tissue, Mr. Cole.

"I never went back to that grave, and if it weren't for Peter Adams, I never would have even thought of the real Alexander O'Connell ever again. Peter insisted that he keep communications with Straus. That we kept updated with his progress. That asshole Straus was convinced that he'd be the one to figure out what was keeping Alexander alive and that he would become rich and famous. Bastard thought that he'd discover some cure for every disease known to man.

"Did you hear anything about William Straus, Mr. Cole? The cop who called me didn't mention his name except to ask if I knew his whereabouts."

"Nothing, and I assume you don't have any idea where he might be?"

"No idea. But I almost hope he is hiding in some god-awful place. I almost hope that Alexander finds him before he finds me. That's how I feel about Doctor William Straus. He's just another sin in this world. Another reason for Alexander Black."

Derek knew that trying to convince Mark Rinaldo to protect himself was futile. He knew that Mark wanted, or felt that he *needed* Alexander to kill him. To purge him from his sins and from his guilt. To reunite him with his wife. "Doctor, I don't agree with your thoughts about not doing anything to protect yourself in case he comes looking for you, but I respect your decision."

"Please don't patronize me with respect. I don't deserve any of that," he said as he quickly reached for and emptied the bottle of blue into his glass.

"Understood. But please understand that I have been hired to protect the O'Connells and that I take my job very seriously. Is there anything you can think of that will help me do my job?"

"Find Doctor William Straus. He knows everything you need to know."

"How about Doctor Stanley Mix and his wife?"

"Leave them the hell alone!" Mark screamed. "They were the lucky ones. They found each other because of this mess. They have a life. A good life. Don't involve them, you hear me?"

"They are already involved, doctor. I'm sure they've been notified about what happened in Piseco Lake. I learned that someone, probably Alexander, had a list of names. Your name and Stanley's name was on that list."

"And Michelle? Was her name on the list?"

"No. It wasn't on the list, as far as I know."

"Then keep it off," Mark said.

"That's really not up to me," Derek said as he stood, knowing the conversation had given him all the information it was going to provide.

"If they know what happened, they are smart enough to take precautions. The police will certainly want to investigate their involvement. But I've already told Stanley to deny absolutely everything. Michelle is involved only because she worked for that asshole Straus. *Leave them alone!* If the police find out that you were looking for them, they'd figure out that Stanley was involved from the beginning."

Knowing that arguing with Mark would serve no purpose; Derek agreed not to contact Stanley or his wife, Michelle. He knew that the police would discover what happened and would find out the names of every player in this drama. Derek knew that anyone whose name was on that list would have to pay. He was determined to protect his clients first, and then do whatever he could to make sure that the people on that list paid their obligations to the law and not to Alexander Black.

As he left Mark's home, Derek again suggested that Mark at least think of getting out of town. When his suggestion was returned only with a slamming door, he headed back to his car. Once in his car, he called the US Airways reservation number and booked the next flight out of Chicago to Albany, New York. He then tried to contact Henry Zudak, but his calls, three of them, went straight to voicemail.

"I hope you are somewhere safe, Doctor Zudak," Derek said.

Chapter 11

The earliest flight Derek could book was scheduled to depart Chicago's O'Hare airport at 9:58 p.m. that same day. As he glanced at the digital clock in his Buick Lacrosse, Derek realized he had time to kill. Time to think. To plan out his next steps. To figure out what he would do if he came face to face with Alexander Black and what story he would give to the police if and when they asked him for details.

In the three years that Derek had been a "freelance detective," he had made several friends on police forces across the country. While none of these friends would ever invite Derek in on one of their investigations, he knew that if he ever got into a situation, they would have his back.

He also knew that he had made plenty of enemies during his three years of freelance work. To many, what Derek did was "real police work" and, as such, should be left to the professionals. He was seen as a danger, an outsider, a nuisance to many police departments. Though Derek never intentionally broke any laws, his freelance status allowed him to cut corners that police detectives couldn't.

"We have protocols to follow, Cole!" he was often told. "You go running into situations, doing whatever you think you should do and next thing we know, our whole case is blown because you didn't follow protocol."

While Derek had made some mistakes when he first started freelancing, those mistakes were never repeated as he gained more experience. He learned better how to do his job while assisting and not interfering with the "real police detectives' work."

Over the last few years, Derek had helped police departments that were often understaffed and overworked to solve crimes that would have otherwise gone unsolved. Though he had only been involved in less than thirty cases since going freelance, his skills were sharp and his reputation was, for the most part, stellar.

Still, the average detective in an average police department wanted nothing to do with any "freelancer."

At least not publicly.

Many of the cases that Derek was hired to solve or resolve were also cases that a local police or sheriff's department was involved in. Though few would ever welcome Derek's involvement in front of others, many would quickly learn to appreciate what Derek could do and how he could help their cases.

"I don't need any credit once we solve this case," he would tell anyone on any police force that would listen. "My credit comes from my client paying me. I can be as invisible as you need or want me to be."

Derek's ability to avoid complying with protocol and "police procedures" gave him a unique, and often times, envied advantage over a police department's officers. When a house couldn't have access gained without a search warrant in hand first, Derek was able to get in without having to wait for some judge to "weigh the rights of the person against the expected and possible evidence that may or may not be found." When a suspect needed to be spoken to and was "less than agreeable," Derek didn't have to honor a request for a lawyer to be present and didn't have to worry about what was being seen on the other side of a two-way mirror.

He was no vigilante, and he tried very hard to follow the police procedures that needed to be followed. But when push came to shove, as it often does in the world of "good guys versus bad guys," Derek took care of business. It was his clients, after all, to whom Derek was responsible. If they needed something resolved, and the desired resolution was legal, Derek would get it done. One way or another, Derek always delivered the desired resolution.

As he drove to the airport, Derek made a few more calls. The first was to the Hertz reservation line, where he rented a mid-sized car to be picked up at the Albany airport.

"And how long will you be needing this vehicle, Mr. Cole?"

"Can we leave that open for now?"

"I'm sorry, sir. We do need a time frame."

"Four days, and if I need to extend or shorten the rental?

"Just call us back, and we'll take care of you, Mr. Cole."

The next call he made was to Verizon's 411. "Name and listing for a Doctor Stanley Mix. I believe they live near or in Rochester New York," he asked.

"I'm sorry," the computerized voice responded, "that number

is unlisted."

"Damn," he said.

He dialed the next number and waited for his call to be answered.

"Hello?"

"Thomas, it's Derek."

"How did your meeting with Rinaldo go? Did he deny everything?"

"He confirmed everything. Listen, you did some research, and I need a little help from you."

"What do you need?"

"Do you have the phone number for Stanley Mix?"

"Yes, but why do you want to call him?"

"His name is on that list you told me about, isn't it?"

"Yes, but I didn't hire you to protect anyone but me and my parents."

"Understood, but if I can make a call and let him know that he should take precautions, I don't think that would take any time away from my primary responsibility."

Derek hated when his clients went "freelance" themselves or grew impatient with whatever time it was taking Derek to provide a resolution. This client had already done too much research. Derek knew that people who do research end up acting on whatever information their research produces.

"Understood. You just find my brother and keep me and my parents safe."

Chapter 12

Derek loved flying. Something about being so distant from the ground. Unreachable with an assumed and accepted reason for being so. He loved passing through the clouds and the feeling of being invisible, if only for a moment. He loved the way the other passengers would tense during takeoffs then feel their stress dissipate as the plane blasted through the clouds.

It was the clouds he enjoyed the most. He wished that planes stayed in the clouds longer. Not just for a brief visit but for the entire flight.

As he sat in his preferred seat (exit row, window), Derek let his thoughts drift as the plane ascended into the clouds. As he looked through the window and saw clouds both distant and near, he imagined her face. Hoping to see some formation that would let him know that she was still with him. Watching over him. He remembered as a child, his mother, lying next to him in their backyard, telling him to look up into the clouds and tell her what he could see.

"Do you see that horse over there?" his mother would say, pointing straight up to a cloud formation. "Give it time, and use your imagination. You'll see it."

"I can see it! And I see a bird" Derek would exclaim. "And

over there is see a whale."

"I see it, too. Can you see any people up there?"

"I don't see any people. Do you?" he asked.

"I see Gramma and Grandpa sitting on a long bench, way over there," his mother said pointing off to the west. "And over here, I see your Aunt Stella."

But Derek, try as he might, could never convince himself to see any people in the clouds. No matter how strong his imagination may have been, he couldn't put heads on top of shoulders and legs beneath a torso.

Derek's parents were as middle-class as one could imagine. His father worked on the Ohio State Campus in the print shop for over thirty years, and his mother worked part-time at the college bookstore. Derek always felt that his parents would always be there for him. Supporting his decision when he told them he was going to join the army, his decision to re-enlist after his four-year hitch, his falling in love with and marriage to Lucy, and his decision to join the Columbus City Police Department.

His parents were with him each step he took, during each phase of his life. When Lucy was killed, it was his parents who tried to console him, to comfort him and to make sure that he didn't allow his grief to drive him so far away from them that they couldn't reach him.

When Derek told his parents that he had quit the police force, his parents only offered support.

"I didn't like you doing that work anyways," his mom said.

"I don't blame you at all, son," his father offered. "There are plenty of opportunities for a young man like yourself that don't involve risking your life every time you go to work. Plenty of opportunities."

But Derek wasn't interested in spending his days in a safe, practical job. He wanted to do what he could to make sure that someone else's wife wasn't murdered because a police force had to follow protocols.

"I'm going to start my own detective agency," he told his parents.

"Like a private investigator?" his mother asked.

"Sort of. But more like a private detective."

"Oh Derek, I'm not sure about that. There are too many bad people out there. Too many for even the police to handle."

He thought of Lucy and the "bad person" who the police couldn't handle. He thought of her face, her pleading eyes, staring at him through the bank's front window. "That's exactly why I want to do this," he said.

It was the way he said it that told his parents that his decision was already committed to and nothing they could say would convince him to take a more practical and safe job.

Starting a "freelance detective" agency wasn't easy at first. Derek had no idea of how to get his name out in the public. He started with Google Ad Words, a dedicated Facebook page and a website that he had custom designed.

Nothing.

For the first six months, the only public interest shown to Derek's agency was expressed by police agencies and private investigators.

"It's vigilantes like you who make it even harder for the 'real' police to do their jobs."

"Don't try to be cute with your title, Mr. Cole. A catchy title won't make up for the fact that you have very little actual police experience."

Derek also received a few emails from prospective clients. All of those turned out to be people looking for some "less than legal" work to be done.

It wasn't until his seventh month in business —when his savings were all but dried up —when he signed his first paying client. Derek was hired to locate an accountant who absconded with over $500,000 from the firm where he was a partner. Following the leads his client gave him and his uncanny ability to read people, Derek located the accountant six days after his services were retained.

"That was some impressive work," his client told him. "The police had no chance of finding him. Their trail went cold two days after the money was stolen."

Derek received fifteen percent of the recovered money. More importantly, he earned a very satisfied client who promised to "spread the word."

Clients then began streaming to Derek. One after another, Derek accepted cases that, for whatever reason, the local, state, or federal authorities couldn't solve. His reputation was building, and Derek was sure that his parents would now be proud of their son and his bold decision to start his own detective agency.

But now he was sitting in a plane, desperately trying to see something in the clouds that he had never been able to see before. He wondered why so many people—other people—told stories of being visited or of receiving a sign. And why he, as hard as he tried to see and to hear, never received any sign that she was still with him.

As the plane rose through and then above the clouds, Derek turned his gaze to the horizon. In the distance, he could see nothing but a blanket of clouds falling ever further from him and a dark sky above. He craned his neck, hoping to see something in the stars that were visible. Somewhere, off in the distance, he knew that the sky and clouds would meet. Maybe there, he thought, is where he would find a sign. A token of hope that she was waiting for him to notice.

She had been gone for over three years and for three years Derek had struggled to remember her face. Not the face he could easily remember by looking at pictures, but her face when her smile was not for a camera, but for him.

The only memory he could easily recall of her face was a poison to him. That final vision of her face, pressed against the glass, the consuming blackness of the pistol held against her temple and, behind her terrified face, his face. The face of the man whom Derek had never seen before and whose face he could recall in greater detail than the face of his own wife.

As he sat thinking about Lucy, he found his fingers tracing the scar on his left cheek, recalling the pain, the depression, the anger that caused the scar. He remembered the look on his mother's face when she arrived at the hospital. How his father looked at him as he leaned against the far wall of Derek's hospital room, seemingly wishing the room was five times the size but still glad he could be there for his son. He remembered the embarrassment he felt when he explained what had happened and how he knew the doctors didn't believe his story.

"Can I get you anything to drink?" a flight attendant asked. She was leaning in close to Derek, closer than she did to any other passenger. She was attractive, no doubt, and she seemed to Derek to be the type of woman who understood the effects her appearance had on men.

"Scotch, on the rocks, please," he answered, shaking the memories from his mind.

"We only have Dewar's. Is that okay?"

"Fine. Dewar's is fine."

"Fourteen dollars, and we only take cash."

"Make it a black coffee and a glass of water. No ice."

Derek retrieved his Moleskine Notebook from his backpack and began reviewing his notes. It had only been a few hours since his first meeting with Thomas O'Connell and after accepting the case, yet he had heard and seen so much. He felt, as he studied his notes, that he was missing something. Something that he needed not to miss. Something that shouldn't be missed.

Whether it was the fact that he was charged with the protection of a family from their own child, born without a heart, or the succumbing nature that Mark Rinaldo adopted as his punishment for his actions over twenty years ago, something was not adding up.

And why was Thomas not concerned about meeting him in a place as public as a park? Sure, the reason he gave was valid, but still someone truly in fear for his or her life would at least seem nervous or uncomfortable sitting out in the open.

"The killer could be anywhere," he thought, trying to dispel his suspicions. *"The fact is that someone killed three people exactly where Thomas said three people were killed. Fact. And the doctor who started this whole mess and who received a message from the assumed killer confirmed his story about his brother. Fact. And since the police are obviously looking for the killer, it wouldn't make sense for the killer to walk around, looking for his next victim in a public park. Opinion."*

The flight attendant returned with two bottles of Dewar's White Label in one hand and a plastic cup filled halfway with ice in the other. "I don't think anyone will miss two little bottles," she smiled. "These are on me."

"And if the pilot doesn't get us out of these turbulence, they may be on me, soon. Thank you."

She laughed a forced laugh and held eye contact with Derek a bit longer than what the joke deserved. "If you need anything else, you know where I'll be."

"Thanks again," Derek said.

After the flight attendant moved on, Derek scribbled some

notes in his book.

- *Find William Straus. Knows more than anyone else.*
- *Contact O'Connells. Why did they leave and not demand that Thomas join them?*
- *Check in on Rinaldo*

He closed the Moleskine Notebook, pushed off the overhead light, leaned back as far as he could, and closed his eyes. He was thankful that his wife's memorized face was not there to greet him as he closed his eyes.

"Where are you, Alexander Black, and what is your next move?"

* * *

The flight from Chicago to Albany, New York took just over one and a half hours. By the time Derek had sucked any remaining scotch from the melting ice cubes, it was time to return his seatback to its upright position. He didn't have enough time to plan out his next move but knew that he would have time as he made the estimated two-hour drive from Albany to Piseco Lake.

As the plane descended back through the clouds, he looked out of the window and again searched in vain for her face. The clouds were soon above him. Where they belonged.

When the plane landed and finished its taxi ride to the gate, the scotch-gifting flight attendant approached Derek.

"I hope you enjoyed the scotch," she said.

"I don't admit to this most people," Derek said as he removed his seatbelt, "but I love free scotch even more than I love cheap scotch."

"Well, if you're don't have to get to anywhere too quickly, I know a few places in Albany that have a whole shelf of cheap scotch."

Being hit on was nothing new to Derek. Though it made him uncomfortable while the "hitting on" was happening, it always made him feel good about himself. He worked hard at keeping his body in shape and knew that so many men took a more relaxed approached to fitness when they reach their mid-thirties.

But flirting also made Derek feel guilty. Though he no longer wore the wedding band that he and Lucy exchanged on the altar, he still felt married. Connected. Obligated, though he hated to feel obligated to someone or to something that he loved.

Lucy was dead. That he knew. He also knew she wasn't going to make a triumphant reintroduction. But she was still there. There in his heart, in his thoughts, in his mind's eye most every time he closed his eyes. He looked for her everywhere at first, not fully believing that something as simple and as abundantly manufactured as a gun could actually steal her away. To rip her out of this life and into whatever comes next.

After a while, he stopped looking for her, knowing that she was truly gone. To where, he didn't know. He often would wonder about what happens after. He hoped for the heaven he learned about in church and the heaven that he was promised from his priest. As the days that separated him from her grew greater, he began wishing that the decision of whether or not a soul is granted residence in heaven was up to the person to whom an individual caused the most harm to when alive. He imagined the bastard, standing before the pearly gates, knocking and waiting for the gates to swing open wide. He loved to picture the bastard's face when Lucy walked out and how he would respond upon learning that his fate now rested in her hands.

But he knew her heart. He knew she would let the bastard in through the gates. Even show him around the place, buy him dinner, and introduce him to her parents if he asked. She was too forgiving.

"You can't let people walk all over you, Lucy," he would tell her. "They take advantage of you."

But he knew that he couldn't change her. And he knew that he didn't ever want to. She made him want to be a better person. She allowed him into her own heaven, showed him around and showed him that what he was promised was already his.

"I wish I could," he said to the flight attendant who was now sitting in the empty seat next to him. "I have a long drive ahead of me and ..."

"Okay," she said and moved down the aisle as if the conversation hadn't happened. "It's your loss."

The flight attendant's response, sudden and swift as it was, caught Derek off guard. Though relieved, he wondered what he might have missed by rejecting her advances.

As he collected his overnight bag from the overhead compartment and began heading out of the plane, he felt his anger begin to build up. He didn't understand why his anger was making itself known, or what prompted it. He just felt it rising much too quickly.

Soon after her death, Derek's anger had a target, a place to call home. But three years after her death, his anger had lost its familiar target. It had no direction at times, no place to land.

He brushed past the flirting flight attendant and walked as quickly as he could up and out of the gangplank. He felt his anger building as he impatiently navigated past other passengers, all moving too slowly. His anger turned to rage when no one was manning the Hertz booth.

Then, as quietly and as quickly as his anger came, it dissolved as a fleeting memory of her face flashed in his mind. The face he wanted and tried so hard to recall. It was there, then gone before he could study it. Though he begged the memory to come back, all that he could see through his efforts was her face the moment before her life was finished.

"Can I help you, sir?" A young man, who had approached the Hertz desk asked. "Can I get you anything?"

Derek saw the clerk through watery eyes. He had grown used to his anger giving way to tears in an instant, but had yet to come up with a reason to give to compassionate others. "Sorry," he offered. "Long day. Damn yawning always makes my eyes tear up. I have a reservation under Cole. Derek Cole."

"Yes, Mr. Cole," the clerk replied. "Your car is all set for you." The clerk reached for the keys. As he retrieved them, both the clerk and Derek noticed a note was taped to the set of keys. "This must be for you, Mr. Cole."

Derek took the keys, separated the note that was taped to the key fob, and read the note to himself. "Welcome to Albany, Derek Cole," was all that was written on the note. "Where did this note come from?" snapped Derek.

"I'm not sure. I just got here at 8:00."

"Can you find out who wrote this note?"

"I could call the person who was working the counter earlier today but not sure if ..."

"Please call," Derek said.

"It's a little late to call now, don't you think?"

Derek glanced at his watch, realizing the late hour. "Listen, I'm going to leave my cell number with you. Please leave a note to have whoever knows who wrote this note to call me. Okay?"

"Okay, Mr. Cole."

"Please make sure that you alert the person who relieves you of my request."

"Okay. Shouldn't be a problem."

"It could be a big problem. A very big problem."

Chapter 13

Derek thought about getting a hotel room to catch a few hours of sleep, and then heading out to Piseco Lake and the cabin of Doctor Peter Straus. But once he was in his rental car, he thought that arriving at the lodge well before most people would be up and moving around would be a better plan.

It was close to midnight when he punched in the address of the lodge that his client had provided him. Once entered, the Hertz Never-Lost system estimated his time of arrival to be at 2:17 AM. It had already been a long twenty-four hours for Derek, and as he started his drive to Piseco Lake, he started to realize just how much had been packed into the space of a single day.

"Let's review," Derek said to no one. "We have what appears to be a baby born without a heart who is whisked away to be cared for by a doctor who has been referred to as an 'asshole.' We have a triple murder that included two doctors who probably cared for the aforementioned heartless baby and another victim who I have no idea about. We have a missing doctor, that being one William Straus, the supposed killer, that being one Alexander O'Connell or Alexander Black, depending on who you ask. Finally, a stranger leaves a note at my car rental place, welcoming me to Albany. And me without a clue as to what I should do next. Sounds like one of my typical cases!"

The directions to the lodge that the Never Lost system provided were spot on. As Derek drove his rented Ford Taurus passed the lodge, he noticed a few lights were on, but he didn't see any cars parked in or near the driveway. Yellow caution tape was stretched completely around the house.

He kept driving several hundred yards past the lodge until he noticed a small pull-off area on the right hand side of the road. Derek pulled his car as deeply into the parking area as he could, taking advantage of the low hanging tree limbs to serve as additional cover. He grabbed his notebook and a small flashlight from his backpack and decided to bushwhack through the woods to approach the lodge.

From the cover of the dense forest that surrounded the lodge, Derek could clearly make out the details of the two-story lodge. The lodge looked like it had been modified from its original build, with the main part of the lodge being a well-crafted log cabin and the modified section being shaped like a two-story dormitory that stretched 50 feet from the main cabin. He counted a total of three windows on each floor of the dormitory, assumingly bedrooms or offices.

One particular part of the dormitory structure was noticeably different from the rest of the structure. While the other windows were full-sized, the section that most interested Derek had very small windows, no more than one foot high. And while Derek couldn't be sure, it looked like the two small windows were barred. He also noticed that there were no windows on the second floor directly above this one area.

As he moved closer to the dormitory, Derek could see bushes were planted around the entire bottom of the structure. A quick flash of his light showed that the entire dormitory was elevated around ten inches off the ground.

He paused to listen to anything that might indicate someone being in the lodge or walking around outside. Hearing nothing, Derek got flat on his stomach, crawled through the bushes and under the dormitory. Once under, he clicked on his flashlight to see if anything looked peculiar. Immediately, he saw that a piece of the aluminum flashing, probably used to keep forest critters out of the dormitory, was partially opened.

He continued his crawl towards the open flashing as his mind began to wonder how many raccoons might be living under the dorm.

When he reached his target, Derek noticed that the aluminum flashing was cut into four by four squares and fastened into the floor joists. But the area of the flashing that was his target was without screws.

"One of three things happened here," he thought. *"One, a talented and gifted raccoon learned how to use a screwdriver. Two, the builders forgot to secure this one piece of flashing. Or three, someone removed the screws."*

He flashed his light across the entire bottom of the dorm, noting that every other piece of flashing was securely in place. He pointed the light from his flashlight to the ground beneath the hanging flashing and noticed a few scattered droppings of wood dust in the ground.

"Whoever removed these screws did so from exactly where I am right now," he thought.

Derek carefully pulled back on the flashing and saw that the insulation that had certainly been in place was removed. A quick shot of his flashlight to the ground revealed some remnants of the removed insulation. He reached his hand up the twelve-inch empty space and pushed gently on the floorboards.

An area of slightly more than two square feet lifted easily from his push.

"Easy access in and out of the dorm," Derek thought. *"Maybe this is how Alexander got out and was able to surprise his victims. But how the heck did he remove the screws from the flashing? He couldn't have done that from inside. Either he got out without being noticed to make his own modifications or someone else helped him."*

As quietly as he could, Derek pulled himself through the opening in the floor and into the dorm. He stood motionless for several seconds, his ears trained on any noise coming from the lodge. After hearing nothing, he clicked on his flashlight.

Chapter 14

Ralph Fox wished that he could sleep. His insomnia was a repetitive challenge he had faced several times during the last ten years of his life. He knew that staying at the lake-front-lodge-turned-crime-scene wouldn't do much good at ending his insomnia, but he also knew that this was exactly where he needed to be.

He had spent the better part of the last few days reading every note and medical record he could find in the doctor's small office. Most of the notes he read made no sense to him, but Ralph had learned not to doubt things he didn't fully understand.

As he made his way through the lodge's rooms, each decorated in the way one would expect an Adirondack lodge would be, Ralph carried a handful of papers and read them out loud, hoping some trapped memory in one of the rooms would explain the mystery contained in the doctor's notes.

Several times, he tried sleeping in one of the six guest rooms; only to be disturbed by a pressing need to "read that last note one more time."

"What we have here, ladies and gentlemen," he said openly to a vacant room, "is a mystery of the highest degree. And like any other mystery, this one has a puzzle piece that, once found, will unravel this whole thing."

But no matter how many times he reread the notes, the puzzle piece remained hidden.

Ralph was a loner, a man more comfortable being spoken about than spoken to. Though he didn't dislike people, he felt that there was an unbridgeable gap separating him from most others. His ex-wife often told him that he lived "contrary on purpose. Always trying to see things differently. Never just getting along just to get along."

And that's what Ralph could never understand: Why people would agree with what others were saying, doing, believing just to have something, real or imagined, in common. He felt lonely at times but also secure in knowing that the few people he called friends were true friends. People he liked because of who they were and who liked him for what he was.

His move from Texas to rural upstate New York was easy. Ralph didn't attach sentimental feelings to things and people who, he believed, would remain the same no matter the distance between them. In upstate New York, as Chief of Police in a small town, Ralph felt that he would be just another face in a scarce crowd. Someone who people would recognize but not feel compelled to speak to. He believed that moving over a thousand miles away wouldn't represent a fresh start, just a continuation of his life, but in a different climate.

It was close to 2:30 in the morning when he heard the sounds. Defying his body shape and his physical condition, Ralph moved with cat-like movements towards the sound. Silently retrieving his

Colt 45 from the kitchen counter where he had placed it while eating the rest of the sub sandwich he had ordered for dinner, he moved without a sound towards the rooms where the dead bodies had been just a few days prior.

He made sure to not assume what or who was making the noise; just find the source and take action as needed. The room's darkness was cut by a well-aimed and trained flashlight, at times covered by a hand, and then revealed in an intelligent and targeted pattern.

Ralph, knowing that the person directing the flashlight was unaware of his presence, held his Colt out two feet behind the flashlight and reached for the light switch on the wall.

Derek was unsure of what he noticed first: the overhead fluorescent lights filling the dark room or the sound of a revolver's hammer being set back into ready position.

Chapter 15

"If you could explain to me what the hell you think you're doing here, and if your explanation is good enough, why, I may just decide not to put a .45 caliber bullet into the back of your head."

"That's a lot of pressure to put on a guy," Derek said as he instinctively raised his hands above his head.

"Maybe so, but since I am the one with the gun, and you are the one with the Maglite, I have to believe that I hold the cards in this situation. That means that I call the shots. No pun intended, said the man holding the gun."

"My name is Derek Cole. Thomas O'Connell, who I believe is the brother of the perp you are looking for, retained my services. If you look in my wallet, you will see a card with the names of four detectives from four different police departments who will vouch for me."

"And I bet that wallet of yours in tucked neatly into your ass pocket?"

"Afraid so. I will use two fingers and will slowly remove it."

"Go ahead, but if I see something shiny and black come out of your ass, I'm not going to give you enough time to shoot me and spoil my evening."

As Derek slowly removed his wallet, he was thankful that his wife had chosen the brown wallet instead of the black one for the birthday gift she bought for him. He tossed it over his shoulder and heard it hit the floor. Ralph bent over, keeping his Colt fixed on Derek, picked up the wallet, thumbed it open, and saw the glossy business card tucked in between a few hundred dollar bills.

"So far, so good, Derek. Now I want you to turn yourself around and give me your undivided attention." Derek turned slowly around, his hands still in the air.

"So, let me ask you, what do you mean by 'your services?'"

"I am a Freelance Detective. My clients hire me to assist them in locating and resolving issues."

"Freelance Detective, you say? Now, I've been in law enforcement for a lot of years. But I have to admit that I've never heard of a 'freelance detective' during my years."

"I have some experience in the detective field. Eight years as an MP with the Army and three years with the Columbus, Ohio police department."

"Yippee for you. But that still doesn't explain what the hell a freelance detective is."

"I am retained by private clients to assist them ..."

"Yup, I kind of deduced that part already," Ralph said, cutting Derek off mid-sentence. "Let's try this a different way. Are you one of them private eyes?"

"Not really, but sort of."

"Well, that certainly clears up this whole situation."

"Sorry to be so vague."

"Is that what you call it? Being vague? I'd be more likely to say you are monkey punting around the truth. To me, 'freelance detective' sounds like something an assassin would call himself or herself, depending on the particular assassin. You an assassin?"

"Not at all. I don't kill anyone. Just locate them, isolate them, render them powerless if needed, and then alert local authorities. Basically, I do what a detective does, but I don't have to worry about following all the protocols."

"When I was down in Texas," Ralph said, pointing the Colt directly at Derek's chest, "I was the fire chief in my town's volunteer fire department. I always use to say there are two types of firefighters: one who follows the rules and listens to the officers, and the other type, who may or may not be as well trained, hell, may even be better trained, but goes off and does things the way he thinks they should be done. Come to think of it, I think I actually called that second type of fire fighter a 'freelancer.'

"Now, here is the problem as I see it, Derek. Freelancers get themselves into bad situations way more often than do those who follow the rules. And when a freelancer gets himself into a situation, me, as fire chief, would have to send someone else in to get the freelancer out of the situation. That means that I have to risk injury or death for one of my rule followers to save the freelancer's ass. Derek, I have to tell you that I don't like saving a freelancer's ass by putting my own ass or the ass of someone else at risk."

"I don't blame you at all. But let me tell you how I see things," Derek said.

"I can't wait to hear your side of things, Derek."

"Let's say that that freelancer's wife is trapped inside a burning building and the other fire fighters won't even try to save her because of protocol. Would you blame the freelancer for running in and at least trying to save his wife?"

"Can't say that I would."

"And if the freelancer was prevented from going in after his wife, who ends up dying in the fire, could you understand how the freelancer may feel about following protocol?"

"I suppose a man might be prone to think ill about any protocol that he thinks prevented his wife from being saved. I'm with you so far."

"Let me ask you, . . Uh, I don't know what to call you?"

"Let's start with referring to me as 'the only man in the room with a gun.' Unless you have something stuffed in your waistband."

"Nothing stuffed in my waistband Mr. 'only man in the room with a gun,' sir."

"Good to hear. Proceed with your story,"

"When I was on the police force in Columbus, my wife was held captive during a bank robbery gone bad. A spaced-out loser with a Glock held her and five others at gunpoint. I knew the bank and knew that I could get in the rear entrance, walk up, and pop the bastard before he knew what I was doing. But, I wasn't allowed to do it. I wasn't allowed to 'freelance.'

"Another ten minutes goes by, with me trying to convince my Captain that I could get in and make the whole problem go away. He kept telling me about the department's 'protocol' and how we needed to wait for a hostage negotiator. Then we heard the shots. Three of them. One for my wife, one for some eighteen-year-old kid, and one for himself. Bastard killed my wife and a kid, then shot himself dead in the head. So you see, Mr. 'only one in the room with a gun' how I may just feel about following protocols?"

"Turn around and face that wall," Ralph said without pause.

As Derek turned, he heard Ralph move closer, and then he felt himself being frisked.

"Okay, freelancing Derek, you can turn around now."

Derek turned to see Ralph lowering his Colt.

"The name is Ralph Fox. And just because I put my trusty peacemaker down doesn't mean that I won't pull it back up if you decide to do something stupid."

"Understood, Ralph."

"You said you were hired by a Thomas O'Connell, did you?"

"Yes sir. He hired me to protect him from his brother, Alexander, who my client believes has already killed three men. The three men who, I have to believe were found in this room."

"I'd say your client is right about Alexander killing people."

Derek looked around the room, noting the bloodstained couch and splatter stains on the ceiling and walls.

"What the hell happened in this room?" he asked.

"Something that was pretty damn fatal."

Derek, relieved from the stress he was feeling when a gun was being pointed at him, regained his level of curiosity.

"Not sure if you or your team discovered this yet, but there is a trap door under the bed here." Derek moved the institutional looking bed to reveal the opening in the floor.

"Son of bitch," Ralph Fox said. "My boys may not be the best in the world with all this police stuff, but you'd figured that all them State Police investigators would have noticed something like this. How did you find this out?"

"Luck, I guess," Derek said. "This leads to a crawl space under this part of the lodge. A square of the flashing had its screws and insulation removed. I can't say for sure, but to me it looks like this was done from underneath, not from inside this room."

"Like maybe the fella who resided in this here room had some assistance?"

"Seems likely to me."

"So, tell me Derek Cole, you said you were hired by Thomas O'Connell?"

"Yes. He is the son of Ken and Janet O'Connell, who I believe you contacted already."

"Yep. Called them the day after my boys discovered this scene. Found their names, and a whole lot of other names in a bunch of files in Doctor Straus's office. Found a lot of very interesting stuff as well. Medical reports, experiment results, names and addresses, and a stack of pictures. Some of them damn pictures are scary enough to scare the stink off a skunk."

"I'd love to have to look at those files," Derek said through a grin.

"I bet you would, now wouldn't you?"

"The story that my client told me, and that was confirmed by a Doctor Mark Rinaldo, seems a bit hard to believe. You find information in those files that referenced a pretty unbelievable story?"

Ralph gestured for Derek to follow him out of the bedroom, through the sitting room and into the hallway. Ralph didn't say a word until he reached the entryway of the lodge.

"Now what I found and whether or not it supports this story of yours depends on what your story is. Doesn't that make sense?"

"I was told that Alexander O'Connell, who may now be called Alexander Black, was reported to have died shortly after birth on account of him not having a heart. I'm no doctor, but I believe having a heart is pretty important."

"Well now, Derek, I have to say that you and I are on the same page with that statement."

"I also was told that the doctors in Chicago told the O'Connells that Alexander died and then formulated a plan to hide him away with a Doctor Straus. Straus ran an institution on Long Island."

"So far what you have said is in agreement to all that I have read and determined as well. But one thing you mentioned caught my attention. I would have asked about it a tad earlier but you seemed pretty excited about telling me the story you heard."

"And that was?" Derek asked, knowing that there was something about Ralph Fox that he liked. Perhaps it was Ralph's confidence in himself, his down to earth nature or just the fact that he hadn't shot him, Derek liked this guy.

"You indicated," Ralph said as he sat in one of the leather chairs that decorated the lodge's entryway, "that you had a conversation with a Doctor Mark Rinaldo. I gave Rinaldo a call right after I spoke with the O'Connells to let him know that we found his name on a bunch of medical reports as well as on a list."

"My client told me about the list. Told me the names that are on it and that two of the names were crossed out in what looked like blood?"

"Their own blood, to be exact," Ralph said. "Now Derek, you have a fine ability to take a conversation down a different path than what was intended. I'll get to that list in a while, but I want to have a bit of a conversation about Doctor Rinaldo if you don't object."

"Sure. Sorry. Lot's to digest with this case," Derek responded.

"As I was saying, I gave Rinaldo a call to find out some details that I may need in this here case and also to let him know that his life may be in danger. Told him that three men, two of them doctors, had already been murdered and that the perpetrator may be fixing to pay him a visit. He didn't shed any light on my case and didn't seem to care about my suggestions that he take some precautions."

"I got the same reaction when I visited with him in his house. He didn't seem to care if Alexander Black, or whoever is responsible for these murders, came after him. He said he deserved whatever happened."

"I always say that apathy is a telltale sign of guilt," Ralph said.

"So is guilt," Derek replied. "Rinaldo confirmed my client's story and told me that he deserves whatever Alexander has in store for him. I suggested that he get some protection, but I don't think he will."

"He didn't," Ralph said, his eyes fixed on Derek's.

"What do you mean?"

"Rinaldo was killed late last night in his home. Had his skull crushed."

Chapter 16

He held the world in contempt. Each person playing their part in a production of a critical mass of fools. Each striving to be counted as part of something that they erroneously perceived to be much greater than themselves. Each of them, nothing more than a variation of a single. Many faces of one. Mindless creatures guised behind pretentious intelligence and assumed superiority. Varying in their degrees, but all striving to satisfy the exact same set of needs.

They were followers, all of them. Each trying to fool themselves into believing in their uniqueness, in their ownership of being special. But actually, they were all the same. Bags of meat, of bones, of repeated thoughts. Shared, stolen, and borrowed thoughts. The same that have been thought for centuries, only altered by evolutionary processes. They were nothing but organisms dependent on each other, yet convinced of their own extraordinary ability to be their own expression. Some chose the comfort of conforming and others the importance of being contrary.

He didn't hate them; they didn't deserve such a powerful emotion. Nor did he pity them, for they were too far beneath him, and he, too far above to consider them worthy of pity.

No. They were obstructions, many of them. Others, potential tools.

Falsely intelligent, deviously blind preventers, and rendered such by their own DNA. They didn't need to be eliminated, only structured. Revealed. Yet he knew that revelation would only be for a very select few. The others would never become aware.

Why did they claim to be something that they could not possibly understand? Fools, all of them. And now they would see. If only through the vehicle of terror, they would see. He knew they would never be able to understand, but at least they would be given the chance to see.

He managed his way through their disorganized and ignorant attempts to domesticate him. Following the prescribed methods used for generations. Manners. Respect. Controlling emotions. Politeness. All of it learned as a bird learns to crane its neck higher than its nest-mates to grab the worm.

Simple and delicate and utterly unaware of the passing moments leading them closer to their own eradication. Finding perceived meaning in his agreement to their requests. Their leaders, nothing more than panderers to idiots. Saying what was to be considered correct and damning those of opposition.

He learned of their created answers to questions well beyond their comprehension levels. Saw them structure and organize these answers. Give them rules, rituals, rewards, all while he understood their reasoned need to stomp out other answers. Crushing threats under the pretense of immortality. One after another, the creators came, each with demonstrated evidence to disproof another's answers and offering a new one.

A parade of comical misery and guilt.

But each answer was folly and each nothing more than a trick of convenience. Born of opportunity and given life through the considered tragic conditions, caused by their own hands. By their own words. By their own dismantling of logic, reason, and tolerance.

Fools, every one of them. Grasping in the air for substance and believing, then testifying that the ether they held was solid. Reachable. Containable. But never malleable. Until another, wiser in the same train of thought, offered more irrefutable evidence.

For every organic spark, they assigned a common name. Each of those given the respect of efficient labeling, elevating himself or herself to a vaulted position. Discoverers of the obvious. The obtuse truth. Patting themselves on their own backs for seeing the blinding light in front of them. Rewarding themselves and those that they felt they needed to be in favor with.

Patience was not a gift, but a choice. For him, the choice was made consciously. Deliberately.

"Feed their imagined ego, and advance towards the only possible conclusion," he would remind himself. *"Trained discipline and calculated steps. One after another."*

It started with books. He learned about their feeble attempts to create an understanding that others could then point to as reference. He knew his captors, his unwitting suppliers, had lacked making the choice of patience. He knew that they were searching through him for their way to become a point of reference.

Doctor Straus and his team began offering him books to read

in order to distract him and to give themselves a break from the constant barrage of his questions. He would ask questions about nearly any topic and would only stop a line of questioning when he realized that he could gain no additional information from his captors.

The books started with history books, as they deemed to be the safest for him to read.

"History of Ancient civilizations?" he asked when, at six, Doctor Straus handed him his first book. "But Doctor Straus, I don't know how to read yet."

"I'll ask Doctor Curtis to provide you some reading lessons. A few lesson should be all it takes before you'll be reading completely on your own."

He took to reading very quickly. Within days, as Doctor Straus had suggested, he was able to manage his way through his first book. His questions tempered, more books were brought to him.

More history. Classic works of fiction. Outdated and replaced science. Mathematics.

The more books he was offered, the fewer questions he asked to the doctors. They were relieved and more than happy to offer him as many books as he wanted.

As other creators advanced in their imagined brilliance, books gave way. Though hundreds were used, invention rendered them debilitating in their pace and in their accessibility.

"Alex," he was told, "I've saved several articles for you to read. Read them then I will test your ability to recall them."

"From the Internet, Doctor Straus?"

"Yes, Alex. These are from the Internet."

He enjoyed the last decade of his life much more than he did the first. His years at Hilburn, were filled with aggressive treatments and invasive tests and sensing the growing impatience of the doctors. They made their expectations of him quite clear.

"Alexander, we have all made significant sacrifices and have put our careers at risk by caring for you. We feel that our requests of you to be a willing participant in our experiments are more than fair. The doctors who abandoned you with us have completely forgotten about you and, honestly, would rather never be reminded of you every again.

"But Alexander, we have cared for you, protected you from the public, kept you warm, fed you, and even granted you the opportunity to gain an education. We have never given up on you and will continue treating you as long as you promise to assist us and to never try to harm any of us. Do we have an understanding?"

"We do, and I appreciate all that you have sacrificed caring for me."

He didn't care if they fully believed him. Their hubris would allow them to believe in their irresistible influence over him. Once he added compliant actions to his promises, they would be controlled.

When Straus told him that "a move to a more secluded, quieter, and much more pleasant environment" was necessary, he agreed to be sedated during the transfer. To sedate him, the doctors couldn't just inject a sedative into his arm but needed him to drink a cocktail of drugs. Once consumed, his cells would transfer the sedative throughout his body, and the effects would be felt. They knew, from multiple experiments, that to sedate him could take as long as three hours. The only fast way to make him unconscious was by shocking him, and that method was too painful and too dangerous.

"If you still do not trust me, Doctor Straus, and feel you need to take this precautionary measure, I will offer no resistance. I am, however, disappointed in myself."

"Why is that?" Straus had asked.

"Though I have tried to demonstrate my trustworthiness and my appreciation for all that you have done for me, if you still lack confidence in my promises, I must have not done enough. Yet."

Doctor Straus had decided, more out of necessity and convenience than out of concern, which he needed to move his patient out of the once friendly and secure confines of Hilburn and up to the Adirondack Lodge that Straus had inherited from his father. The state of New York was continually slashing its funding to institutions like Hilburn and, twelve years after his patient had arrived, Straus received notice that Hilburn was scheduled to be closed within one year.

Having nowhere to continue to treat, examine, test, and hide his patient, Straus hired a contractor, who promised confidentiality in exchange for payment in cash, to make several modifications to Straus's lodge in Piseco, Lake New York.

"I need an addition put on," he told the contractor. "I plan to start renting out rooms to fellow doctors who need a quiet place to relax. However, I also need a suite of rooms designed to ensure maximum security."

"Plan on keeping criminals in your lodge, doctor?" the contractor from Connecticut asked.

"I believe our agreement includes confidentiality but does not require full disclosure. Am I correct?"

"Tell me what you want, and it will be done."

His patient was nearly thirteen-years old before the modifications were completed at the lodge. The timing was perfect, as the state of New York informed Straus that many of the buildings that comprised the Hilburn campus were already being leased to start-up companies. The main building was to remain open until all the patients were placed in community group homes, smaller state-run facilities, or psychiatric hospitals. What happened, however, was that some of the patients that once called Hilburn home were simply released into the public and left, for the most part, to fend for themselves.

Most of the Hilburn staff were offered transfers or early retirement packages. Straus and his core team were all given the choice of transfer or to accept a rather healthy severance package. Curtis and Straus took the severance while Lucietta accepted a transfer to a state hospital in Manhattan.

Straus's favorite nurse, Michelle Pettingal had resigned her position when Alex was only three years old. Though she never admitted it, Straus learned that she had married Doctor Stanley Mix and had moved somewhere in Upstate New York. Straus tried to keep track of Michelle as his desire to "have" her remained. But that desire eventually faded, and Michelle became nothing more than a pleasant memory.

On her last day of work, Straus made sure that Michelle would honor her commitment of keeping the story of Alexander Black quiet.

"I won't say anything, doctor. Honestly, no one would believe my story, and I would rather just forget everything about this place."

The outlook of being forgotten struck Straus deeply. After all he had done for her, how could she simply "forget" him? He had suspected that Stanley Mix and she were keeping in contact but never thought their contacts would turn romantic.

"I hope you keep your promise, Nurse Pettingal," he said to her as she handed in her staff badge and completed her exit interview. "But I do hope that you retain some pleasant memories of our time here together."

His time in the lodge, though confined to two rooms for the first several months, was when he began designing, testing, and refining his plan. While he continued acting as the willing associate to Straus and those who remained a part of his team, he continually looked for opportunities to expand specific knowledge. He knew that, despite his intelligence, he would be lost in the world. He lacked the skills needed to blend in, to properly engage others, even to find sustenance. He knew that his plan needed time, and time demands patience.

The first time he was allowed to leave the walls of the lodge was at night. The night sky was brilliantly clear. He sat on the damp grass behind the lodge and stared up at the stars for well over an hour, saying nothing and remaining perfectly still. He had read about stars, about constellations and the folk tales surrounding them. He had studied the moon and the planets, and had read several books filled with theories and speculations about the universe. As he sat, staring up at the night sky, he grew more convinced that life could not be learned from a book. That no matter how talented a writer may be, describing the simple light of a star with words was as futile as him trying to escape and live in the world he had only read about. That night, he decided how his plan would conclude. He also decided that the first steps of his plan were still many years away.

Over the years, he often asked to be allowed to walk to the shore of Piseco Lake. Each request was denied.

"There are too many risks involved, Alexander. While we have grown to trust you, we don't trust what others may do if they see you. I hate to have to remind you of this, but your appearance, Alexander, you don't look like the others."

He knew what he looked like, and he knew that his appearance would certainly disturb the public. He had been told, countless times, that the public would never understand him. They would, out of fear, restrain him and subject him to tests, much more severe and invasive that what he had grown accustomed to.

As the years rolled past, he continued to expand his

understanding of the world outside of the lodge. Occasionally, he earned the reward of going outside, feeling the sun warming his face, watching a storm cloud releasing its anger, or seeing the stars, reminding him of their mysteries.

As Straus had planned, the lodge became a popular place for big city doctors to spend their vacations. During the summer and fall months, it was common for Straus to have at least one guest staying in the guest rooms, one floor above his rooms. Each guest was told the same thing about him.

"I have a patient who lives here year round. He is an especially challenging and interesting patient; highly agoraphobic, paranoid, and extremely private. He pays me to ensure that he is left alone. I ask that you understand and respect his wishes and that you do not enter the first floor hallway. I assure you, he is as harmless as a butterfly, but his emotional stability would, I fear, crumble if anyone he hasn't learned to trust makes contact with him."

The few times that all of the lodge's rooms were filled with guests, he was sedated and either kept in his bedroom or relocated to a rented cottage in the nearby hamlet of Oxbow Lake. The days in the cottage were usually spent unconscious and always included an armed guard who liked to promise him that he would not hesitate in the use of his gun.

"I don't know what your story is, and I don't care. If Straus wants to pay me to babysit you for a few days, so be it. But I promise you that if you try anything, your head will explode."

He was strapped to the cottage's bed and secured with enough rope and wire to make any attempted escape impossible. And all the while he would lie in the bed, his babysitter would sit a few yards away, pointing his high-powered rifle towards his head and telling him what a freak he was.

As unpleasant as those days were, he used them as opportunities to study and to learn. The more exposure he had to the world and to those who lived in the world, the closer he became to fulfilling his plan. For him, the passage of the years did not bring him closer to his own end but rather to his own beginning. The more agreeable he was, the more rewards and privileges he was given.

Several weeks before his plan was launched, Straus awarded him with a privilege that seemed too perfect in its timing.

"Alex, I know how much you want to go outside. To go feel the lake as you have wished for. As long as you agree to my terms, I will allow you to walk with me to the lake. But I assure you, if you do anything that I even remotely think is an attempt to leave, I'll shock you."

"Why would I try to leave, doctor? Where would I go?"

They had learned of the impact that electricity, of being shocked, had on him. They were amazed at how quickly and how powerfully the slightest jolt would drop him to his knees.

"I need you to attach this to your ankle. Make it tight."

"What is it?" he asked.

"It's a training device for dogs. I'm sorry, but if you want to earn more privileges, you have to agree to my terms."

"Which ankle?"

Straus waited a few hours until Jacob Curtis joined him at the lodge. He wanted to be sure he had a backup in case his patient was able to subdue him.

"Jacob, I need you to make sure that no one is around. I want to take Alex outside, but I don't want anyone seeing him. All I need is for some local to start talking about the 'gray guy walking around Straus's lodge.'"

Jacob Curtis was gone for no more than a minute before returning.

"Can't see anyone. Rain is keeping people inside, I suppose."

Once Straus confirmed that Alex had tightly placed the shock collar on his ankle, he reminded Alex of his expectations.

"Now Alex, this is a privilege. I hope you understand the risks I am taking."

"I do, Doctor Straus."

"It's raining out which will make the shock from that collar a bit more severe, so I really hope you don't do anything to warrant its use. Just stay with Doctor Curtis and me, don't speak to anyone who may show up, and, for God's sake, don't try to run or swim away."

"I can't swim, Doctor Straus, and I have nowhere to run to and nothing to run from," he answered.

The gray sky matched his complexion. The light rain that was falling felt wonderful against his sensitive skin. Together with the two doctors, he walked down the narrow path that led to Piseco Lake's shore. Once at the water, he bent over and splashed water onto his face and arms. He loved how the cool water sent shivers racing throughout his body and wondered how it would feel if his whole body were submerged. He knew that he could easily jump into the water and remain submerged for hours, but he also knew how quickly Doctor Straus would press the button and send a shock throughout his body.

"Alex?" Jacob Curtis called from a few yards away. "I don't like how quiet you are."

"I am just enjoying this immensely, doctor. Nothing to be concerned about."

He had felt shocks before. Doctor Lucietta was the first to use them as treatment many years ago and was also the one who first discovered how they debilitated him. Shocks were not only painful for him, but they disrupted his thoughts and ability to function for days.

They allowed him to stay at the water's edge for nearly twenty minutes before suggesting they "head back and get in out of the rain."

"Very well, Doctors. And thank you for this privilege," he complied.

Neither he or the doctors saw the young man approaching them, but there he was, smack dab in the middle of the road separating the lodge from the lake. He seemed like the nervous type, the type that Straus would enjoy having as a patient. And had Straus been alone during this encounter, he might have offered his business card and a suggestion that the stranger contact him for an appointment.

But now was not the time to advance a career. Straus and Curtis stood as if they were catatonic as the young man stood staring at the gray man walking up from the path. As the stranger moved closer, Straus thought that he looked familiar but couldn't place the face.

"Good day," the young man offered, his eyes now less intense. "Not the best day for a hike, is it?"

"Just a short walk to the lake. No hiking today." Curtis said.

"Well, stay dry," the young man said.

"You too," Curtis said. "We should be getting inside now. Take care."

The young man stared at Alexander, and the doctors noticed that he was staring back at the young man. There was no look of terror on the young man's face, only intrigue.

"You must excuse us," Straus said. "Our patient hasn't been feeling well. We need to get him back into his bed. Good day."

"Hope you feel better," the young man said as he continued his trek down the road.

When he was far enough away, Straus whispered with an intensity unfitting for a whisper, "Inside. Now!"

But his patient just stood, not moving. He was looking at the stranger getting smaller with distance.

"Alex, inside now, or by God, I'll press this button."

"I doubt that, Doctor Straus. Doing so would create a scene that may attract the attention of that strange young man as well as the attention of anyone who may be glancing out of their windows. I am not planning on doing anything foolish. I just realized that the man I just saw was the first person I've heard speak besides your team."

"Well," Straus said, collecting himself and shifting his gaze to see if any neighbors were looking out of their windows, "I appreciate your behavior, Alex. I truly do. And I also appreciate how you must be feeling. However, I know that you are fully aware of what people would think and do to you if they ever found out about you. With that in mind, Alex, why don't we return to the safety of your rooms? I promise that the next time you earn the privilege of coming outside, we will do a much better job at making sure you will have your privacy. Sound fair enough?"

"Fair enough, Doctor," he said as he shot a final glance towards the stranger who was now almost out of sight. "I must admit that that man's reaction to me was not as drastic as I would have thought. Not like you suggested reactions would be."

"You have no idea how he may be reacting. Imagine if he ran into you alone? Trust me, Alexander, that reaction is far from what you should expect. Now let's get back inside where it's safe."

It was time for his plan to begin.

Chapter 17

"This doesn't make sense," Derek said. "The timeframe. The note left for me at the car rental desk. It doesn't make sense."

"Now Derek," Ralph said as he walked over to the counter to retrieve a fresh Arthur Avenue cigar and a book of matches, "this whole case is stuffed to the rim with things that don't make much sense." Ralph paused, introduced flame to his cigar's end and was soon billowing out grayish smoke into the humid air of the Adirondack lodge's entry way. "But, before we get further into discussing the finer points of this case, you said something that caught my interest."

Derek had stood up and was tracing the scar of his left cheek gently with his fingers. He knew he was tired and that his mind wasn't as sharp as he needed it to be. As he paced the entry area of the lodge, he struggled to piece together the time frame of the last several hours.

"Are you planning on pretending that I am not here in this same room as you or are you just building up something brilliant in that freelancing mind of yours?" Ralph said.

"I'm sorry. What did you ask me?"

"Actually I have yet to ask you anything, but I am planning to as soon as you appear ready to be asked a question."

"I just can't figure this out. I must be missing something. But, go ahead and ask me your question."

"You said during your little ramble a moment ago about some note that was left for you at the rental car desk. I sure would like to know what that note said and who gave it to you."

The smoke from Ralph's cigar was quickly replacing the fresh mountain air. Derek moved over to the main door, opened it, and took a deep breath of non-cigar smoke filled air.

"The note just said, 'Welcome to Albany, Mr. Cole,' and I have no idea who wrote it. The only person who knows that I flew into Albany was my client."

"Any chance your client left that note?" Ralph asked, thankful for the open door but not as thankful as he was for the finely crafted cigar he held between his stubby and overly hairy fingers.

"Possible, but it doesn't make any sense. If he left the note for me then he did so assuming that I would suspect it was him."

"Someone else must have known about your travel plans?"

"American Air and Hertz. That's about it."

Ralph checked the time on his watch. "What time did your flight leave Chicago?" he asked.

"Just before ten last night."

"And when did your plane land?"

"Around midnight. Got to the Hertz desk twenty minutes after that. I asked the clerk who the note came from but he had no idea. Think it could have been Alexander? But, how the hell would he know I was headed to Albany and was renting a car from Hertz? Had to have been my client or someone my client told that I was coming here. Must have been."

Ralph drew softly on his cigar and watched Derek struggle to figure things out. For his entire working career, Ralph had been in law enforcement. He had developed an ability to read people that others who worked with him both envied and were cautious of.

Though he knew that allowing Derek access to information about the case would violate nearly every rule in the book, he also knew that his department lacked the resources and experience to solve the murders. The state police were involved and certainly didn't need Ralph's or his department's assistance, but Ralph liked to see things through himself. He never liked when another department, be it a federal, state, or city department barged in and took over an investigation.

As Derek continued his thought-laden pacing, Ralph felt that Derek could be trusted and that there was something about him, something that made breaking the protocols, rules, and standard operating procedures worth the risk.

"Well, let me ease your mind about one of the options you have. It wasn't Alexander, and I'll show you why."

Ralph waved a single hand towards Derek, inviting that Derek follow. They walked deeper into the lodge, through the great room that in the daylight would offer spectacular views of Piseco Lake and the surrounding mountains. They finally came into a small, windowless room. The room was decorated with countless pictures of who Derek assumed to be William Straus.

Ralph took a seat behind the blonde wood desk that was entirely too large for the small room, opened a desk drawer, and pulled out a four-inch thick manila folder.

"I have made a few mistakes in my career," Ralph said as he held the folder out in front of him, "and I sure do hope that what I am about to do here is not gonna be another one. Whether or not it is a mistake is entirely up to you, Mr. Cole."

"Is that the case file?" Derek asked.

"Not exactly," Ralph said as he dropped the heavy folder on to the desk, sending dust into an immediate flight.

"This here is a little something that those state police investigators overlooked. Now, I'm thinking about showing you some very interesting things I've found in this folder, but I need to make sure my impression of you is accurate."

"Ask me anything you want."

"You see, Mr. Cole, I wasn't a 100% forthcoming about my feelings on freelancers. Fact is, I often wished I could bend the rules a tad. You know, here and there."

"In my experience, you're not alone," Derek said in a measured response.

"Now I may have actually bent some of those rules over the years but always did so when my instincts suggested that them rules needed a little flexibility. So since I am pretty much alone on this investigation, and the state police see me as someone just to keep informed, I am going to include you into this investigation."

"I appreciate your trust."

"You need to catch some shut eye?"

"Eventually, but I'm more interested in seeing what's in that file first," Derek said as his eyes grew hungry at the idea of reading the contents of the file.

"Well, I do. So I'm going to leave this file right here on this goofy-looking desk and go find a place to sleep." Ralph stood and hitched his pants over his belly. "I want to show you a few things first that I want to pay particular attention to." Ralph opened the file and thumbed through a few sheets until he pulled out a group of photographs. "You take a good look at these, and I'll bet you'll understand why I don't believe your mysterious note leaver wasn't Alexander."

As Ralph quietly left the small office, Derek moved to the more comfortable chair behind the desk. He gave a quick glance at Ralph.

"Thanks for not shooting me earlier," he said.

"Well, I imagine that would have not been an enjoyable event for you. But, there's still time, I imagine. Still time."

As Ralph left to search for a bed that would be kind enough to allow him a few minutes of sleep, Derek dropped his eyes to the series of photographs lying on the desk in front of him.

"Holy shit balls!" he said.

The picture on top of the pile was of a young man who, to Derek, seemed to be posing for his autopsy pictures. The man in the picture stood over six feet tall and was standing against a wall. As he stared at the photograph of the man standing naked against the off-white wall, his eyes captured Derek.

Baby blue, yet dimmed, surrounded by yellowish-gray skin where white should have been. Eyes too large for a man, and too blue. If not for the spark of something in them, Derek would take these eyes for those of a dead man.

Lifeless. Cold. Vacant.

The man's eyes were they only bit of life's color in the picture. The man's skin was a horrible shade of death; gray mixed with hints of purplish blue. He was completely bald, and though the photograph was obviously taken from a digital camera then printed out on an ink jet printer, Derek could make out whispers of eyebrows, so faint as to remind him of an infants. Soft brown and stretched to a point of comical sparseness. Above each eyebrow were two, nearly perfect circles of much darker skin. They looked like old, healed burn marks and made Derek think of the pictures of electrodes he'd seen pictures of before.

The shade of death the man wore on his face was a theme carried throughout the rest of his body. Though some areas of the man's body- his elbows, back of his hands, and knees - were a darker shade of death, the man was colorless.

There was very little fat on the man. Muscles, seemingly defying the death motif, were visible. A classic and envied six-pack was clear in the man's abdominals. Biceps and deltoids both well developed and prominent. Muscles lined the man's thighs and appeared to have been carefully carved to show each of their assigned functions. His genitals hung softly and assumed a much darker variation of gray. Unlike the rest of the photo subject's body, his genitals appeared to have never developed.

"I see what you mean, Ralph," Derek said out loud, somewhat hoping Ralph was still awake and within earshot. "This guy showing up in an airport would certainly be remembered." Derek received no report back from Ralph.

As Derek scanned the photograph again, he paused when his eyes met the man's smile. The thin lips curled just slightly at their corners, parting enough for Derek to see that they hid nothing. Though he couldn't be certain, the way the lips fell inward and the lack of anything white behind them, suggested that the man was toothless.

As he flipped through the remaining pictures, each of the same subject, Derek noticed that each picture was dated and each date marked the same day of the year. June thirtieth. There were twenty-two pictures in the stack, each taken on June thirtieth of the last twenty-two years. The only picture that broke the sequence was the very first picture that was dated July 4, 1992.

This picture showed a baby wearing the same alarming shade of death-gray. He was lying in a crib. His eyes, baby blue then, held an unsettling gaze back at the camera.

"This is not a good-looking baby," Derek said.

Derek quickly scanned the printed photographs again and noticed that the first thirteen were taken in a different place than the last nine. In those, the subject stood, naked and gray against a painted concrete blocked wall. In the remaining nine, the person stood against an off-white and typical-looking sheet-rocked wall.

Derek collected the photographs into a neat pile and set them aside. He wanted to see what else of interest was in the over-stuffed folder that sat in front of him. As he began to thumb through, Derek noticed several smaller pictures, all black and white, bound together by a rubber band that was showing its age with cracks and a visible loss of elasticity.

Derek removed the tired rubber band and thumbed through the twelve or thirteen pictures that the band faithfully bound. Each was of an attractively shaped woman and was obviously taken without her being aware that a camera's lens was trained on her. The woman was captured in many positions; bending over what looked like a crib, standing with folded arms looking at something in the non-captured distance, sitting at a small desk writing notes. Each picture was of the same woman dressed in a white nurse's uniform, and each was taken from what Derek assumed to be a hazy window.

The pictures were not dated, but all seemed to have been taken the same day, for the subject's uniform and hairstyle remained consistent. The last picture in the lot was of the nurse holding the gray baby. Her backside was the obvious target of the photograph, but the eyes of the baby as the nurse held it over her left shoulder were what sent a disturbing shiver through Derek's soul.

The eyes were certainly the same eyes of the subject of the other pictures, but they seemed different in this one picture. They seemed aware that they were being watched. To Derek, the eyes looked angry about an interruption. A presence that, though seemingly unnoticed by the nurse holding him, was clearly known by the baby.

"Michelle Pettingall, I assume?" Derek thought and began to wonder what kind of man Straus was to have taken these secret pictures and to have kept them in a file for over twenty years. The thought of what Straus may have been doing while looking at the pictures caused Derek to drop them and then to rub his hands clean on his jeans.

"Sick bastard," he thought of Straus.

Next to review were the hundred or so medical notes. Some were printed and many were handwritten in a journalized format. As his eyes were growing weary,

Derek flipped through the notes and only paused to read a few. Those he read continued to affirm his client's story and to affirm Derek's initial impression of Doctor William Straus.

Patient arrived today. Initial examination confirmed diagnosis of Doctor Adams et al – No heart. No breathing. Skin color=gray. Reflexes very sharp. Doctor Lucietta to run lab tests on pooled blood, skin cells, and muscle tissue. Results in two days. 7/4 1992 DWS

Patient slept 14 hours. Lung activates upon sleep. Cell regeneration tests inconclusive. Cell transfer ability noted 7/8/92 DWS

Patient displaying unusual levels of awareness for age. Eye tracking and environment awareness remarkable 7/10/12 DWS

Derek thumbed through the stack of notes and reached one that explained the dark patches above the eyes of Alexander. He assumed that the initials after the notes were to indicate which doctor was doing the note taking.

Patient did not respond as expected to shock. Small voltage caused extreme reaction. Highly sensitive to electricity. 2/5/2002 DBL

Derek continued reading notes that seemed to stand out from the rest.

Patient displaying unusual strength. Electricity continues to be the best method to subdue. Highly effective, but need to send low dosage only! 5/17/2003 DBL

Patient move complete. Suite secured. Memory tests to resume in two weeks. 9/3/2005 DTC

Encountered stranger during outdoor activity. Patient behaved well due to threat of "dog collar" shock. Limit future outdoor activities to evenings and rainy days. 7/9/2013 DWS

Test results positive!!! A breakthrough at last. Dr Curtis running third round of test against HIV virus to verify results. 7/1/2014 DWS

Derek placed the final note back into the folder, realizing that there were no more notes dated after the last one. And there would be no more tests or notes, ever. He leaned back into the soft, leather executive chair, rested his head back and let his mind mull over the pictures and the notes. His mind, however, had enough of thinking, and soon Derek was sound asleep.

When he opened his eyes, Derek saw that Ralph was sitting

across the desk from him and seemed to have been waiting for Derek to wake up.

"How much reading did you get done before you fell into la la land?" Ralph asked.

"Enough to know that Alexander probably would want to stay out of public as much as possible and that the doctors, Straus, Curtis, and Lucietta, used Alexander as a lab rat."

"Did you happen to read that last note? The one about the big breakthrough?"

"I did. Kind of suggests they were on to something with the HIV virus."

"Yup. And I went through every other file in the file cabinet over there," Ralph said as he nodded to Derek's left, "and didn't find a single mention of anything related to HIV or any other virus."

"Any idea where Straus is?" Derek asked after a short pause.

"Now that is an interesting question right there, Derek. And one that I truly wish I had an answer to."

"I take that as a 'no.'"

"Some townsfolk reported that they saw the doctor's car tooling down Route 8 and moving at a pretty good clip about the same time we figured the murders took place. State police put out an APB on Straus and his car but ain't nothing come of it yet.

"I'd really like to talk to that Straus guy. Especially since your recent investigative find of the trap door under Alexander's bed. Sure would like to find out why he wasn't among the victims we found in this lodge."

"You liking Straus for an accomplice?" Derek asked.

"I sure do find it peculiar. The timing of everything, that is. The last note says something about a breakthrough. Two of Straus's fellow doctors found all dead in that room. Straus's car seen tooling out of the area. And your discovery of the trap door. Lots of reasons to be interested in Straus, I'll admit."

Derek paused and began thinking about the note left for him. He wondered if the Hertz clerk had discovered where the note came from. As had become his habit, Derek slowly traced the scar on his left cheek absently as his thoughts drifted to planning his next step.

"I noticed that scar while you was sleeping. I've seen plenty of scars in my day. Spent two years in the Army as a medic. Yup, I sure have seen plenty of scars. But that little beauty you're sporting, I find to be interesting."

Derek dropped his hand to his lap and asked, "Why do you find it interesting?"

"Funny thing about scars," Ralph said looking down, "see enough of them and you can tell what caused them. It ain't much of my concern, but I have to say that your little reminder there is an exit wound. Something went through that cheek from the inside of your mouth."

"You do know all about scars, Ralph."

Ralph, knowing that his curiosity about Derek's scar was satisfied, and not wanting to find out what drove his guest to create the scar, stood up abruptly.

"I do not know about your digestive system, but mine is telling me that it needs something to do. Now, this town may be small, but it has one of the best diners this side of Texas not four miles from our exact location."

"Sounds good. Any place to get cleaned up first? I have an overnight bag in my car that's parked up the road a bit."

"I took the liberty of moving your car down closer to us. Didn't think you'd mind all that much. And since you left your keys and wallet out in the kitchen, why, I thought you were all but requesting me to get your car."

"Thanks. Have any trouble finding it?"

"One of my officers spotted it around an hour ago. Gave me a call and told me where it was parked."

"I do apologize again for breaking into this place. And again thank you for holding off sending a bullet into my head."

"As I said before, there's still plenty of time for that. But right now the only thing I am thinking of is to getting some eggs and toast into my belly. Go get your stuff from out of your car so you can get yourself all prettied up like a good city boy."

As Derek began walking out of Straus's office, he felt his cell phone vibrate in his pocket. A quick check of the caller ID told him that the call was from a 518 area code number.

"Derek Cole."

"Mr. Cole, this is Amanda from the Hertz car rental office in the Albany airport. I got a message from another Hertz team member about a note that was left for you when you picked up your rental?"

"Yes," Derek said. "Do you know who left the note?"

"I wrote the note for you. I received a phone call a little after ten last night. The man on the phone just said he was a friend of yours and to write a note welcoming you to Albany. I'm sorry, but I don't know the man's name."

"Can you tell me what his voice sounded like?" Derek asked, hoping for some clue.

"I'm sorry, Mr. Cole. I really don't recall the man's voice. Will you be needing anything further, Mr. Cole?"

"Any way to trace the call through your system?"

"Again, I'm sorry, Mr. Cole. We really have no way to trace any incoming calls. We do appreciate your loyalty with Hertz, and if you should need anything regarding your current rental, please don't hesitate to call. Have a great day!"

Ralph heard enough of the conversation to know that Derek received no information about who left the note for him. While knowing would have made his case less of a mystery, Ralph could tell that the mystery surrounding the note was bothering Derek much more than it was bothering him.

Ten minutes after getting the call from Hertz, Derek and Ralph climbed into Derek's rental car and headed out for breakfast.

"Now, I know I told you this diner is but four miles away. And that is the truth of the matter. However, I'm gonna ask you to add some miles to that and drive around a bit."

"Something you need to see or do?"

"If you are going to be my freelance assistant on this case, you need to get a lay of the landscape. I'd like to start by showing you where our third victim, Roger Fay, lived."

"Sounds fine to me."

As Derek backed out of the crushed stone driveway of Straus's lodge, he took notice of the large maple tree wrapped with police tape almost directly across from the driveway.

"I take it that something fatal happened at that tree?" Derek asked as he stopped his car near the tree.

"Yup. As far as we can tell, that tree is where Roger Fay was killed. Looks like old Roger had a knife plunged straight through his neck. Damn knife went a few inches deep into the tree itself. Lots of strength to do that."

"Then his body was dragged into the lodge?"

"More likely it was carried. There are no drag marks, just a whole bunch of blood splatters. Like the blood had fallen from a few feet above the ground. We found Roger all dead and pretty close to naked on the floor next to them other doctors."

"Naked?" Derek asked.

"Folks who saw Roger walking that day said he was wearing some cowboy type of hat and black boots. All of them items were taken off by what I assume to be the killer."

"Did you know him?"

"Probably met him a time or two. My officers tell me that I had, but I don't recall. I know he was some type of a writer who lived up here year round. Just killed by being in the wrong place at the wrong time, we reckon."

The route to Roger Fay's home included a short time spent on

New York State Route 8. When Derek's car reached the intersection of Route 8, Ralph spoke.

"This is Route 8. Our Doctor Straus was seen turning right out of here and speeding down that way," Ralph said pointing to his right. "Ain't no use us heading that way and following him, as I'm sure you'd agree, so take a left here."

As Derek turned his car onto Route 8, he asked Ralph why he hadn't seen a car parked near the lodge last night, though Ralph was obviously there.

"I do like to be close to my work. But mostly I stayed at the lodge last night because the state police didn't want me to. They thought I'd sully up the scene. But I figured, since I am the man in charge that I'd go ahead and do what I damn well pleased. I had one of my officers bring my car back to my house yesterday afternoon. I figured that if Alexander or anyone else involved in this here crime had to get back inside the lodge that they'd be more likely to do so if they thought there was no one around. Turns out the only person who showed up was some freelancer."

The route to Roger Fay's home was just under a mile away from the maple tree across from Straus's lodge. Derek turned off Route 8 and onto a road that followed the shoreline of Piseco Lake and then circled back towards the direction of the lodge. When they reached the trailer park that Roger Fay called home, Ralph had Derek pull his car over to the side of road in front of Roger's doublewide but suggested that they not do any outside investigation.

"Ain't nothing we gonna learn by traipsing around his old

trailer. State police wasted a whole lot of time looking for any clue that connected Roger to Straus and came up with a handful of nothing. I just wanted you to start piecing together the events and time frame of our murder. Go ahead and drive straight for a bit. This ain't the way to the diner still, but I want to show you something that I find very peculiar down the road a stretch."

Derek continued driving down the road as his mind began retracing the timeline of the murders. He tried to imagine what Roger Fay had seen or done to get himself pinned to a tree. His imagination failed him again.

It was just over two miles past Roger Fay's home when Ralph told Derek to pull over to the side of the recently paved road and onto the hard-packed dirt shoulder. Without saying a word, Ralph opened up his door, pulled himself out, and started walking across the road. Derek followed quickly behind.

"Tell me what you make of this," Ralph said, pointing to an outcropping of large rocks on the side of the road. The rocks were set back twelve feet from the road and seemed to be in the same position they had been for the last million years. Painted on the rock in red was an image of a heart.

"Looks like some local kid wanted to spray paint a message to his girl and was interrupted," Derek offered, not sure why Ralph seemed to think that the spray painted heart may have been important.

"That may be true, but the neighbors all say that they hadn't seen this graffiti before a few days of the murders. And if you head on back down this little trail right next to the rocks, you'll see something else that I find a bit interesting."

The small trail that started right beside the rock formation seemed to be made several years ago. Weeds and ground plants had recaptured much of the trail, making the task of keeping on trail a bit of a challenge for Derek.

With Ralph trailing behind and breathing much heavier and louder than Derek thought the simple hike demanded, Derek navigated his way through the overgrown path for roughly one hundred yards before Ralph breathlessly called from behind.

"Now if you pause a moment," he said as he used a trailside tree as support, "and take a look around, let me know if you see anything peculiar."

Derek glanced around the trail, then off towards the dense undergrowth that bordered the trail. He knew that Ralph wouldn't have asked him if he saw anything "peculiar" unless Ralph felt that there was something that he found to be "peculiar."

A second before Derek was going to report that he couldn't see anything of interest; he noticed a small, white birch tree twenty-feet off the right of the path. On the tree was spray painted a small, red heart. The image was small but stood out clearly against the white, paper-like bark of the tree.

"Think that's a trail marker?" Derek asked.

"Head on over, and let me know what you think," Ralph answered, still challenged to capture his breath.

Derek hopped some small bushes and bounded over to the

white birch tree. Once there, he noticed a small pile of twigs and leaves just behind the marked tree.

"Okay to see if anything is under this pile of sticks and leaves?" he called to Ralph.

"Isn't any reason since I know exactly what's under it. Get on over back here, and I'll tell ya what I found."

When Derek returned to the path, Ralph had found his breath, though his brow streamed with sweat.

"Damn hot out here. Muggy as all hell. You'd think that an ole Texas boy would be accustomed to heat and humidity but, damn if this upstate New York heat doesn't get me every time."

"So," Derek pushed, "what was under that pile?"

"Same thing that is still under that pile, actually."

"And that would be?"

"A small backpack. And in the backpack, which I am sure that you're about to ask, is a .380 caliber Smith and Wesson semi, a well folded map of the area, three vanilla flavored Power Bars, a pair of Nike sneakers, socks, a clean shirt, long pants, and a towel."

"Not sure how smart it is to leave a gun out here for anyone to find," Derek said.

"Guns are funny, Derek. They ain't much good with no bullets and the firing rod removed. That gun has been modified. I guess you could call it a custom."

"Someone left the gun without bullets?"

"No, there were bullets there. Hollow points. A full box of fifty of them, plus six loaded in the magazine. I took the liberty of removing them."

"Get any prints off the bullets or the gun?"

"Clean as a virgin's nightstand," Ralph answered.

Ralph pointed further down the path.

"Keep on walking that way for another click. You walk your pace, and I'll do my best to keep up."

Though Derek wanted to talk more about the hidden backpack and the two painted hearts, he figured it was more important to keep on Ralph's good side, and he turned to continue walking the path.

Five minutes later, the path ended at the shore of Piseco Lake. Directly across from the end of the path was the lodge of Doctor William Straus.

"Interesting," Derek said, though Ralph was still too far behind to hear.

A few minutes later, Ralph's breathing could be heard. He reached the end of the path next to Derek and sat down on a large rock that Derek hadn't noticed was marked with a small, red heart.

"And beneath this rock that is now holding up my fat ass," Ralph said, "was a flashlight, not unlike the type I found you waving around the lodge last night."

"This whole path is a bit 'peculiar' I'd say," Derek said.

"Very much so," Ralph answered. "Now, I want to hear your ideas about this path, the objects on this path, and the three small hearts painted on the rocks and tree. I have my thoughts, but I am very curious to hear what you think."

Derek thought of how his father would always ask him to

share his thoughts about difficult to understand questions that Derek had growing up. Derek would share his views before his father would share his thoughts. When Derek asked about why his grandmother had died, his father asked him, "Derek, everyone has their own ideas of why people die. What are your thoughts?" And while Derek never felt the need to replace his father with another "father figure," the way Ralph spoke to him made Derek feel comfortable and at ease.

"Well," Derek started, "the fact that this trail is directly across a narrow stretch of the lake from the lodge, is marked at both the beginning and end and has some supplies stashed along the route, also near a marker, I have to think that Alexander used this route to escape after murdering the three men. Since Fay was murdered outside the lodge, I imagine that Alexander was headed towards the lake to either swim to this point or to use a boat that may have been stashed on the lodge's side of the lake. Did you or the state police find any canoes or small boats drifting around the lake?"

"Not a-one," Ralph answered, his smile showing his obvious satisfaction with Derek's summation.

"Now the fact that the flashlight and backpack were obviously never collected," Derek continued, "leads me to believe that Alexander didn't make the swim over here, that he got lost, or that he had another means of escape. I also am more convinced than ever that Alexander wasn't acting alone."

"My thoughts exactly," said Ralph. "I had one of my officers take a look at the underside of the lodge while you were still dreaming of lollipops and rainbows this morning. And he agrees that the screws were pulled out from outside, just like you suggested. Now that tells me that either Alexander got outside without anyone noticing or that someone else helped him get out."

"If Alexander was able to get outside, he could have been the one who planted the supplies on this trail."

"Entirely possible," Ralph said. "But I don't think so. You see, as soon as I discovered this lovely path, the painted heart symbols and the supplies, my little brain immediately told me that these were arranged by someone else. Someone who was planning on assisting Alexander in the murders and his escape. Someone who knew the timing of it all. These hearts painted along this path look too new to have been out in this weather too long. They are as fresh as a schoolyard bully's mouth during recess."

"Straus?" Derek questioned.

"I do not know who helped Alexander, nor do I know why. But I do know that wherever Alexander is, he didn't get there by himself. And, while I don't know for certain, I also believe that whoever called in that note of yours to the rental car place, is the someone who can answer all my questions."

Chapter 18

Henry Zudak needed to breathe. He had to alert someone, anyone about what was happening. He heard, though he couldn't be certain of the exact words used, that Mark Rinaldo was dead. That shocked him more than he thought it would. After all, he knew that Alexander Black had escaped after killing three men inside of William Straus's lodge, and that one of the victims was Henry's old co-worker, Peter Adams. Henry also knew that his name was found on a list with a bunch of other names that he recognized and that two of the names, Adams and Curtis, were crossed out in blood. He knew that Alexander would be looking for him and for Mark, but, still, the shock of hearing that Mark was dead was hard to handle.

Then there was the more pressing issue of breathing. He certainly had enough experience remembering how to breathe when stressed. The months after the whole "O'Connell incident," as he began to refer to it as, found him suffering from near-constant panic attacks.

The psychologist he met with told him that panic attacks are nothing more than his body not knowing how to process an overload of stressors hitting it all at once. He prescribed a mild sedative to help Henry through the more troubling attacks and suggested that Henry learn some "yoga breathing exercises" to help manage the more "palatable" attacks.

Henry was certain that he packed his sedatives when he hurriedly threw his suitcase together, and he knew exactly where he placed the plastic amber-colored bottle when he unpacked that very same suitcase just two days ago.

"On the sink, next to the toothpaste, behind the folded washcloths," he thought to himself. If only he could reach them from where he was kneeling. Though he wasn't sure that the pills would really do him any good, the thought of getting to them at least gave him something to shoot for.

A goal.

An objective beyond his primal objective of breathing.

He knew he couldn't talk and ask whoever it was standing behind him holding the rope tightly across his windpipe for a quick time-out. He had tried screaming to get the attention of anyone who may be in the room next door or even out in the hallway, but his scream was locked deep in his lungs.

And as black speckles began to fully cloud his vision, he accepted that breathing would not be something he would be doing anytime soon. Certainly not in time to save himself.

As the black speckles began to flash at their outer edges, Henry gave up the goal of getting to his pills and turned his thoughts to his wife. Her name was Abigail, and she would soon be getting back to the hotel room. He wished that the last thing he said to her had been *"I love you"* instead of *"Make sure that no one follows you back from the store, and please don't forget to pick up some Fritos."*

"Damn," he thought as the black speckles covered his entire vision. *"Damn."*

Chapter 19

Derek and Ralph had just finished ordering breakfast when Derek's cell phone began to vibrate. Glancing at the caller ID, he saw that his client, Thomas O'Connell was calling.

"It's my client," Derek said to Ralph. "Should I take the call outside?"

"Well, if it's all the same to you, I sure would like to hear what that client of yours has to say."

Derek knew that Ralph was sticking his neck out by allowing him to be part of the investigation, and though Derek believed that maintaining his client's confidentiality was of high importance, he also didn't want to make Ralph think he was keeping information from him.

"How about we step outside, and I'll put the speaker phone on?"

"I like the way you think, Derek Cole."

Derek answered the call and quickly told Thomas to "hold for one second" while he and Ralph made their way out of the small diner and into Derek's rental car.

"Okay, Thomas. I'm back. Had to get somewhere quiet. Is everything okay with you?"

"Fine. What did you find out in Albany? Did that ass-backwards police chief get in your way?"

Derek glanced at Ralph, apologizing for his client's remarks. Ralph blinked an eye and nodded his head towards Derek's cell phone.

"No problem at all. Have you heard from your parents yet?"

"Yes, and that's one of the reasons I am calling you. My father called me around 11:00 last night to tell me that he and my mom are safe and sound in the Bahamas. I assume you don't want to know which island they are on nor which hotel they are staying at?"

"Correct. If I need to know, I'll find out. Did you talk with both your parents?"

"Yes. Why do you ask that?"

"Just want to make sure they're both safe."

"I spoke with my mother last evening after they got to their resort and with my dad just a few minutes ago."

"Perfect. You were saying something about your father?"

"Yes. He knows where I am staying and knows I'm safe, and since he and my mom are together and very safe, he wants you to call him and give him updates on your progress."

"Fine. Text me over the number where I can reach him." Derek glanced at Ralph who was still holding his gaze on Derek's cell phone. "You probably didn't hear yet, but Doctor Mark Rinaldo was killed late last night."

"Oh, I did hear," Thomas said. "I won't tell you where I am, but just know that I can get Chicago news and Chicago police radio on my cell phone. What I heard was that his head was bashed in, unlike what happened to Zudak."

"What happened to Zudak?" Derek asked. Ralph lifted his gaze and met Derek's eyes.

The questioning look in his eyes let Derek know that Ralph had no idea what happened to Henry Zudak.

"Looks like my brother has crossed off more names. Zudak was found in a hotel outside of Chicago. I guess he was strangled to death. His wife found him dead in their hotel room."

"If it's your brother who killed these two, that means he is in Chicago and is probably actively looking for you. You need to assure me that you are in a very secure location and that you have an exit strategy in case your brother pays a visit."

"If you saw where I was and knew who was around me, you wouldn't worry at all."

Ralph shot a strange look to Derek and mouthed, *"who was around me?"* to Derek. Derek shrugged his shoulders and made a mental note to try to find out more about Thomas's location if and when knowing became important.

"Listen Thomas, I'll call your father as soon as I can, but I need to know if you let anyone know that I was headed to Albany?"

"No one. Why?"

"Did you call Hertz and have them leave a note for me, welcoming me to Albany?"

"Hell no," Thomas said. "If you got a note, that means that someone else knows you are on the case. That really concerns me."

"Me too," Derek said.

"Any idea who it could have been who left that note?"

"I have a short list of possibilities," Derek said.

"Well I'm sure my name is on that list, but I promise you that I had nothing to do with it. I hope you believe me."

"I do," Derek said honestly. "Wouldn't make sense for you to hire me only to set me up."

"Listen," Thomas said after a short pause, "I need to get running. Please make sure you call my father and keep me informed about any developments. I assume that you will be headed back this way soon?"

"You text me his number, and I will call. As far as my next steps with this investigation, I will let you know when I figure it out. You stay safe."

"Talk with you soon."

It was the relaxed tone of Thomas's voice that most worried Derek. While he was happy that his client believed he was safe and protected, Derek couldn't help but wonder why Thomas seemed to be a man without a care in the world. Maybe his attitude was the curse of being the only child of wealthy parents, or maybe his parents were overly protective since they had already lost, or thought they'd lost, their other son, and had no interest in ever losing letting anything happen to Thomas.

Whatever the reason for Thomas's apparent relaxed nature, Derek assumed that a relaxed attitude was better than a paranoid one, though the latter seemed to Derek to be more appropriate.

The two men walked back into the diner just as their food was being walked over to their table.

"I've always had good timing when it came to food," Ralph joked. "So, you headed back to the Windy City?"

"I don't know," Derek said. "I'm surprised that you didn't hear about Zudak."

"Shouldn't be," Ralph said as he shoved a folded piece of toast, heavily dipped in egg yolk into his mouth. "*You* should understand the filters involved in police work. See, once the state police took over my investigation, they started handling all communications between other departments. I know they contacted Chicago, and I also know that Chicago is gonna send any intel back to the state police. Hell, they probably don't even know that some police department of a tiny town is involved. And that is just fine with me!" Ralph paused to drink a swallow of coffee and to take another bite out of his toast. "So when something happens in Chicago, the powers to be out there call the powers that be here, that being the state police, and I get filtered out. I betcha I get a call before too long from the state police letting me know about Zudak and any details that they deem me worthy of knowing. Till that happens, I focus on what I can focus on. And that is solving this mystery."

"The fact that two of the doctors whose names were on the list you found at the lodge were killed in Chicago confirms that Alexander is not working alone," Derek said.

"Well, I think we agree on that matter. But how do the murders in Chicago prove that?" Ralph asked.

"I highly doubt that Alexander learned how to drive a car while he was held up in those rooms of his. Which means that for him to get to Chicago as quickly as it appears he has, that he either took some form of public transportation or was driven there. And based on those pictures of him in that file, I don't think the public transportation option is likely. And, while I don't like to make any rash assumptions, I am liking Straus as the accomplice."

"Now that is something that I'd like to hear more about. You're figuring that Straus is the guy behind this whole mess. You keep talking, and I'll get to eating. Don't mistake my not asking questions as me not paying attention. My mamma told me never to speak with food in my mouth, which I plan on having for the next few minutes."

As Ralph gave his focus to the plate of food in front of him, Derek began talking about his suspicions.

"First off, Straus is a major player in this whole Alexander Black thing. It was his lodge where Alexander was living and his lodge where three men were killed. Now why in the world would those doctors be at his lodge and Straus not be there? Second, his car is spotted speeding away from the crime scene around the time the murders happened. Based on what I've read about Alexander, I highly doubt that Straus, who must be in his fifties, could have defended himself against someone strong enough to drive a knife through Roger Fay's neck and three inches deep into a tree. Third, that whole path and supplies mystery almost certainly points to someone helping Alexander. And fourth, what I found outside under

Alexander's bedroom convinces me that either Alexander was able to go outside at will or that someone else removed those screws and made the hidden trap door. And if Alexander was allowed to go outside at will, then he wouldn't have needed a trap door.

"Also, the fact that no one seems to know where Straus is, and yet his body hasn't shown up floating in some lake *and* his name hasn't been crossed off the "death list," makes me think that he is alive and also makes me very, very suspicious."

Ralph finished the last bit of coffee in his mug and signaled to the waitress that he needed another cup. Without a word to Derek, he returned his focus to what was left of his breakfast and resumed his task of quieting his hunger.

"Well?" Derek asked. "Any thoughts?"

"If I had disagreed with anything you were saying, I promise you I would have made my differing opinion known."

"But there are other options, don't you think?"

"Other options?" Ralph questioned.

"Think about it, why does it have to be that Roger Fay was just in the wrong place at the wrong time? He knows the area well, and I read a note in the file that suggested that some stranger had a run in with Alexander and the doctors outside of the lodge one day. Maybe Roger wanted to see what the heck was going on in the lodge after getting a good look at Alexander. Isn't that an option?"

"I suppose it is," Ralph answered.

"And my client, Thomas O'Connell. Who can say that he's not the one who is helping out Alexander? Or his mother, his father, or any of the people on that list? Let's not forget about Brian Lucietta. Did you speak with him at all?"

"I was able to track him down. Seems the good doctor took an administrative position in a psychiatric hospital in Manhattan. I called him at this office after all hell broke loose. He didn't seem worried in the least," Ralph said.

"Guess I should add him to my list of suspected accomplices."

"I don't think so. Not yet, anyways," Ralph responded. "From what I dug out about Lucietta, he is more concerned about his legacy than he is for his life. I betcha he and Straus made quite a team."

"Is he taking any precautions?"

"Don't know. He just cut me off and asked me to let him know if I felt that his life was in danger. Pompous son of a bitch just cut me off and wished me a fine day."

Derek's head was swimming. In most of his cases since going freelance, he only had one person to track down. One person to find, alert authorities about and to worry about. While Alexander Black was certainly Derek's most obvious concern, the cast of potential characters who may be helping him was only being decreased after a body was discovered.

"And why is Michelle Mix's name absent from the list?" Derek barked, frustrated by the realization that the list of confusing items about the case was still not complete. "Maybe she has something to do with this whole thing."

"I thought the same thing. In fact, I have yet to hear you say anything that I can't honestly say that I haven't thought of," Ralph said with his breakfast plate cleaned and his mug refilled with black coffee. "But I do have to say that Fay is not a suspect."

"Why is that?"

"First of all, while I didn't know the man, those who did tell me that he was more of a loner and a loser than an accomplice to a few murders. Second, him being all dead doesn't help put Alexander out in Chicago. His car is still parked in his driveway. Plus, he kept a journal. And, while I am not a fan of going through a dead man's personal thoughts, I did read his. And from what I read, he wasn't the person who met Alexander outside of the lodge. Furthermore, you'd think that if he was scheming something that he'd at least make some mention of it in his diary. Not a peep or an innuendo about anything suspicious."

"Okay," Derek said after a short pause. "Your points make sense. I'll scratch Fay off my list of suspects," a somewhat relieved Derek said. "How do you feel about the nurse Michelle?"

"I do find it interesting that she didn't make Alexander's list. And when I called her and her husband, Stanley, she didn't sound all that concerned about Alexander being on the loose. When I told her that he'd killed two doctors already, the only thing she asked me is whether or not Straus was one of the victims. I found that a bit odd."

"Have you contacted them since?"

"Nope. Did try, though. Calls went right to voicemail."

"As far as my client goes, I suppose that I'm just being too suspicious. It doesn't make any sense for him to hire me if he is working with the man I am trying to stop."

"Also a good and fair observation," Ralph said as he folded his short, thick arms across his chest. "And what about your client's parents?"

"Not sure. I've never spoke with them. If they are in the Bahamas, then they probably shouldn't be on my list."

"Well, I did speak with them," Ralph said. "And I'll bet you dollars to donuts that he would have arranged for all them doctors to be killed if Alexander wasn't doing it already. Boy, was that man pissed off."

"Wouldn't you be?"

"Yup, I sure would be. But not the type of angry that your client's dad was, though. I'd be mad as hell, but he seemed to me the type of mad that drives people to do things they may not normally do."

"And the mother?"

"Cried most of the time on our call. Kept saying that she should've known that her baby didn't die. She sure was upset and genuinely shocked. He stayed shocked for only a minute or two before he started with that special type of anger I told you about."

"I'll take your word for it and keep him on my list."

The waitress walked over and handed the check to Ralph. She gave a quick smile to Derek before returning to her spot behind the counter.

"I'll take care of that," Derek said.

"Take care of what?" Ralph said. "The check? Now Derek, you do insult me. I consider you to be my guest, and if my mother up in heaven is looking down on me and sees me letting a guest pay for a meal, she'd find a way to haunt me for months."

Once Ralph paid the breakfast bill, and the two men were back driving in Derek's rental car, Derek asked Ralph to give Stanley and Michelle Mix another call.

"I'll tell you what," Ralph said. "We get ourselves back to that lodge, you call your client's father, and then I'll give the Mixes another call. Sound fair?"

"Sounds good."

Derek gave a quick glance at his cell phone and saw that he had received a message from his client.

"Thomas must take orders well. His text message includes his dad's cell number and a reminder that his dad wants updates right away."

"I'd sure like to listen quietly to that call, if you don't mind?"

"Not at all."

Derek and Ralph arrived back at the lodge ten minutes after breakfast was paid for. Parked in the driveway of the lodge were three New York State Trooper cars.

"Either something is about to be filtered down to me, or we have ourselves yet another problem," Ralph said.

Chapter 20

"Add a new officer to your team, Chief Fox?" Captain Jared Smith asked as Ralph and Derek were walking up the driveway to the lodge's front door. Smith was a twenty-two year veteran of the state police and believed that rules and protocols were in place for damn good reasons.

"Not that my department is any of your concern," Ralph said through a smile, "but this is Derek Cole. Good friend of mine and an experienced private detective."

"You haven't shared any case information have you?" Smith asked as Ralph reached the front door of the lodge. Instead of giving way, Smith stood, with arms on hips, blocking access to the inside of the lodge. "Ralph, I asked you a very simple question."

"Now, I have not known you all that long, Captain Smith, but I have to believe that simple questions is about all you can ask."

"I've been hired by Thomas O'Connell to protect him and his parents from whomever killed the men in this lodge," Derek answered, hoping to ease the palpable tension in the air. "Chief Fox has not divulged any case information, despite my repeated requests. Perhaps you can help me with my case, Captain?"

"I don't even want you near this scene," Smith said to Derek though his eyes were fixed on Ralph's. "Nothing personal, but I prefer to work with professionals, not people who pretend to be something they aren't."

"Well now, that attitude of yours is concerning," Ralph said to Smith. "So concerning in fact, that I've changed my mind. Derek Cole," he said to Derek while extending his hand, "as the Chief of Police of the town of Arietta, New York, I'd like to extend you an offer to become a temporary officer of my department."

Smith stood shaking his head, clearly not impressed with Ralph's impetuous way of managing a police force but also fully aware that his position with the state police did not give him any authority over how Ralph, or any other department chief, ran their business.

"What you do with your little department is your problem, not mine," Smith said as he cleared the entrance into the lodge. "I came by to do a bit more investigation and to let you know the latest developments. Can you and your newest officer give me ten minutes of your time, or do you have to run over to HR and fill out some new employee forms?"

"I suppose we can spare you the time," Ralph said, moving into the lodge and over to his zip lock bag containing his cigars. "Shall we sit right here, or would you be more comfortable elsewhere?"

Over the next ten minutes, Captain Jared Smith let Ralph and Derek know that both Mark Rinaldo and Henry Zudak were killed in the Chicago area.

"Chicago PD found no notes on either of the bodies."

Smith then discussed the statewide search for Doctor William Straus.

"Straus's car was captured on several traffic cams. Seems that he headed back down towards Long Island. We have images of his car on the Tappan Zee, the GWB, and at a stop light on the island."

"He have a house or an apartment on the island?" Derek asked.

"Ex-wife lives in Stony Brook. Our people met with her and believe her story that she hasn't seen or heard from Straus in over a year. He did have a leased apartment on the island, but his neighbors say they haven't seen him in several weeks. We went through the apartment wall to wall. Didn't find anything. Straus has a son, but he moved to Kentucky. We contacted him, but he stated that he hasn't spoken with his father in six years."

"Thinking he's hiding out somewhere on the island?" Ralph questioned while drawing deeply on an Arthur Ave maduro.

"Trail goes cold. Based on the direction he was traveling when we last caught an image, he is either on the island, or he continued heading south. We have departments up and down the coast keeping a sharp eye out for him."

"Well, we sure do appreciate you keeping us informed and up to date, Captain," Ralph said. "But we already knew about Rinaldo and Zudak. Word travels fast in today's age."

"I figured you might have found out through whatever communication methods you have, but I wanted to keep you up to date. And there are a few other things that I'd be surprised that your network has informed you about."

Derek straightened his back and silently hoped that Ralph wouldn't say anything that would either delay or prevent Smith from telling them about the other developments in the case.

Ralph stood silent.

"We had three pings to Straus's cell phone. Three pings of interest, that is. He made a call to the main number here at the lodge at zero-9:33 the day of the murders. Call was never connected. Next we have a call received from the lodge thirty-six minutes later. That call lasted less than five seconds. The last ping we discovered was from Straus's cell phone to a hospital in Manhattan. Traced it to a Doctor Brian Lucietta, whose name should sound familiar since it was on the list found at this crime scene. We contacted Lucietta, who is either very stupid or very smart. He denied talking with Straus and contends that he hasn't spoken to him since they stopped working together at Hilburn Psychiatric over ten years ago."

"Ain't surprised by any of what you said," Ralph said. "Either Straus called this lodge to find out if the murders were all taken care of, meaning that he was involved in their planning, or he wanted to see if Curtis or Adams would pick up the phone."

"And the call back?" Smith asked.

"Either from his accomplice or from someone who wanted to know where he was headed to so that he could take care of Straus as well."

"Do you find the fact that no list was found on either Rinaldo or Zudak interesting?"

"I do, indeed. I do find that peculiar."

"We haven't been able to contact Mix. He's either gone very dark, or his body hasn't been found yet."

"I was actually planning to give them a call," Ralph said. "In fact, since we're all here together, how about I make that call right now?"

Ralph retrieved a folded sheet of paper from his wallet that sat bulging in his back pocket. As he dialed the numbers read from the sheet of paper, Smith told him to put the phone on speaker.

"I doubt that anyone will answer, but just in case, I'd like to hear every word said."

As the connection was made, and Ralph's cell phone's speaker reported rings, Derek glanced down at his iPhone to both make sure that he hadn't accidentally deleted the text message from his client that contained Ken O'Connell's cell number and to check for any other messages that may have come through. The text from Thomas was still there, along with a notification of five missed calls and four voice messages.

"Ain't gonna answer, seems. But, the fact that it is ringing tells me that Mix's cell phone is on. Isn't that correct, Captain Smith?" Ralph asked as he closed his flip phone and buried it back into the front pocket of his khakis.

"If you are suggesting that we try to ping his phone, we've been trying that for the last two days."

"Any reason why you can't locate his cell phone?" Derek asked, after having checked the missed calls and not recognizing any of the numbers of the missed calls.

"Verizon suggests that Mix may be in an area with poor coverage. His phone may ring on our end, but he may not be receiving any notifications. His phones are both somewhat current Samsung models that have been on his account for over a year. They are not burner phones, so he isn't trying to hide using technology."

Derek thought about calling his client's father with Ralph and Smith but felt that doing so may violate his confidentiality clause he signed and lived up to with every one of his clients.

"There's one more thing that I think you two will be interested in hearing," Smith said, talking more to Derek than to Ralph. "Ralph said that you were hired by Thomas O'Connell to protect him and his parents from whomever is going around killing people?"

"Yes," Derek confirmed.

"Before I ask why you thought coming all the way up to Piseco Lake instead of staying around your client was a good way to offer client protection, I want to ask what your client told you about his parents. Specifically, his father. Where they are, anything they plan on doing, etcetera."

"My client told me that his parents flew to the Bahamas to get to a safe place. Just this morning, my client told me that he had spoken to his mother last night who told him that they landed safe and sound and were headed to whatever resort they are staying at. My client also told me that he spoke with his father early this morning. He said that his dad wants to get updates directly from me regarding my progress with the case."

"And have you called him with an update yet?" Smith asked.

"Not yet."

"Can you give me a valid reason why you don't call him right now so that we can all speak with him?"

"I have a reason, but you probably won't like it," Derek said.

"Try me."

"I believe in client confidentiality. What my clients say to me is for my ears only."

"That may be a good policy, but didn't I just hear Chief Fox hire you as an officer for the Town of Arietta Police force?"

Derek knew enough about how police departments work to know that withholding case information wasn't widely approved of.

"I am afraid that I may have to resign my position with the town," Derek said to Ralph who just smiled back.

"Then I may have to arrest you for obstruction of justice," Smith said, clearly tired of the game Ralph and Derek were playing. "There's a damn good reason I need you to call Ken O'Connell and a damn good reason why I need to hear exactly what you say to him and what he says to you."

"And that reason is?" Derek asked, knowing that he would have to make the call and violate his own code of confidentiality.

"Janet O'Connell was the only O'Connell who got on that plane to Nassau."

Chapter 21

Her hair needed to be colored again, or at least she thought so. Her husband would say that she looked beautiful no matter how successful those pesky gray hairs were in their mission to take over as much territory as possible. But she wanted always to look her best for him. Especially now. Especially with everything that he was dealing with. She knew she wouldn't be able to visit the resort's fitness center but could balance things out during their stay at the resort by eating a little less.

He deserved her looking her best.

She was standing in front of the mirror in the bathroom just off from the bedroom of their two-room suite. Standing there, separating strands of hair to more closely inspect her roots.

"Darn gray roots," she whispered, careful not to disturb her resting husband.

He was sleeping, still tired from the impromptu car ride the other day. She knew that him feeling tired was all part of his disease, and she knew that more horrible side effects would soon become an even larger part of his everyday life.

The lethargy was okay. Easy to put up with. A few naps each day handled those well. The pain in his abdomen, though mild now, would soon be presenting a different level of interruption. He would have to take more oxy to keep it under control, which meant more cloudy thinking and even more naps.

As she quietly completed the root inspection, she finished getting dressed then walked into the darkened bedroom, listening to hear the slight snoring sounds he was still making.

"Good," she thought. *"He needs more rest."*

Silently, she walked out of the bedroom and into the living room of their suite. From there, she poured herself a vodka tonic (heavy on the vodka), and walked outside and onto the small balcony that overlooked the Saint Lawrence River.

She sat, checked her cell phone and, once seeing that she had missed another call, placed it back on the small glass table beside her after removing the battery.

"Not now," she said. "I'm not ready just yet."

It was only then, only after knowing that her husband was sleeping comfortably, that Michelle Mix allowed herself to cry.

She had married Stanley Mix nineteen years ago and had what many friends and family considered to be the perfect marriage. Though she was unable to get pregnant, the volunteer work she had time for thanks to Stanley's income filled the need that not having her own children created.

She met Stanley when she was working with William Straus in that "awful place" that she never liked to talk about. It wasn't long after meeting him that she reluctantly began to allow herself to fully heal after losing her first husband.

Stanley was wonderful. He was patient and understanding. He

never pushed her to do, say, or feel anything that she wasn't ready to do, say, or feel. Michelle often told people that falling in love with Stanley was something about which she had no decision.

He loved her more than she thought possible, and she grew to love him back with an equal intensity. She felt her fears and resistance to falling in love again melting away with each passing day. She tried her best to ward off the feelings but was unable to maintain her defenses for very long. And when Stanley told her that she didn't have to work another second longer at Hilburn, her defenses collapsed.

It was almost exactly two years after they had met that day at Hilburn that they were married. A small ceremony, with only a handful of friends, Stanley's mother, and a Catholic Priest were there to witness the marriage. But everyone that they met after being married was witness to the love they shared.

Stanley's skills as a surgeon afforded them a lifestyle that many might envy. A beautiful home overlooking Lake Ontario. Cars, never older than two years, in their garage. Yearly three-week vacations to their condo outside of Lahaina on Maui.

All that was nice. Wonderful, in fact. But both Michelle and Stanley would have given it all up if doing so would allow them to stay together for a few more years. Everything; the house, Mercedes, the condo, the expensive art hanging on their living room walls, the forty-foot Sea Ray; all of it would have been gone in a second if there was a trade offered.

"Everything you have in exchange for the cancer being gone.

Deal or no deal?" she wished someone offered.

But no one ever made the offer. No one ever could. All that was offered was a grim prognosis.

"I'm sorry. We'll treat the cancer as aggressively as your body can tolerate, but we can't cure it. All we can do is to extend the time you have left."

Though they tried to figure out what caused his stomach cancer to explode into existence, having no history of cancer or digestive diseases in his family's history, Michelle always knew the cause. She knew that her husband was one of the "good guys." The type that would never intentionally harm anyone, and someone who would always go out of his way to lend a hand.

Michelle knew that it was the guilt of what Stanley had willingly become a part of that created the acidic environment that allowed the cancer to flourish. She knew that what Stanley, Mark Rinaldo, Henry Zudak, and the bastards at Hilburn did to the O'Connell family and to Alexander was the cause of Stanley's cancer.

When she learned that Mark, Henry, Peter, and Jacob had been killed by, supposedly, Alexander Black, she knew that Alexander would be looking for her husband. She had no interest in her husband being the next person whose name got crossed off. There was no way that anyone would take her husband away from her a second before his time was up.

No way.

When she heard from that police chief that her husband's

name was on some list and that they needed to get protection until the suspect was apprehended, she knew that what she did six months ago had come back to haunt her. But learning about Stanley being on the list pissed her off. After all, wasn't it her call that made everything possible in the first place? Wasn't it she who let Ken O'Connell know what happened over two decades ago? Sure, she made the contact out of her own guilt and to remove whatever traces of guilt that were still creating the environment for cancer to grow in her husband's body; but it was she and no one else who did what should have been done the day Alexander O'Connell was born.

As she pulled the final sip from her glass, Michelle listened again for any sounds coming from the bedroom. All was quiet except for the wonderful slight sounds of her husband's breathing.

She remembered clearly the day she contacted Ken O'Connell. As clearly as she remembered the day she and Stanley were married, and as clearly as the day Stanley told her that he had inoperable and terminal cancer. It wasn't a rushed call, one made with a mindset of bargaining with God for her husband's life. It was a call she had wanted to make for years. She just couldn't risk what would happen to her husband if the O'Connells took legal action. And she knew they would. Ken O'Connell told her so when she did finally make the call.

"I will make damn sure that everyone of you bastards are put in jail for the rest of your pathetic lives," he screamed at her. "How the hell could you keep this from us?"

She had no answers for him. No excuses for what the doctors

at Saint Stevens had done, or for herself keeping quiet for over twenty years. She didn't even try to explain why William Straus never alerted anyone. She didn't care how the O'Connells decided to deal with him. She didn't care about defending Brian Lucietta or Jacob Curtis in the least. To her, Straus and his entire team were criminals with doctorate degrees.

She never told Stanley that she had told Ken O'Connell. Nor did she tell Stanley that Ken told her that they would make Stanley and all the doctors pay for what they had done. And she never told Stanley that only he, Brian Lucietta, and William Straus were still alive.

Michelle was surprised that Ken O'Connell didn't do anything that even remotely seemed like what he promised he would do after she told him the whole story. No one ever called from any police department. No one from any medical ethics board ever paid a visit. No governmental oversight committee member ever sent an email requesting clarification on a matter of particular importance.

Nothing happened.

Though Michelle truly didn't care what actions Ken decided to take, she was surprised when nothing seemed to happen. So surprised, in fact that two months after her first call to Ken O'Connell, she called again.

"I know what everyone did was awful. Unforgivable. And I honestly feel that everyone should pay for what we did to your son. But, Mr. O'Connell, whatever actions you are planning, I ask that you leave my husband alone. He's sick. Very sick. He doesn't have much time left, and I know that whatever you may have planned to do won't be nearly as bad as what his guilt is doing to him already."

"I'm afraid, Michelle Mix, that your logic is flawed. But take heart," Ken O'Connell said, "based on what I've learned through my personal research, you played only a reluctant role in the doctor's evil scheme. I have no issue with you. However, I'm afraid that your husband was too involved for me to just ignore. Maybe he will die before I've decided exactly what I will do. If so, I will regret how long it took me to execute my plan. But knowing that, as you say, his guilt is what is killing him, I will take comfort in that belief."

For Michelle, what had happened to the other doctors was nothing more than the way O'Connell chose to take out his anger and hatred. She didn't feel guilty about what happened. She knew that once she told the truth that her only focus in life would be to protect Stanley and to make his final weeks of life filled with as much love and as little pain as was possible.

While she never heard from Ken O'Connell and had no concrete proof that he was somehow behind the murders, she knew in her heart that he was involved. She also knew that a man of Ken O'Connell's resources would be able to know if her husband were still alive, and he probably could access those same resources to find where she and Stanley were hiding.

But Stanley wasn't hiding. He had no idea why his wife packed the car with enough clothes for a week. He didn't understand why she told him that they were going away for a surprise vacation. He knew that he had chemo treatments scheduled and going away would mean that those treatments would be missed. He began to think that Michelle had a conversation with one of his doctors and learned that the treatments were not working, and that putting him through the misery of additional treatments would serve no purpose. Stanley didn't know that he was hiding at all but thought instead that his wife didn't know how to tell him that he didn't have much time left.

But he knew. He knew the second the diagnosis was given to him, and he knew without any doubt the second after the first CAT scan showed his cancer had spread. He knew that he chose the aggressive treatment option for Michelle's sake. She had already lost one husband to a tragedy, and Stanley was willing to do whatever he could to delay her losing her second husband to another tragedy.

He had fallen in love with Michelle the second he saw her standing next to William Straus in that urine-smelling institution. He felt that he had to overcome his fears of getting hurt and had to let her know, somehow, how he felt about her. And when he learned that she felt the same for him, his life became complete.

He often wondered how it was possible that his being a willing participant in everything that happened with the O'Connell baby had resulted in delivering the greatest thing in his life. He never forgot what he and his fellow doctors did with that baby, though once Michelle had left Hilburn, they never talked about it. He felt that talking about the baby would somehow destroy everything good in his life. The memories of those days haunted him, but he vowed to himself to never mention Alexander Black ever again. Especially not to Michelle.

He hoped that somehow Michelle had very selective amnesia and had forgotten that it was he who had delivered the heartless baby to Hilburn. He feared that if he mentioned those first days to her that her amnesia might evaporate, and she would realize what a monster of a person she had married.

He kept everything buried deep inside, and though the memories often tried to escape, he was resolute in his convictions to keep what he had been a part of hidden.

The only time that Alexander Black was mentioned after Michelle left Hilburn was the night after he told her that he had cancer.

"Maybe my disease is my punishment," he told her.

When Ralph Fox called Michelle and told her about the murders, she didn't react the way Ralph probably expected her to react. The fact that people she knew had been murdered and that her husband's name was on a list of probable victims just increased her determination to keep Stanley safe. She knew that ignoring the repeated calls from Ralph Fox and from the number her caller ID told her was coming from the New York State Police, was probably making them suspicious about Stanley and her. Yet she didn't care what anyone thought.

When she read about Mark Rinaldo and Henry Zudak being found dead, she didn't care. They were distant memories for her, and while they were close with Stanley, he didn't need to know that they had been murdered. He didn't need to know anything that was going on around him.

Each morning since receiving that first call from Ralph Fox, Michelle would replace the battery in her phone, certain to leave it in for only the time it took to check for messages. Then the battery was pulled so that no one could trace where she and Stanley were. She paid for the resort room and every purchase she made using cash.

Leave no clues.

She thought about contacting Ken O'Connell and pleading with him to leave her husband alone.

"He doesn't have much time left," she would tell him. *"Killing him won't give you any feeling of revenge. He's dying because of what he did to your son. Isn't that enough?"*

But she never called. Calling wouldn't stop anything. Her husband was going to die. Soon. And there was nothing she could do about it except choose the cause of his death.

She thought for a fleeting moment that perhaps Alexander Black killing her husband would allow him to avoid the pain that would certainly be coming. But that thought was banished. Though she knew she couldn't prevent his cancer from killing him, Michelle knew that she could prevent Stanley from being murdered.

And that was exactly what she intended to prevent.

As she heard him stir in the bedroom, she wiped her eyes clean of the few tears that had formed, adjusted her hair and clothes, and prepared the smile that would greet her husband to this new day.

Chapter 22

"If he didn't get on the plane, then his wife is in on whatever it is he's been doing," Derek said, still shocked.

"And maybe their son, your client," Smith said. "Though I have a feeling that this is all Ken O'Connell's plan, and his wife is just going along with things to keep him happy. His son is probably in the dark."

"Y'all have any idea where Doctor William Straus is?" Ralph asked.

"No idea. Derek?" Smith asked, nodding at Derek.

"No idea. But if he's not involved in assisting the O'Connells, he is probably hiding somewhere and isn't likely to reveal his position anytime soon. Have you been able to contact Stanley or Michelle Mix?"

"Called the cell phone registered in their name. No answer. I checked with their service provider, and they told me that their phones haven't pinged any towers since the day after the bodies were discovered here. Either they have pulled the batteries or have disabled network data and location services. Or, they've been visited by our suspects, and their bodies just haven't been discovered yet."

Derek glanced again at his iPhone and saw that he had received another text from his client. It read, *"Have you called my father yet???"*

"I assume that you want me to call Mr. O'Connell now?" Derek asked Smith as he sent a message back to his client stating that he was about to make the requested call.

"Not yet," Smith said. "We first need to get things set up so we can get a location on O'Connell's cell. I'll need to borrow your phone for a few minutes. When you do call, you just need to do and say exactly what I tell you to say. If he asks you a question that we haven't prepared an answer for, look at me, and I will write out what you need to say. Do not even think of going freelance on his, Cole. I know that freelancing is your thing, but it will not be tolerated. I hope you understand."

Nothing was making sense to Derek. In every one of his previous cases, there was a line that needed to be followed. Every line had a starting point and an end point. The starting point was created when someone did something which made someone else upset, concerned, or downright pissed off. The end point was providing the client a satisfactory resolution. Connect the two points with as straight a line as possible, get paid, and move on.

But with this case, Derek didn't know what or where the starting point was or what ending would be considered a desired resolution. While he did work closely with police departments in many of his cases, this case had now found him under the control of the authorities. He was expected to do exactly what Captain Smith wanted him to do and to suppress his own instincts.

As Smith stood, arms crossed, waiting for him to comply,

Derek decided to do what Smith expected. Then, as soon as possible, he would get as far away from Piseco Lake as possible and run his case the way he knew the case should be run.

"So," Derek said, "how long till I can make that call?"

"Twenty minutes," Smith said.

Smith left Derek and Ralph alone in the entry room. There, the two men sat in absolute quiet. Both were processing the information that they had just learned from Smith, and both were wondering how Ken O'Connell came to learn about Alexander Black.

"We seem to still have some pieces missing to this jigsaw puzzle," Ralph said, breaking the silence that had lasted several minutes. "But this new information also puts some pieces together nicely."

"Like what?" Derek asked.

"Seems to me that Straus isn't running because he is helping Alexander Black, but because he must've seen what Black did here and didn't want to have his body added to the pile. And wherever he did run off to is somewhere that he feels will be as far away from Black as possible. To me, this new info rules out everyone but the father from the list of suspected accomplices. You see things any different?"

"Not sure yet," Derek said. "I mean, until we know if or how the father may have found out about Black, we can't assume to understand his reasons for not flying off to the sunny Bahamas. He may have stayed back to make sure his son – my client – is safe or to talk him into flying to the Bahamas with him. We don't know. Way too many options. And until I know his reason for staying and exactly where he is, Straus is still a suspect. Maybe he got tired of hiding Black and made a deal with Ken O'Connell. *'Everything you ever wanted to know about that day you thought your son died but were afraid to ask'* sort of deal. Maybe Lucietta is involved somehow. I don't know. But what I do know is that I need to find William Straus. Now more than ever."

"You think your client knows what his daddy has been up to?"

"Something tells me that he has no idea. Not sure why I feel that, but I do."

"Didn't you tell me that his daddy suggested that your client hire you?"

"He did. According to my client."

"Then why would your client's daddy suggest that you get on the case if he's the one you're looking for?"

"I don't know. Maybe he thought that we wouldn't find out that he never left town or maybe he wants me involved for another reason. I don't know."

"Well, you're about to find out," Smith said to Derek as he walked back into the lodge's entry room.

After spending ten minutes telling Derek exactly what to say and what not to say, Smith handed Derek his phone back.

"Remember, you need to keep him on the call for at least ninety seconds and, whatever you do, don't tell him that you're with any police agency and make damn sure that you act like you believe he is on some beach in the Bahamas. Clear?"

"Clear."

The phone rang twice before being answered.

"Ken O'Connell."

"Mr. O'Connell," Derek said. "This is Derek Cole. Your son asked me to give you a call about the case I was hired to assist with."

"Took you damn long enough to call me," Ken barked. "I trust that you understand that while my son contacted you, the money you've received came from me. That makes *me* your client, and if I want something from you or need you to do something, I expect your full compliance. Is that understood?"

"Understood. How can I help you?"

"Where are you right now?" Ken asked.

"Sitting in my car down the street from Doctor William Straus's lodge in Piseco Lake New York," Derek delivered his instructed response.

"Have you contacted or are you working with any of the local police?"

"I've met Chief Ralph Fox but am not working with him. He'd prefer that I just stay out of his way."

"And that's what I want you to do as well," Ken said, his voice sounding somewhat relieved. "I don't know why the hell you felt it was important to be up in that area in the first place, but I am not going to tell you how to run your investigation. I am, however, going to tell you what I need you to find out from this point forward."

"And that would be?" Derek asked.

"Find William Straus, Brian Lucietta, and Stanley Mix. I need you to find them and keep them safe. I want to punish those assholes for what they did to my family. Not that I wouldn't be glad if they were killed, but I want to make them suffer in a court of law and in prison."

"I understand. Do you have any suggestions as to where Straus and Mix may be holding up?"

"If I knew that I wouldn't need you, would I?"

"Just trying to save you some money, Mr. O'Connell. The longer I spend on this case, the higher your bill."

"Don't worry about my bill. In fact, I've arranged to have another payment transferred to your account tomorrow."

"Much appreciated," Derek said.

"I want you to call me twice a day, every day with updates. Call me at 8:00 a.m. and 8:00 p.m. Understood?"

"Absolutely. How long do you plan to stay in the Bahamas?"

"I'm not in the Bahamas, Mr. Cole. Never got on that plane. Never intended to. My wife is down there, and my son believes that I am with her, and I need you to assure me that you will not tell anyone that I am not where everyone thinks I am."

"Where are you?" Derek asked.

"Chicago."

Chapter 23

"Chicago?" Derek questioned. "If the police find out that you're in Chicago, then you're going to quickly become a very sought after person."

"You think that I'd actually leave town without my son?" Ken responded.

"Which son?" Derek asked.

"Don't be a smart ass, Cole. You know I'm talking about Thomas. I found out about what the doctors and Saint Stevens did six months ago. I've been planning exactly how I was going to get my revenge when I got a call from Ralph Fox, telling me that Alexander Black had killed three people and had listed my family on his hit list. I'll tell you that I am not at all upset that those bastards are dead. Wish I had the courage to kill them myself. But now that Alexander has made his intentions clear, I am focused on keeping my family safe and making damn sure that Straus, Lucietta, and Mix don't get killed before I can send them to prison.

"Mix is dying of cancer. He doesn't have much time left, or so I've been told. I need you to find him first. I want to look him in his eyes and let him know what a waste of humanity he is. I want the last thing he hears is a jury finding him guilty and the last thing he sees is seen through steel bars.

"Find him, Cole. Whatever it takes, and whatever it costs. You find Stanley Mix before Alexander does."

"How did you learn about what happened with Alexander?" Derek asked.

"I got a call from Mix's wife, Michelle. Told me everything that happened. Every last detail. Also told me that her husband Stanley was dying of cancer. Then she tried to convince me to just leave him the hell alone and that his guilt is what caused his cancer. I told her that I couldn't care less about what caused his cancer or how long he had to live. I let her know that I would find a way to put all of those assholes in prison and make damn sure that the whole world knew what they did."

"If you found out six months ago, why didn't you go to the authorities then?"

"If someone called you out of the blue and told you the same story, would you believe it right off the bat or would you do some research?"

"Research, but not six months of it."

"It took longer than you might imagine to verify her story. They covered their asses pretty damn well. The state of New York had zero information on Alexander Black since Straus kept him hidden in some closed-off ward in a now-closed psych hospital. It took a while to pick up a trail, and that trail leads straight to the lodge you are looking at right now.

"Once I discovered that the story was true, I started planning my next steps. Only thing was my next steps were interrupted by what Alexander Black is accused of doing."

"Did you ever see Alexander? I mean, did you ever go out to Piseco Lake to verify?"

"Mr. Cole, I am a man of resources. No, I never went out to Piseco Lake, but I hired a few people who did all the verifying I needed. I received pictures of Alexander and copies of his entire file two weeks ago."

"Mr. O'Connell," Derek said, "I strongly suggest that you make your location known to the local authorities. Your name was on that list as well for whatever reason, and if the state police or Chief Ralph Fox find out you never boarded that plane, they will come looking for you and will have some targeted questions."

"You worry about doing what I am paying you to do, and I'll take care of myself. I know that my son is safe, but that doesn't mean that he will stay safe. Find Straus, Lucietta, and Mix. And if you happen to find Alexander Black, give him a message for me."

"And that message would be?"

"To leave my family the hell alone. Call me at 8:00 your time. Got it?"

"Got it."

Chapter 24

William Straus was conflicted. He didn't know what to concentrate on. His thoughts flipped between congratulating himself for his cunning and the intense fear that he knew demanded more of his focus.

When he received the call and heard the demands expected of him, Straus knew he had to respond with caution. Though he offered no resistance, he calculated how he would respond. He practiced which words he would use, how to use them, when, and even the tone of voice he would present the rehearsed words with. But he also planned his approach, and that planning, that calculation was why he was still alive.

The caller was viciously clear.

"Be at your cabin no later than seven in the morning. Alexander and I will be waiting for you. Do not alert anyone about our meeting. Should you have previously scheduled guests planning on arriving, let them keep their schedules. If you decide on inviting anyone else who you feel might give you some negotiating advantage, don't. You know exactly what this meeting is about and can probably correctly assume our demands. However, if you fail to comply or choose to modify your expected response, our demands will be satisfied in a different manner."

William Straus had no intentions of making a risky move. He would comply fully. Do what was asked, exactly as directed. But he also would have his own "Plan B" and "Plan C" ready to be implemented. Before any plan was set into motion, Straus designed a prequel.

He stopped his car a full half-mile down the twisting, tree-lined road that housed his lodge. It was still dark when he shut his BMW off and disappeared into the thick woods. The closer he got to his lodge, the slower and quieter he made his pace. When he was within a safe viewing distance, he opened his gym bag, pulled out a long sleeve shirt and sweat pants, and put them on over his Jos A Bank gabardines and crisp, white pinpoint Oxford. He found a low bush that afforded excellent cover and crawled beneath its concealing bows.

Once situated, he glanced at his watch.

"Six-thirty," he said to himself. "Perfect."

From his position, Straus could see the back end of a sedan, unfamiliar to him, parked in the stone driveway of his lodge. His angle of view did not allow him to see the plates nor the make, but he knew whose car it was.

Ten minutes after he arrived in his perch, Straus saw a car slowing, then turning into the lodge.

"Curtis and Adams," he whispered.

He watched Jacob Curtis and Peter Adams enter the lodge after pausing to consider the strange car parked in the driveway. He knew they were planning on being in attendance when Straus told

Alexander the good news, but he didn't expect them till well after ten.

It was perfectly still and quiet for several minutes before Straus saw the main door of the lodge swing open. Standing in the doorway was a bloody Alexander Black. The morning sun was still struggling to ward off the dark shadows, but Straus could see, even from one hundred feet away, the blood dripping from Alexander's hands.

"Shit!" he thought.

The decision to leave and to execute Plan B was made instantly, but he knew he had to remain unseen and unheard. He needed a distraction. And as he glanced further down the road, he saw his needed distraction headed straight towards Alexander.

He didn't know the man, but Straus recognized him. He remembered having seen him walking by his lodge before. His name didn't matter. All that mattered was the fact that he looked to be speaking with Alexander, which meant Alexander would be distracted.

As quietly as he could, Straus crawled backwards, keeping his gaze fixed on Alexander and the familiar stranger as they spoke in the middle of the road. When he was free of the bush and could stand, Straus began to quicken his pace. Before he turned his back on his lodge, Straus saw Alexander plunge a knife deep into the man's neck.

He sprinted back to his car.

He made no attempt to keep quiet. He wheeled his car into the road, hastily made a two-and-a-half-point turn and gunned his engine towards his escape route.

Had he just followed the instructions he was given, Straus was sure that the blood dripping from Alexander's hands would be his. If he had trusted Alexander's assistant, he would have no ability to implement Plans B and C. No, if he had been a sheep like most others and had just done what he was told, he would be dead.

As he slowed his BMW to a speed less likely to raise suspicions, Straus grabbed his phone, removed the battery, and tossed it into his back seat. He then removed the Plan B driving directions from his center console and prepared to turn off State Route 8.

He had spent a considerable amount of time planning his alternate route, making certain that if Alexander and his accomplice were to try to follow him that they would be hard pressed to keep up with the frequent turns. Within an hour after leaving his lodge, Straus pointed his car south and headed towards New York City.

His first stop would be to see Brian Lucietta. He had to let Brian know what had happened.

"Brian," he said while standing outside of his car in Mercy Hospital's employee parking lot, "both you and I need to protect ourselves. If what O'Connell told me is true, he and Alexander are not planning on making everything public but in exacting revenge."

"William," Brian Lucietta said, "you're running scared from two people who, unless I've missed something, are not career criminals. If what you believe you saw at your lodge actually happened, the police would have them in custody within a day. Two at the most. I'm staying right here and keeping things business as usual."

"I'm going to Hilburn. Ward C is impenetrable. I'll keep in touch with you and with the news and won't come out until I know Alexander and O'Connell are either dead or behind bars."

"You're overreacting. What you should be more concerned about is explaining to the authorities why you kept Alexander hidden all these years."

"I've already figured that out," Straus replied.

"Shouldn't you share your story with me so that we are on the same page?"

"As far as you know, Alexander was just another patient, and you had no idea of the circumstances behind his arrival to Hilburn or departure."

"Keeping me safe, are you, Will?"

"Keeping things clean, Brian. My story is the only one that is ever heard, if things come to that point. The more you deny, the better."

"And with Jacob and Peter out of the way, that only leaves the doctors from Chicago to deal with," Brian said as he checked an incoming text message on his cell. "I have to get back. You keep in touch, and let me know if there's anything else I need to know about your story."

"I have a plan for the good doctors from Chicago."

"Good enough," Brian said as he extended his hand to Straus.

"I do think it unwise for you not to take precautions," Straus said as he shook Brian's hand.

"I still carry my Taser. Just in case."

Doctor William Straus was now safe, hidden in a place that he knew better than anyone. A place where no one would look for him, but from where he could keep fully informed of Alexander and his accomplice's doings. Behind the locked doors of Ward C on the second floor of the vacated Hilburn Psychiatric Institution, he sat surrounded by a month's worth of supplies. He had everything he needed, and now only ventured out of the protective confines early in the morning and late at night.

The rooms in Ward C had no exterior windows. The steel and brick construction blocked the WiFi signal from the tech startup company that was housed in the old Hilburn supply building that stood fifty feet from the walls of the main Hilburn hospital building. Straus would carefully listen for any noise outside of the only door that led from the "hub" of Ward C to the hallway. After hearing nothing for at least three minutes, he would unlock the door and quietly make his way down the southern hall to a window that faced the old supply building. There, Straus was able to log on to the tech company's WiFi signal on his iPad, access news streams, check emails, and respond to any that he considered to be "critically important."

He was certain that no one knew that Ward C was no longer vacant and knew that the only time a visitor would enter the abandoned main hospital building would be if a possible tenant was interested in seeing the available space. Over the years, three of the four buildings of the Hilburn campus were converted. The tech company occupied one building, another was converted to a warehouse, and the third was converted to small offices for start-up companies looking for inexpensive office space. While there were many companies interested in the three story main hospital, no tenants had been found. Rumors of the hospital being haunted were well known in the area, and local police had to increase their watches to keep out amateur ghost hunters and teenagers looking for a thrilling night.

Straus didn't believe in ghosts and was able to easily dismiss the occasional sounds he heard during the night as echoes from the nearby roads or kids, loitering in the parking lot. There were some sounds, however, that gave Straus pause. Sounds that sounded eerily familiar.

His first night back in Hilburn, Straus thought he heard a crackle of electricity coming from the first floor where doctors like Brian Lucietta would perform "therapeutic shock therapy." Later that night, Straus was certain that he heard the voice of a particularly disturbed patient calling for him. The patient died on the second floor from asphyxiation, though the exact cause was never determined.

Though the sounds startled Straus, he passed them off as his nerves getting the better of him.

"I've never read an obituary that claimed ghosts as the cause of death," he chuckled to himself. "Empty halls distort sounds, and a nervous mind can turn the wind into a blood curling scream."

It was at the window where Straus read about the two doctors murdered in Chicago. He read about Rinaldo having been killed by "severe blunt force trauma to his skull" and about Zudak being strangled in a motel thirty miles west of Chicago. He also read the details of the murders at his lodge and of the police search for "Doctor William Straus, wanted for questioning."

There were no emails worth his response and nothing from Brian Lucietta. The only email that he did find interesting enough to be saved and read several times, came from an unknown Gmail account. He assumed that someone, probably Alexander or O'Connell, had accessed the computer in his study at the lodge, had learned his email address and had contacted him. The message was simple, concise and well written;

"Your name still appears on my list. I'd like to remove it, soon."

Part of his Plan B called for three stops. The first being to visit with Brian Lucietta, to both make Brian aware of the happenings at the lodge and also to instruct him to deny knowledge of Alexander Black. The second was to a grocery store, where, using cash, Straus bought a month's worth of food, water, and supplies. The final stop he made was to his home on Long Island. There, Straus collected boxes of files, his Smith and Wesson .380, two boxes of tactical bullets, and several changes of clothes. He needed nothing else and felt confident that, if after his food and supplies ran out, he would be able to sneak out to gather more if the situation with Alexander Black had not been resolved.

Straus had thought of nearly everything to include into his Plan B to ensure his safety and protection. The one thing Straus had not planned for was the battery of his iPad running low. He kept a car charger adapter in his BMW that was concealed in one bay of the loading docks two floors below him. If the iPad's battery died, Straus decided a trip to the loading dock might also give him the opportunity to drive to a nearby hotel, for a shower and to "borrow" a pillow, another missing item from his plan.

Chapter 25

"I have no idea how you got into my office, but I do suggest that you leave immediately." Brian Lucietta was certainly startled when he walked into his office, turned on the overhead lights, and felt the hard shove that sent him sprawling onto the floor. But Brian didn't believe in staying startled long. He quickly found his footing, and when he realized that he had no clean path to get out of his office, he stood to confront his unwelcome guest.

"I will give you three seconds to turn around and walk out of my office before I take action."

"And what action are you prepared to take?" his guest asked.

"Three, two..."

Brian's countdown, though short, was made even shorter when he felt the probes dig into his body. He had only enough time to look up in terror before those two small, shiny barbs released an eruption of pain.

The electricity seized his muscles together in a tight, contracted, and painful way. His brain was scrambled with electrical impulses. As he fell to the floor, Brian felt his jaw tightening, clenching, and grinding his teeth together. Had he expected his jaw to clamp shut so tightly, he would have been certain to move his tongue back and away from the crushing power of his teeth. But he had no warning.

The contractions lasted only three seconds, and when they stopped, his pain evaporated. But not the pain of his severed tongue. He felt blood pouring from his tongue, into his mouth, and flowing down his throat. He coughed to move the blood from his airway and out of his mouth. Along with a disturbing amount of blood, his cough also caused a two-inch long strip of his tongue to launch from its home. Brian watched it land inches from the boots standing a few feet from his prone position.

"This is a remarkably effective tool," his guest said. "I was pleasantly surprised to find it in your top desk drawer. Remarkably effective. And in case you were worried, I had the foresight to wear rubber gloves, in case the electricity travels through the handle."

As Brian tried to stand, he heard the popping of the current again. He didn't understand why he hadn't noticed the popping when the first jolt of electricity was delivered and hoped that he would never have to hear it again.

Three seconds of searing, contracting, exhausting pain, then, nothing. Complete absence of pain. He felt his body soaked with sweat and could feel the blood still pouring from within his mouth. He raised his head and locked eyes with his attacker.

"Peeez, wha u wan?" he mumbled; his tongue screaming for no movement.

"I am sorry, Doctor Lucietta, but it seems that you are very poor at speaking with a shortened tongue. Please, try it again. I will listen more closely."

"Wha u ewe wan rom e?"

"Sounds like you are asking about my intentions? Nod if I heard you correctly."

Brian nodded his head as more blood was sprayed into the air by a painful cough.

"Fair question," his attacker said. "All I want to know is where I will find William Straus?"

Brian raised his hand and pointed to a picture hanging on the far wall of his office.

"Here?" his attacker asked. "I will find him here?"

Brian nodded then heard the popping sound again.

When the current stopped, Brian's body was convulsing. His legs and arms were uncomfortable, but the pain in his chest was what Brian was most concerned with.

"I've never used one of these Tasers. I had no idea a cartridge was needed in order to deliver the voltage," Brian's attacker said. "I must commend you for your forward thinking. Having a cache of additional cartridges hidden in your bottom drawer: Brilliant."

His attacker popped in another cartridge, squeezed the Taser's trigger, and sent another round of shock treatment into the body of Doctor Lucietta. Without pause, he slammed in another cartridge, squeezed the trigger again but heard no report of the popping noises that signaled a passing current.

"Three successive doses," the attacker said. "Your Taser is good for three doses. Not that you will need to know that information, but it is a good bit to have."

Brian was unable to move. Though the only pain he was feeling was his severed tongue and the fading discomfort in his chest, his muscles were spent. He saw that his attacker had moved across the office and was carefully inspecting the photograph that contained the location that William Straus would be found. He knew this was his chance. He knew he had to reach the door and the safety that the hallway just beyond his office door would provide.

Brian summoned every last bit of his energy and forced himself onto all fours. His arms screamed and shook violently as he demanded that they pull him towards the door. His legs offered no assistance to his arms and were nothing but dead weight needing to be dragged across the office floor. His eyesight was spinning and his thoughts, muddled. But he felt himself moving. Moving towards the door and to safety. His closed one eye to better keep to his course.

His senses were muted except for his smell. As he struggled to reach safety, Brian's stomach turned at the foul smell that was filling his nostrils. Though he couldn't be certain, he believed he has no more than four feet from the door. Four more feet before he could spill himself onto the hallway floor where someone would certainly see him and call for help. His body was sending random signals to his brain so Brian wasn't sure if the sharp, stabbing pain he felt when he was two feet from the door was something new or just his muscles continued reaction to the stun gun.

But when he saw the blood flowing down his arms and onto the floor, Brian knew that the pain in his neck wasn't a side effect. The next thing he felt was a continuation of this new pain. But this continuation was deeper. Slowly reaching through his neck, into his throat and then, the long, thin knife finished its journey.

His arms went numb as they folded beneath his weight. He could feel nothing; no pain, no twitches, no blood running its way down his body.

"I made it," he thought as his eyes clouded over, and he felt shallowness in his chest.

"Thank you for the information," he heard his unwelcome guest say as if speaking from deep inside a tunnel. "Good night, doctor, and, again, thank you."

Chapter 26

Derek's departure was sudden. No more than five minutes after his call with Ken O'Connell ended, Captain Smith gave Derek his clear expectations then made sure Derek's car started and headed away from Piseco Lake New York. When Derek was no further than three miles away from the lodge, he pulled his car over to the side of State Route 8, pulled out his cell phone from his pocket, and redialed the last number called.

"Ken O'Connell."

"Ken, it's Derek Cole."

"Problem?"

"Unfortunately, there is, and the problem is yours," Derek said. "The last conversation we had was not as private as you would have liked."

Derek explained the circumstances of their last call. He explained that Ralph Fox and Captain Jared Smith from the state police heard that Ken was not in the Bahamas but was in Chicago, the same city where two murders had just taken place.

Ken was silent as Derek explained that while he could have refused to make the call in front of others, learning that Ken hadn't made the flight to the Bahamas made him very suspicious. Ken O'Connell said nothing when Derek explained what he had found beneath the bedroom of Alexander Black and how it seemed highly likely that Alexander had an accomplice. Derek tried to describe what he'd seen on the trail, marked with freshly painted hearts and stocked with supplies. He explained how the timeline of the murders in Chicago demanded that Alexander had either learned how drive and to steal a car (though no cars were reported as being stolen in the area) or Alexander was given a ride.

"You've seen the pictures of him," Derek said. "The chances that anyone would have pulled over and picked him up if he were hitchhiking are highly unlikely."

Derek shared his thoughts that Straus may be the accomplice and told Ken why he suspected Straus. He also told Ken that while he thought it was careless and suspicious that Ken never got on the plane and admitted that he learned the truth about Alexander Black, he still didn't suspect Ken O'Connell had anything to do with the murders.

"You are my client, and I take my client relationships very seriously," Derek said. "As soon as our last call ended, I knew I had to call you and let you know that the conversation was not a private one."

"Derek," Ken finally spoke, "I don't blame you at all. I should have expected something when I noticed that you were speaking to me on your speakerphone. Doesn't matter, though, I guess. I didn't have anything to do with any murders or helping Alexander escape. As far as I'm concerned, I won't do anything differently than what I was planning on doing, even though I will have to keep an eye out for police. I still need you to find Mix, Lucietta, and Straus, and I still want you to call me twice a day.

"Cole, I do appreciate you letting me know about our first call. And don't worry about pissing me off. The fact that you called and let me know says more to me than you can imagine. Listen, I have a call scheduled in one hour with some of my other hired resources. If they have come up with anything, I'll call you right away. In the meantime, what are your plans?"

"Honestly, I don't know which way to head. I could drive out to Rochester and start trying to track down the Mixes, or I could head down to Manhattan and try to locate Lucietta. As far as Straus and Alexander go, I have to believe they are in the Chicago area. If they are together or if Alexander is acting alone somehow, that means that they, or he, will be looking for you and your son."

"Thomas is on a boat in the middle of Lake Michigan, along with three of my 'special forces' team members. I'm not worried about him," Ken calmly said.

"Special Forces?" Derek asked.

"Cole, I have been fortunate in my business dealings. I started with a used car lot on the south side of Chicago when I was nineteen years old. I turned fifty last year and opened my eighteenth car dealership the day after my birthday. I've also branched out to a few other endeavors, all of which are profitable. I will tell you this, Cole; everything I do is above board. Nothing illegal. At the same time, my success in business has made me a target on more than one occasion. I told you that I have many resources, including some ex-military professionals who handle personal security for my family and me. Nature of the game, I suppose, but considering what's happening now, I am damn glad I have my Special Forces team on payroll."

"If Thomas is out on Lake Michigan, how is that I've been able to contact him whenever I needed to?"

"Each morning and evening, the boat moves close enough to shore to pick up a cell signal. My team knows exactly what they are doing, when to do it, and how to do it."

"Wish I had a team like that sometimes," Derek joked.

"As long as you are working for me on this case, my resources are at your disposal. In fact, I have two private investigators assisting in your efforts. One is getting close to finding Stanley and Michelle Mix, and the other is busy locating Straus. I don't have anyone looking for Alexander, however. I figured that he'd either show up or the police would be focusing their efforts on finding him.

"Listen, Cole, I do appreciate you being honest with me, and I need you to know that I am being honest with you. If you think that I am somehow behind these murders, you need to tell me right now. I can't trust someone that doesn't trust me."

"I think we are on the same page," Derek said.

"I need you to *know*, not to just *think*."

"I can't tell you that I am without my suspicions yet. There are too many variables and coincidences to rule out anyone. Hell, I even wonder if I had somehow had something to do with these murders."

"I guess that's fair enough. I have to run. That call is coming in soon, and I have some other matters to attend to. I'll call you if my resources come up with anything important. If you don't hear from me, call me at 8:00 tonight. Agreed?"

"Agreed. Stay safe, Mr. O'Connell," Derek added.

"Call me Ken, and you stay safe as well."

It was no more than five minutes after his call with Ken ended that his cell phone rang again. This time, the caller ID told Derek the caller was from the Piseco Lake area. "You left so damn fast that I didn't even get your cell number. Had to do some research to find it," Ralph Fox slurred.

Though Derek had left Ralph just a few minutes ago, it sounded like Ralph was at least an hour into a happy hour. "Miss me already, Ralph?" Derek said.

"Not entirely, but I do think it wise that you and I maintain a certain level of ongoing communications regarding our shared case. And since I believe I made you a member of my team, I do believe the chain-of-command position that I have affords me the ability to expect an open line of information sharing with you."

"I told Ken O'Connell that he was on speaker phone and that you and Smith heard everything he said," Derek said.

"I figured you would," Ralph said, his voice now sounding clear and solid "I noticed a change in your face when O'Connell said that he was in Chicago. Bet you no longer like him for these crimes?"

"I'm still not sure, but his reasons for not getting on that plane make sense to me. To me, he's someone who had a horrible injustice happen to him and someone who wants to deliver his own type of justice to the doctors."

"Honestly," Ralph said, "I don't blame him at all. Now since we are sharing like a couple of school girls here, I do feel compelled to let you know that Captain Smith is going to keep an eye on your movements. He ain't got the resources he'd like to have you trailed, but part of the reason he took your cell phone was to allow his smart people to trace your whereabouts. Ain't sure if he can tap your calls, but he is going to know where you are at, most of the time."

"That's good to know. Thanks Ralph."

While he was still talking with Ralph, Derek heard the familiar "beep" of his cell phone, alerting him to an incoming call. "Ralph, I have another call coming in. I'll get back to you later."

He ended the call with Ralph and answered the incoming call.

"Derek Cole," he said.

"Derek, it's Thomas. Did you speak with my father yet?" The sound of wind and rain could be heard in the background.

"I did. He's fine. Just wants me to keep him informed. He told me that you are on a boat out on Lake Michigan. Seems like a pretty safe place to be."

"Didn't think you wanted to know where I was," Thomas said through a soft chuckle. "And I have two of his goons around me at all times. My father tends to go overboard, pardon the boating pun."

"He seems like a smart man. You just make sure you don't fall overboard. That lake can get rough, and it sounds like it's raining out your way."

"Little summertime storm. We pulled in close to the marina, so were not a sitting target out in the middle of the lake. Listen, I called you because I was just given some more information that you probably need to know."

"Shoot," Derek said.

"My father's goons are pretty well connected, as you might imagine. They have friends working in police departments all over the country. This isn't confirmed yet, but there was a doctor murdered in the same hospital that Brian Lucietta works. Happened a few hours ago. Middle of the day. And before you ask, they don't have anyone in custody."

The likelihood that Alexander had at least one accomplice was now a certainty for Derek. The fact that six murders had occurred in three different parts of the country, each separated by at least six hours of driving, made the possibility of one person acting alone virtually impossible.

"Thanks for the update," he said to Thomas.

"I don't know what my father wants you to focus your efforts on, but I figured you'd be interested."

"The more I know about all the players, the better."

"That's all I have. I'll be heading back out beyond cell coverage as soon as this storm passes, so I will be out of range for a while," Thomas said.

"Stay dry," Derek said as he ended the call.

Derek slowed his car down to the reduced thirty-five speed limit as he approached the small Adirondack town of Speculator,

New York. Feeling hungry, he started looking for a quiet place to eat, think, and to process the events of the day. Off to his right, he spotted a small pizzeria and deli that only had two cars parked in the lot in front.

Before he could shut off his car, his cell phone rang again.

"Derek Cole," he said, amazed at how many times his normally quiet cell had rung in the last twenty minutes.

"Alexandria Bay. River's Edge Resort," the voice of Ken O'Connell said. "My resources tracked the Mixes down. They made reservations under the name 'McClury,' and checked in last night." The excitement was abundant in Ken's voice.

"I'll head up there now," Derek said. "I found out that my cell phone location is being traced, so I will turn it off as soon as this call is done."

"Fine. If you can't contact me by 8:00, call me whenever you can, no matter the time. I just want you to identify Stanley and Michelle and confirm that they are in the resort. Understood?"

"Understood. I'm going to grab some lunch, pull up the directions, and head up to find them."

"Don't engage them. Just identify them, and contact me right away. If they leave, I need you to follow them. I'll email you their pictures so that you can mark them."

"Sounds good." Derek pulled into the parking lot of the pizzeria, turned his car off and sighed deeply. While his suspicions about Ken O'Connell remained, he felt like he, Ken, and Thomas were all working together towards the same goal. Derek never wanted to become friends with his clients. He intentionally made decisions to prevent learning too much about his clients as well as letting them know too much about him. As he sat in the parking lot, listening to Ken's altered instructions, he wondered, if things were different, if he and the O'Connells may have enough in common to become friends.

"I hear that the Chicago area is getting some storms. Hope your weather clears out soon," Derek said, cutting off his thoughts and giving the conversation a logical ending.

"Weather? There's not a cloud in the sky around the whole area."

Chapter 27

His head was swimming. Each time he reached a conclusion, another thought changed the course of his thinking and suggested an alternative. As he drove the three hours the trip to Alexandria Bay would take, Derek rode in absolute silence.

His phone was turned off and stuffed inside of a lead- and aluminum-lined bag that prevented any signals from getting out or into his phone. Though he usually would spend his windshield time listening to music at the highest volume a car's system could pump out, the radio in his rental car was silent.

"Not raining in the Chicago area," he thought to himself. He had confirmed the weather report using his My Radar app on his iPhone before shutting it down. The only place of interest that was experiencing a "summertime storm" was the greater New York City area. Chicago and almost the entirety of Lake Michigan were enjoying a beautiful summer day.

"How could he be in New York if he has his father's ex-military people watching him? Is it possible that the whole family is involved in these murders and that there are no 'goons' protecting Thomas since he doesn't need protection?"

The miles passed. Each mile marker bringing Derek further away from clarity.

Derek had grown comfortable with silence, though he still would prefer to have someone to be with in most situations. Someone to talk with. Someone to enjoy the silence with. Lucy made him comfortable with silence. When they first met, Derek felt compelled to always keep a conversation going. Failing that, Derek would whistle, sing softly to himself, or have either the radio or television on in the background to break up the absent silence.

"We don't always have to be talking, you know," Lucy stated. "You don't have to worry about keeping a conversation going *all the time*. Sometimes I just like to sit with you and not have to say anything."

"But everyone always says that communication is the key to a lasting marriage," he rebutted.

"Sometimes, the best way to communicate is just to be with me in silence."

He tried to just sit and not talk with her, but he found it harder than Lucy expected.

"Have you ever considered that maybe, just maybe, I am really interested in hearing what you have to say?" he asked one evening after sitting next to Lucy on their couch silently for over an hour.

"Have you ever considered that the reason you always want to talk with me is that you are afraid of what I might be thinking about when not talking?"

Lucy was talented at reading people, especially Derek. His attempts to keep his fears and insecurities hidden were in vain. If he asked a strange question, she always could figure out what Derek was really trying to uncover.

"Until you learn to listen more than you speak, you'll never make a good detective," she told him once after he found out that he didn't get the promotion with the Columbus Police Department he was expecting. "God gave you two ears and one mouth. Use them in that proportion."

Derek worked on being comfortable with silence. After a while, he actually grew to look forward to times when he and Lucy could just sit together and digest their days in silence. As long as she was in the same room as he, Derek could go hours without muttering a single sound.

"It's nice. Isn't it?" she asked one night. "To just be together and not have to always struggle to think of something to say."

Derek glanced at his wife as he sat across their living room and raised his index finger to his lips.

"Shhh," was the only response he offered in answer.

Lucy smiled.

Derek remembered that night. How they laughed together. How they talked about starting a family some day. About their upcoming vacation to Maui and how Lucy would someday be able to stop working as a children's counselor and be able to stay home and raise their kids. He remembered how they made love that night and how wonderful it felt to just hold her. There was no way of knowing that the next day, Lucy would be dead.

As he continued driving through the twisting roads of the Adirondack Park, Derek could clearly see and hear the events of

Lucy's final day.

The call came in over his police radio while Derek and his partner, Bill Manner, were on routine patrol. They responded along with at least twenty other patrol officers, lead investigators, Derek's lieutenant and Captain, and the two hostage negotiators.

The call came through as "10-42, 10-43b, First Metropolitan Bank. 423 North Main." Officer Manner new to the police force asked Derek what the codes meant.

"Robbery in progress, and shots fired. Looks like we are headed to a bank robbery."

When Derek arrived on scene, his Captain approached him. The look on his face was one that sent immediate concern warnings to Derek.

"Officer Cole, I need you to stay back from the scene."

"What's happened?" he asked, his voice dripping his fear.

"Your wife is in the bank with the gunman. He's already shot the kid she was with. Hostage negotiators are trying to establish communications with the suspect now. You need to stay back."

"Captain, I know this bank like the back of my hand," Derek pleaded. "I do security for them on my off days."

"Officer Cole, I need you to stay back and let the experts handle this."

"If he's already killed one, why wait and give him time to shoot someone else? I could get in the back entrance without him ..."

"Cole," his Captain interjected. "I need you to let us handle this one. You running in through the back door with your level of emotional involvement will probably end poorly. Let the experts handle this."

Derek could see into the bank through the front window and could make out five, maybe six people all prone on the floor. Towards the teller counter, he could see the gunman holding a woman in front of him with his gun pressed to her temple.

"This is detective Allen Green," a voice boomed from a patrol car's loudspeaker. "I'm here to make sure that no one else gets hurt."

"Leave me alone," a muffled voice was heard screaming from inside the bank. "These bastards took everything from me."

"Why don't you put your gun down, walk outside, and you and I can have a conversation about what happened to you? I promise that no one will hurt you, and if someone in the bank did something to hurt you, I'll promise to give you justice."

The front window of the bank exploded as the gunman fired three shots from his Glock .40 caliber into it.

Derek could see that the gunman was moving closer to what remained of the window, screaming words that Derek couldn't understand.

As the gunman reached the unbroken windowpane, his human shield's face became clear.

"Captain," Derek yelled. "That's Lucy!"

"Stand down, Cole. Our sharpshooter is clear to take the shot as soon as he can. Stand down."

"Captain, I can be in that bank in twenty seconds without him knowing."

"Cole, are you seriously suggesting that I allow you to go freelancing into that bank and risk having you screw up and getting yourself and your wife killed?"

"He'll never know I'm there until it's too late," Derek begged, his eyes now locked with Lucy's. "Please, Captain. I can end this."

Before his Captain could talk, the gunman screamed. No words, just a primal sound at the top of his lungs. Derek could see the fear in Lucy's eyes. She stood, her faced pressed against what remained of the cool windowpane as the gunman began grunting, breathing in heavy pants, and sending his spit onto the windowpane.

"Captain," Derek said, his eyes never leaving Lucy's, as the gun fired.

He watched her fall to the ground in a lump of death, her head exploded out on one side, and her eyes instantly glazed over.

He never heard the next few shots. The gunman turned and opened fire on his hostages before then turning the gun on himself.

No one tried to hold him back as Derek sprinted across the parking lot and in through the shattered glass of the bank. He knew she was gone before he fell beside her and held his dead wife in his arms. He cradled her, saying nothing. Gently rocking her and whispering "shhh" into her ear.

"It's all quiet now," he said as he kissed her bloodied forehead. "No more questions."

No one asked Derek to release his hold of his wife. They worked as silently as they could around him, as he sat cradling her body. He sat holding her for nearly two hours before someone told him it was time to let her go.

"Derek, we have to get Lucy cleaned up. She wouldn't want to stay out in public like this. Come on, let me help you up. I promise that we'll take great care of her."

Derek could never remember who convinced him to let Lucy go. As he softened his hug, he gently rested her back on her side, the way she always slept. He brushed the blood-soaked hair away from her face, kissed her then collapsed beside her.

The days following Lucy's death were a blur of wakes, funerals, impossibly silent nights, and a slowly diminishing stream of friends parading through his front door. The days blended into weeks before Derek's bereavement and personal time had expired, and he was expected to return to duty.

"There's no rush, Cole," his Captain told Derek on his first day back. "If you need more time, say the word."

"Didn't think you cared about what I had to say, Captain," Derek said.

"Come again, officer?"

"You know what I mean," Derek said as he brushed past his Captain and into the officer's dressing room.

Though his Captain never said, Derek knew that he felt that he had wronged Derek. While Derek was desperately trying to save his wife and put an end to the bank robbery, his Captain played it by the rulebook.

It was no more than three months after Lucy had died that Derek's life began to spiral out of control. His performance while on duty was becoming "reckless and haphazard."

"You're behavior of late is putting yourself and others at risk, Officer Cole," his lieutenant told him. "I understand, the whole department understands what you must be going through, so if you feel you to take some more time, just let us know. We'll work something out for you."

"What about my behavior specifically concerns you?" Derek asked.

"Last Thursday, it was reported that you ran into a home with a reported domestic situation. You know that domestics are the most dangerous calls we receive."

"Does your report say what happened after I 'rushed in?'"

"Just because you prevented the husband from causing more harm to his wife, doesn't justify your actions. We have protocols and procedures to follow."

"Like those we followed that day at the bank?"

Three weeks after his conversation with his lieutenant, Derek was placed on "temporary leave with full pay and benefits." The department knew that Derek was a quality officer, who had shown tremendous potential from day one. They also knew that his errant and dangerous behavior would eventually get him or another officer killed.

"How long do I have to stay away?" he asked the Chief of Police when told about his temporary assignment.

"Until you feel fully ready to be a part of this department again, or our counselors believe you are ready to return to active duty."

All departments make occasional mistakes. Some forget to process paperwork correctly. Others make the mistake of not reading an arrested person their rights. Other departments neglect to ask an officer placed on leave for their service weapon. Derek left the department, drove to the nearest bar. Then, after several round of scotch, he drove himself and his modified Glock home.

The tears were streaming down his face as he sat holding a picture of Lucy in his arms. Beside him, on his nightstand, sat a bottle of Johnny Walker black and his fully loaded service pistol.

"I need you here. With me," he cried. "I promise to be more quiet. And I promise to never let anyone hurt you again."

He pulled hard from the bottle of black and danced his fingers over his pistol.

"I can't see your face," he sobbed, dropping the framed picture to the floor, sending shards of broken glass sliding across the hardwood floor.

He reached for another tug of black. As he slammed the near-empty bottle back on the nightstand, his hand held firm to the bottle as his gaze held firm to the gun.

"I can't see your face."

He released his hold of the bottle, grabbed his Glock, and shoved the barrel into his mouth. Between his sobs and desperate cries, he began to squeeze the trigger. Two pounds of pressure, his eyes closed, hoping to see her face. Three pounds of pressure, his mind was filled with the horrible images of her face pressed against the bank window. Four pounds of pressure, he saw a flash in the corner of his eye. He quickly turned his head as his finger delivered the full five pounds of pressure needed to fire the Glock.

He remembered nothing when he woke. His ears still held the ringing and his left side of his jaw and face felt as if they were on fire. He saw doctors and nurses standing over him, assuring him that "everything will be okay, Derek." He slipped in and out of consciousness, each time trying to remember what he had seen that made him turn his head as the bullet left the chamber and blasted its way through his left cheek.

He woke again to see his mother sitting by his hospital bed and his father leaning against the far wall.

"Oh Derek," his mom said. "Everything is going to be just fine. Mom will see to that."

Derek was in the hospital for only four days until he was released. His parents willingly agreed to have Derek stay with them until he was fully recovered and assured the hospital that they would make absolutely certain that Derek attend everyone of his sessions with his psychologist. Beyond having three of his molars blasted out of his head and an exit wound scar on his left cheek, Derek was amazingly uninjured.

"I know you don't feel it son," his father told him the afternoon they brought Derek to their Columbus Ohio suburban home, "but you are one lucky buck. Now, you know I'm not good at talking about feelings, but if there's anything you want to talk about, you just let me know. Anytime. And that goes for your mom, too."

The sessions with the psychologist were an embarrassment for Derek. He knew full well that he was inches away from killing himself and survived only because of a slight head turn.

"I don't know what I saw," he said to his psychologist. "Maybe I didn't see anything and just chickened out. I don't know."

"Do you wish you hadn't turned your head?" she asked, slowly twitching a pen held in her hand.

"I don't know yet, but I think I'm still here for a reason."

"Let me help you find that reason, Derek."

Three months of sessions later, and Derek was cleared to return to the police department.

"I know this won't be easy on you, Cole," his Lieutenant said on Derek's first day back to the police department. "But I can tell you without question that everyone here is on your side and is as happy as hell that you're back. Now, if there's anything you need, you just let me know."

"I quit," Derek said, finding his lost smile as the words effortlessly came from his mouth. "I came back today just to let you know that I quit."

"Cole... Derek... hold on a minute. Maybe you need some more time. Time to think this through."

"I had all the time I need, Lieutenant. What I don't have is my wife. And though I know that your protocols and procedures didn't put that bullet through her brain, they allowed it to happen. I can't work for a place that puts policy before people."

"Now Cole, you are starting to sound like someone that we

need to be careful of. You're not planning…"

"I'm not a criminal, and I'm not insane," Derek interrupted. "I won't bother you or this department at all. I know what I want to do with the rest of my life and believe me, I won't be any concern of yours, this department or any of your policies or procedures. I have no issue with anyone in this department, or on any police force across the country. I just can't be a part of one anymore. I can't be part of something that I blame for Lucy's death."

Chapter 28

He was very good at keeping things in their proper places. Didn't matter what needed to be put into place; tools, information, or people: everything needed to be in their right place. The moment after the shock and disbelief of what Michelle Mix had told him had worn off, he started putting things where they belonged. The first matter to attend to was to understand how something like this, something like his son, could have happened.

"Explain to me," he said to a trusted doctor friend of his, "to what extent genetics can play in the development of a baby."

"A tremendous extent," the doctor had answered. "Be more specific."

"I've read about children being born missing limbs or organs. Does some birth defect like that indicate a weakness in the gene pool?"

"Not always. The human genome is fragile. Many things can go wrong during the fetus's development. Many things. In fact, the vast majority of us are born with an alteration from the original genes. Fortunately, most deviations are not severe enough to be called a 'defect.'"

"So my twins, being born with only one heart, that doesn't necessarily indicate that my genes are faulty?"

"Nor does the condition of their birth indicate that your wife's genes are damaged. What are you getting at?"

"Is it possible," he continued ignoring the question asked, "that the other baby born alongside my son, Thomas, was nothing more than a genetic error?"

"I would have a problem calling the other baby an error."

"But is it possible?"

There were so few people he trusted and even fewer that he felt were strong enough to warrant his trust. He had built his empire, though considered small to some titans, based from his uncanny ability to read people. To judge them worthy of his trust. Weaknesses were quickly identified and, if needed to strengthen his position of leverage, exploited. When he discovered a strength in someone, strength in a trait or skill that exceeded his own, he formed a partnership.

His wife, strong as she was in her compassion, was little more than a convenience for him. She agreed that her place was beside him, smiling, supporting, looking her best, and keeping quiet when she should. From her, he drew comfort knowing that his son was being cared for and shielded from the mass of morons that filled the earth. But she could not be trusted beyond what she had been vetted for.

He had no reservations about telling her what he had learned from Mix's wife. He expected her to allow her emotions to direct her actions, but he also knew that he could easily control her expressions.

"No," he told her, "that is not the way we are going to handle this. Running off with emotions messing up your thoughts will accomplish nothing. For God's sake, imagine what the doctors would do to Alexander if they knew we were on to them?"

Controlling her emotions had grown too easy. A simple smile now and then. Sending a cheap bouquet of flowers. A trip to wherever. A night staying at home. Simple.

He had no concern that she would break the agreement with him. She would keep quiet and let him figure it all out.

"I feel so heartbroken for him," she said. "My son, our son, locked away like some lab rat. We need to bring him home soon. Please tell me that you will bring him home?"

"Just stick to the talking points and timeframe I gave you. You'll have your son home with you before long."

He knew she'd follow the plan. The few times in the past that she thought an idea of hers was better than his had always turned out poorly for her. She had too much to lose, and he knew it. She loved the life his plans had given her, and she wasn't about to risk losing everything. She knew her place, and while she didn't agree with many of the methods her husband employed to get things done, she was comfortable in her place.

He couldn't say that he still loved her, nor would he say that he despised her. She served a purpose, and he felt she served it quite well. What she couldn't do well, or wasn't willing to try to improve on, he had others do for him. All were paid handsomely for discretion.

Hiring Derek Cole was a stretch for him. He hadn't the time to properly and thoroughly research Cole's background, but the urgency of the events at the lodge in Piseco Lake demanded that he make a fast decision. The little that he did find out about his newest contractor suggested that Cole had the skills and abilities he needed to complete the job. He also uncovered what he would feel to be a tremendous weakness, one that may have to be further explored if Cole decided to live up to his "freelance" title.

Cole had abilities, that he knew for certain, but he sensed a streak of morality in Derek that could prove disruptive. Keeping Cole on task probably only demanded frequent payments and promises of additional income generating opportunities. But still, he needed him focused to one objective.

It was focus that he appreciated the most. While so many around him shifted their focus from one intention to another, achieving so little while advancing but inches in thousands of different directions, he remained on point. A single mission. One desired outcome. His flexibility allowed for course alterations, but nothing would be tolerated that pulled him off point.

The team members he assembled were all chosen for specific talents they possessed. Derek was chosen for his faithfulness and honesty. His brother had hired Derek to complete a sensitive job and raved about how well Derek completed the task.

"Cole is your guy," his brother told him after being asked about resources able to maintain confidentiality while following specific instructions. "He's on his own, meaning that he understands how important it is to keep his clients happy. He probably knows that if he pisses off the wrong client, his career is done."

"Well, let's hope he doesn't piss me off or more than his career will be over."

Chapter 29

It was the idea of freedom he liked the most, being able to look out his window without reminded concerns of being seen. The doors were all his to command. His promise to keep inside was not a lock, a collar, or an iron barred window. It was just a promise, an understanding that the plan needed his cooperation in order to continue.

Multiple plans needed multiple understandings. The coordination of each plan, itself in need of a plan. He fully knew that his partners would be calling on him, one in person and the other through emissaries. Each would be expecting that their plans were being followed to the letter. Though his brother's plan lacked direction, it was the easiest to follow. All that was needed was for him to be free, then to follow his brother's lead. The events at the lodge and the murders in Chicago had now rendered that plan obsolete. He knew his brother was scrambling to formulate another plan, but he had no further interest in learning of it.

His father's plan, which had been focused solely on gain, was being dismantled piece by piece. His father had shown a surprising level of patience, which gave him pause. He wondered if he had misinterpreted the emotions driving his father's plan and wondered, if only for a moment, if the prescribed and detailed steps contained an emotion beyond simple greed.

The plan he devised was of singular focus. One governing principle. One driving objective. There were times, multiple times, that he felt pulled to believe that his father and his brother were right and that their motives included a better life for him. He dreamed of what his life could become, with a family by his side to buffet the harsh winds of ridicule, of accusations, of fear. His dreams were consistently interrupted by the memories of Straus telling him "no one would, no one could ever accept him."

He was too different. Critically unique. "A subject to be studied. To be understood. To be feared." His brief time in the world had slammed that truth home. He would never be seen as "one of us," no matter how determined a family might be. And he grew to understand that, despite their assurances, that he would never find comfort in a non-judgmental embrace. There would be no comfort for him. No chance for shared laughter, the recollecting of made memories, or wishful longing that future plans award.

He largely ignored the looks and glances of others, though he questioned his ability to make his appearance less conspicuous. Blending in, it seemed, would be much harder than he had anticipated. Perhaps impossible. The color of his skin and the deep, foreboding color that surrounded his eyes both was too much to conceal.

Though insignificant to him, their remarks struck him hard. Callous insults, not intended to advise, but only to remind him that becoming a part of the critical mass was impossible.

"Take a bath, dude!"

"First time seeing the sun?"

"Ever hear of dentures?"

"Freak."

He had been warned by Straus and by his team. Repeatedly told that the best place for him, the safest place, was behind the walls they provided. He had listened but had not believed that in a world of billions that he would be noticed. Singled out. Laughed at. He never thought that he would cause others to alter their walking paths to steer clear of him. To be the person that caused others to stare in bewildered shock.

As he retreated back to the apartment that his father had rented to serve as a safe house, and after closing the door behind him, he wished, if only for a moment, that it was his door back at the lodge. He wondered how it would feel to cry. To feel the release of a deep sigh followed by a release of emotions. He could not draw a breath, and he could only imagine releasing stress and anxiety by paying attention to his breaths.

He had read about the importance of deep, conscious breathing in some of the books he was allowed to read and had often tried to mimic the descriptive formula. But he found no release, no benefits.

He stood, leaning his back against his motel room's door, knowing that he was utterly alone. There was no one who would ever accept him for what he was. And he knew that his decisions to exact his revenge would prevent anyone from ever accepting him for who he was.

He felt more trapped now than ever before. It used to be steel reinforced doors, barred windows, and captors holding Tasers that kept him from freedom. Now he realized that it was his own being that was his captor. He didn't choose to enter this world in the manner that he did, yet he would always be punished for his arrival. When his father first made contact, he thought that maybe he would have the chance at a normal life. He knew that he would need to be very flexible with his defining of normal, but it was *his* father. He had taken the time and expense needed to find his son. Soon after, his brother accepted his offer to meet. Perhaps to form a relationship the way long-lost brothers often do.

When he learned of his father's plan, he knew his dreams were in vain. His father only wanted him to be the pawn in his plan. The vehicle that would bring in revenue. His brother's plan, so quickly determined to be one made without thought, was more focused on exposing truths than becoming a family.

Alexander's plan, however, included no financial considerations. It did not include a news conference, during which reporters, hungry for scandal, ripped the medical profession apart and launched exposes on the treatment of those in psychiatric institutions. He hated his plan, but following it had quickly proved to be his only choice.

As he leaned against his door, wishing for abilities he had only read about, his phone rang. He had only two phone numbers to memorize. Two people in the world who knew that he could be spoken to. Two souls among billions that wanted to hear his voice.

"Hello father," he whispered. "I'm not surprised you're calling me."

Chapter 30

It was after his normal dinnertime before Derek reached the small town of Alexandria Bay, New York. Finding the resort was easy, though the summer tourists made navigating the small Alexandria Bay streets a challenge. He checked into the resort and was told how fortunate he was that they had a cancellation and that he would be getting a river-view room with a balcony.

"The views of the seaway are spectacular," the desk clerk insisted.

"Awesome," Derek said. "And can you tell me how close my room is to the McClury's? They're good friends."

"Let me check," the clerk said as she fumbled her fingers across the computer's keyboard. "We just installed a new server, and I am not super familiar with it yet."

Minutes passed.

"You are on the fourth floor, and your friends are on the third. You'll probably be able to see each other from your balconies."

"Great, and thanks again for the upgrade," Derek said.

Derek quickly made his way up to his fourth floor balcony room, dropped his overnight bag onto the king-sized bed, and walked out onto the balcony. It took Derek only a few seconds before he spotted Doctor Stanley Mix and his wife, Michelle. The couple was sitting on their balcony, and though Derek's balcony was a hundred feet away, he could clearly see that Stanley didn't look well.

He could see that Stanley was completely bald by the afternoon sun reflecting harshly off his head. His shirt was baggy and revealed his bony shoulders beneath its cover. Michelle was leaning towards her husband, elbows on her thighs and a smile filling her face. He couldn't hear what they were saying, but whatever the topic of their conversation was, Derek was certain it had nothing to do with Alexander Black or any of the O'Connells.

Derek made his 8:00 call to Ken, but received only Ken O'Connell's voicemail. He was glad that Ken hadn't answered as he was unsure what he was planning on telling his client.

The next morning, Derek sat on his balcony and watched Michelle Mix sitting alone on her balcony, crying. Derek made sure that Michelle wouldn't notice him as he sat in quiet confusion, watching. As he sat observing them, wondering what he would tell his client if Ken answered the scheduled 8:00 a.m. call, he saw Michelle stand quickly and move into their room. It was several minutes before he saw motion. Slowly, even more slowly than Derek expected, he watched Michelle help her ailing husband out on to the deck and into one of the lounge chairs. After Stanley was seated, Derek watched as Michelle caressed his face and kissed him on the forehead. She held his hand as she spoke to him, with a smile flooding her face. She then turned towards the room, held up five fingers, smiled again, and disappeared into the room.

Derek quickly moved into his room, put on his sneakers, and headed down to the lobby of the resort. He felt he needed to see Michelle and hopefully speak to her before checking in with Ken O'Connell. Though he had no idea what he would say if given the chance to speak with her, he felt she deserved to know who he was, who we worked for, and what his charge was.

Once in the lobby, Michelle was easy to mark. Though in her fifties, she possessed a comfortable elegance. Her shiny, dark hair and well-conditioned body made her look much younger from a distance. But as Derek drew close and could see the effects of her husband's illness etched on her face, he knew that cancer affects loved ones as hard as it affects those stricken with the disease.

"Michelle Mix?" he said when he was close enough to Michelle but far enough away from others to hear. "My name is Derek Cole, and I've been hired by Ken O'Connell to verify your location. I want to let you know that I'm going to tell Mr. O'Connell that you checked out of this resort before I arrived."

Michelle's deep eyes just stared back at Derek's. She said nothing, but nothing needed to be said.

"I've checked in under the name Robert Mendelsohn and have reservations for another night. I know your husband is ill and weak, but I am willing to help you two move into my room. I'll take care of checking you out."

"Why are you doing this?" she said as tears reluctantly filled her eyes.

"You don't deserve what my client wants to put you through.

Honestly, I don't know what your husband deserves, but whatever it is that he does deserve, I think he is already experiencing it."

"Will Ken believe you?"

"He will. I can be a very good and convincing liar."

"My husband is hungry. Can we move after he eats?" she asked, revealing how vulnerable she felt her position was. She recognized that all Derek need do is to contact Ken O'Connell, let him know that he'd found them and within hours, the little time Stanley had left in this world would be spent in a living hell of embarrassment, police questioning, possibly being arrested, and who knows what else. Michelle knew what Derek was offering was her only chance to spend the rest of her husband's days with him in relative peace.

"Of course," Derek answered. "And I would like to fill you in on what has happened over the last couple of days."

"No offense, Derek, but I don't really want to know. I know that Alexander Black escaped from wherever Straus held him captive, and I know that he's killed several people."

"I'm not sure who did the killing, actually."

"I hope I'm not being rude, considering all that you are offering to do for my husband and me, but, please, I don't want to know."

"Fair enough," Derek said. "Bring up your breakfast, enjoy it with your husband. Then, move your things to room 421," he said as he handed over the credit-card style room key. "If you need help moving your things, tell me now because I am leaving as soon as you head up to your room."

"No," Michelle said, shaking her head. "I'll be fine. But how long is your room reserved for?"

"One more night but I'll see now if I can extend it a few more days. How long do you think you need?" As he asked, Derek wondered if the more appropriate question would have been *"how much longer do you think your husband has left?"*

"I'm not sure," Michelle said. "A few more days should be fine. I don't know. I do know that we can't stay here forever."

"If you give me your cell number, I will text you updates."

"Fine," she said. "But know that I only check my messages early in the morning and only for a minute. Two at the most."

"Understood."

Derek wrote down Michelle's cell number on the back of his hand and assured her that Ken O'Connell would be told that she and Stanley had checked out early in the morning and that he was unable to track them.

"Thank you," Michelle said, her eyes offering all the gratitude that Derek needed. "I can give you cash for the room if you'd like."

"No thanks. Give me two minutes to see how long I can extend my room reservation," he said as he turned away towards the front desk. "And, Michelle?"

"Yes?"

"I know that neither you or your husband are proud of the role you played with Alexander Black, but I also feel that you don't deserve Ken O'Connell's revenge or Alexander's. Take care of your husband, and remember to take care of yourself as well."

Before Michelle could respond, Derek had moved away.

She stood and watched him speaking to the man at the front desk. A minute later, Derek turned, held up four fingers and mouthed, "Four nights. God bless."

The clerk then waved to Michelle who waved back. Derek mouthed the words, "You're all checked out."

"Thank you," Michelle silently said to Derek, then turned towards the elevator. "Thank you, Derek Cole."

Chapter 31

"If I knew where they were going, I would have followed them. They must have left very early in the morning. I was up at five, and they were already gone."

The lies were effortless for Derek. It was not because he was familiar with being untruthful, but this ability to be overly creative with the truth came from his own experience. Though he knew nothing about Michelle and Stanley Mix, he saw a familiar pain in her eyes. Pain that needed to be helped.

"Did you get a look at Stanley?" Ken asked during his and Derek's call.

"I did. He doesn't look well at all. I don't think he has much time left," Derek answered.

"They may have checked into a nearby hospital. Spend the day checking out any hospitals in the area and don't neglect to call on some Canadian ones as well. I believe you are just a boat ride away from Canada."

"Yes sir," Derek said as he pulled his car into drive and headed south, away from Canada. "Any important discoveries since yesterday?

"My resources are telling me that Lucietta may have been murdered in his office yesterday afternoon. Nothing confirmed yet.

Police are keeping things quiet now. Too many connected murders. They probably don't want the public to know what the hell is going on."

"If Lucietta is gone, that leaves Straus and Mix as the only remaining doctors on Alexander's list."

"As well as my family. Do not forget that we are on that list, Cole."

It was the way Ken said it that stirred something in Derek. Almost a request masked as an order.

"Don't forget that we are on that list."

"I haven't forgotten. And honestly, I don't think my services are best used chasing down dying doctors. I should either track down Black or be by your and your son's side."

"I have other resources for protection. You know that," Ken's voice was sounding irritated. "Alexander is unique, but even unique criminals get caught sooner or later. Until he is caught, your focus should be on finding Stanley Mix. I hope that is clear."

"It is clear," Derek said.

"Good. My resources have also provided me with a possible lead to Straus's whereabouts. They are following up today. I hope to have Straus in my sights by the time we chat this evening. I expect you will have Mix locked down as well. Once we have all the players, we go public with the whole story. Maybe that will bring Alexander out of hiding as well."

"Probably a good plan," Derek said. "So where do your resources think Straus is?"

"Straus is no longer your concern. My information sounds rock solid, meaning that the only missing player is Stanley Mix. Find him and keep him under watch, Cole. The second you locate him, contact me."

The tone in Ken O'Connell's voice was unmistakable. He wanted Derek to find Stanley Mix and to leave everything else to his "resources." But Derek had questions.

"Have you spoken to Thomas lately?" he asked, knowing that the question may anger Ken.

"If you are wondering if Thomas is safe, he is. If you are wondering anything else, I think you need to remind yourself of your objective."

"I am charged with his safety as well," Derek said. "I just have some concern I have after speaking with him yesterday."

"And that concern is?" Ken asked, not caring to hide his impatience with Derek.

"He told me that it was raining out, but when I checked the radar on my phone, there weren't any storms in the area. You confirmed it as well when I asked about the rain."

"It's a big lake, Cole. Not sure if you've ever spent time on any of the Great Lakes but an isolated rain storm is not at all uncommon."

"I know that. But ..."

"Listen, Cole," Ken said. "I need to follow up on other pressing matters. I appreciate your concern for my son, but he is well protected and is exactly where he should be. Call me the second you pick up Mix's trail."

Without any more words spoken, Ken ended the call. Derek sat in his car awhile, his iPhone still pressed to his ear. He let his mind wander.

"Exactly where he should be?" he thought. *"Why wouldn't Ken show even the slightest concern that his son may not be where he expects him to be? "*

Before he could answer his own questions, his iPhone rang, startling Derek as the phone was still pressed to his ear.

"Derek Cole," he answered.

"Now I thought you weren't gonna have your phone turned on."

"Chief Ralph Fox," Derek said, smiling. "I figured you'd miss me, but didn't think you'd call me so soon."

"I guess you're like a toe fungus. Growing on me."

"Not sure if that was a compliment."

"Well, compliments and insults are determined by the person receiving them," Ralph said.

"I'll take it as a compliment then if it's up to me."

"So, what did you find out so far?"

"I found Mix. He doesn't look good at all. I spoke to his wife Michelle today and told her that I had no intentions of telling Ken O'Connell that I found them."

"Not being a good employee," Ralph said, his respect for Derek's choice obvious in his tone.

"I'd fire me. Also spoke with Ken a minute ago. He told me

that Lucietta might have been found murdered."

"That man must be a man of influence."

"He has plenty of resources," Derek said.

"Well, Lucietta was murdered, right in his office and right in the middle of the day. No one saw or heard nothing. Looks like he got hit with his own Taser a couple of times before having a knife pushed through his neck. Coroner said it wasn't a painful death, but it wasn't quick, either."

"I guess that leaves Straus and my clients on the 'hit list.'"

"And Stanley Mix, but I am sensing that you are gonna be doing some protecting of him."

"I'll do what I can," Derek said softly.

"Well, there are two things you need to know about the Lucietta murder. One, the killer or killers left another one of them notes. All the names of the deceased crossed out in Lucietta's blood. Names not crossed out still include your client, his dad and mom, Stanley Mix, and the elusive Doctor William Straus.

"Now, the second and more interesting thing is what the NYPD detectives shared with your buddy, Captain Smith. Turns out that the finger printing guys didn't find any prints that didn't belong in the office. But, they did find something interesting."

"And that would be?" Derek asked.

"The killer was wearing latex gloves. Now, I don't know how familiar you may be with latex gloves, but some of them gloves have a powder sprinkled on 'em to make 'em easier to put on. I bet that you've seen that little puff of white when your doctor snaps his gloves on and tells you to bend over."

"Funny. And, yes, I know about the powder."

"Well, the killer was particularly interested in one picture that poor old Lucietta had hanging on his wall. Left glove prints and some of that aforementioned powder on the frame and glass."

"What was the picture of?" Derek asked.

"It was a picture of Straus and Lucietta standing in front of Hilburn Psychiatric Hospital down on Long Island."

"O'Connell told me that his resources had a good lead on where Straus might be. Unless my client's resources include someone on the NYPD, I think he may be involved."

"I think I lied to you when I said I had two things of importance," Ralph said. "There's one other thing. Captain Smith's tech people did some more investigating on that call you made with Ken O'Connell. The tracers showed that his phone was around Chicago. But what they found after doing more digging is that while his cell phone was in Chicago, your call was automatically forwarded to another phone."

"He is definitely involved if he is covering up his location," Derek said. "Now I am even happier I lied to him about Mix. There's something else I should share with you."

"What we have here is a mutually beneficial relationship," Ralph said.

"When I spoke with Thomas O'Connell yesterday, I could hear a storm in the background. He said it was just a passing storm, but when I checked the radar on my phone, there wasn't a cloud in the sky where he is supposed to be."

"Smells like we have a family affair going on here."

"If what I am thinking is accurate, they hired me to track down Mix, Lucietta, and Straus and not to protect anyone. Now that Lucietta is dead, and they have a lead on Straus, all they are concerned about is me finding and securing Mix."

"Yup," Ralph responded. "I bet you feel like you were used."

"Sure do. But now I am going to finish this thing."

"Heading to Hilburn, are you?"

"Damn straight."

Chapter 32

The NYPD detectives and officers searching for anything unusual on the Hilburn campus could find nothing. They walked every foot of the main hospital, entered every room that wasn't locked, and inspected the outside of the main hospital looking for any signs that someone, or some people, could be hiding inside.

The steel reinforced door on the second floor was the only room that couldn't be broken down or that the superintendent of the campus couldn't locate a key for. The police pounded on the door and listened quietly for any noise coming from the other side of the steel door.

Nothing.

After two hours, the lead detective, Mark Smith, called off the investigation. He assigned a patrol car and two officers to "stay back and to watch the grounds closely for anything or anybody moving around."

Workers, employed by one of the companies with offices on the Hilburn campus, began to filter out of their offices to see what the commotion was. After all the police cars had left, a few walked over to the patrol officers to see what was happening at the old hospital.

"Nothing to be concerned with," an officer said dismissively.

"But if you do see anyone trying to gain access to this building, we need you to contact us right away."

"Does this have anything to do with that doctor murdered yesterday?"

"Just precautions. Had reports that someone of interest may be holed up in this hospital. Again, if you should see anything peculiar, call us."

Straus heard the footsteps, the voices, then the banging on the door. It took a few moments for his heart to calm when he realized it wasn't danger knocking, but the police. He assumed that some police presence would remain behind, keeping a close eye on the hospital. He also knew that opening the door and letting them in would lead to his reputation, his career, and his life being dragged through the mud.

He had his own plan that had been working flawlessly up to this point and fully trusted that his cunning and sharp mind would keep him safe. Keep his name clean and respected.

The fact that police had arrived told Straus to expect Alexander and O'Connell to be arriving soon. Lucietta must have said something to someone or had left some evidence behind that led them to Hilburn. No matter. Worst case scenario and Plan C would eliminate the possibility of Alexander Black ending his life. And Plan B was still working just fine.

Straus sat silently on the bed where Alexander Black once rested, keeping absolutely still. He waited for well over an hour after hearing the footsteps move down the hall before he risked standing and walking to the door to capture a better listen. With his ear pressed to the cool, steel door, he heard nothing but an occasional scurry of a mouse moving about in the hallway.

Still, he stood, ear pressed to the door for ten minutes, believing that if anyone were standing outside, their resolve to keep quiet would end before his.

There was no sound.

He glanced towards his iPad, sitting on the desk in the "hub" room. Its battery was drained. He thought about his car, hidden brilliantly in the loading docks, and about the charger that was sitting on the passenger seat. He wondered if the police had somehow found his car, then dismissed the possibility.

"If they found my car," he thought, "they wouldn't have left. They would have broken this door down."

But would taking the risk to get to his car and the all-important charger be worth possible exposure? He knew he was blind without his news stream and realized that the fact the police showed up told him that something significant must have happened.

"Get a decent charge on the iPad only," he thought. "A shower and a pillow will have to wait."

The locking mechanisms on Ward C's door were far from quiet. The dead bolt slid noisily into its home. The steel bars screamed from lack of use as Straus twisted the handle that freed them from their locked position. The echoes of metal scraping metal reverberated down the hallway, scaring away whatever mice and rats that may have chosen the second floor south hallway as their home.

But when he slowly opened the door and saw the fading stream of light trickling in through the window at the hallway's end, Straus was relieved to see no welcoming party.

He closed the door behind him as he made his way down the hallway. The stairway that led down to the first floor and then to the old office of the loading dock supervisor was no more than fifty feet away. Again, he paused to listen and only heard faint sounds of voices and an idling car coming from outside. He moved quickly to the stairway door that, thanks to his cunning mind, had been left open to assist in a quicker escape if things came to that.

The stairway was dark, not graced by any window's filtered light. When he had arrived back at Hilburn, Straus did his best to remove any large debris from the steps, being careful not to make it seem that the stairs were still being used. Slowly, he made the dark journey down the first flight and paused when his feet hit the landing.

Still no sounds.

He moved down the second flight with more confidence and when he reached the landing, he stuck his head out into the first floor hallway to see and to listen.

The hallway was empty and quiet except for discarded papers, broken glass, empty bottles of cheap liquor spilled carelessly about, and a few folded mattresses that he assumed were the resting place of the homeless who used the hospital as shelter during the cold Long Island winter days and nights.

There was nothing else to see or to be concerned about.

Straus drew his body back into the stairway, allowed his eyes to readjust to the dark, and then proceeded down the next two flights of stairs. When he reached the lower level, he again paused to make sure that no one was where they shouldn't be. After a minute, he walked towards the loading docks, using his hands to feel for familiar landmarks on the walls. When the walls opened into a large area, he shuffled his feet, feeling for the three-foot drop that would lead to the storage and warehouse area of the docks.

His car was not as brilliantly hidden as he had thought but certainly concealed enough to avoid being spotted by a lazy flashlight. As he made his way to where he parked his BMW, Straus kicked a few empty bottles, sending them bouncing across the rough concrete floor.

There was no reaction to the noise.

"If that doesn't alert someone, nothing will," he said out loud.

He removed the boxes that he had stacked up around his car, opened the driver's side door, and sat down. He had turned off the overhead light when he parked the car, again to aid in his concealment. He had also left the keys in the ignition and made certain that he had a straight shot out of the dock if he encountered an emergency situation.

His plan was working flawlessly.

He reached over, picked up the car charger, connected it to his iPad. He then turned the key to "on," plugged in the charger, and smiled as his iPad reported that it was receiving a charge.

"Fifteen minutes," he said. "Twenty, at the most. Just get the battery over ten percent."

Five minutes after his iPad started to charge, its screen came to life; filling his car with a dull, gray light. Straus quickly held the iPad to his chest to cover the light, but the iPad's illumination was present long enough for him to see the person sitting in his back seat through his rear-view mirror.

Chapter 33

Derek wasn't concerned about Captain Smith tracking him. He figured that Smith would be too busy trying to prevent another murder than to worry about some freelancing detective.

He searched for and found the address for Hilburn Business Center, plugged the address into the Google Maps app on his cell phone, and headed south. The computerized voice of Google Maps told him he would arrive in just over four hours.

He dialed Thomas O'Connell's cell number and listened as the ringing ended with Thomas's voicemail message. Next, he dialed Ken O'Connell's cell and again, heard his call answered by a voicemail message. His final call was to Ralph Fox.

"Well, hell, I just spoke with you. Now what do you want to ask?"

"Any way you can get Janet O'Connell's cell number?"

"I suppose doing so is possible. What are you planning?" Ralph asked.

"I want to find out how many O'Connells are involved in this case."

"Give me a bit to get her number. Your buddy Captain Smith ain't been around, but he did leave his files behind."

"Thanks, Ralph," Derek said.

"Yup. You just make sure you don't go running into any situations that are likely to get yourself all dead. Hear me?"

"Freelancing is tough work sometimes, but I'll be smart."

Ten minutes after hanging up with Ralph, Derek received a text message from Ralph with Janet O'Connell's cell number. Derek dialed the number and hoped that he wouldn't hear another voicemail message.

"Hello?"

"Janet O'Connell?" Derek asked.

"Yes. Who is this?"

"My name is Derek Cole. I've been hired by your son, Thomas, and your husband to assist in locating the doctors that perpetrated the crime against your family twenty-two years ago. Janet, I need to ask you some questions. Is that okay?"

"If you are referring to the doctors who told us that our son Alexander died after birth, then you can ask any question you want," Janet said, her voice stern and crisp.

"I know this may be hard to understand, but I think Alexander Black is being assisted by your husband and your son. Have they told you anything that might lead you to believe that they are assisting Alexander in these murders?"

"They would never!" her voice assumed the tone of someone intentionally revealing their being offended. "How dare you suggest such a thing. My husband is paying you, isn't he?"

"Yes, he is."

"Then as his employee, you should be showing more respect. I can assure you that I will make my husband aware of your accusations and will see to it that whatever payment you are expecting is not sent."

"I am not making accusations up from my imagination, ma'am. If you'll listen to me. I am concerned that your husband and your son are in danger."

"My son is on a boat out on Lake Michigan, being well looked after by my husband's employees, and my husband is quite busy working with his lawyers in Chicago."

"Neither is where you believe they are, ma'am."

Her voice was hesitating, suggesting doubt. "And just how do you know that?"

Derek went on to explain everything that had happened from the time he met with Thomas in Grant Park to the last call he had with Ken O'Connell. He told Janet about what the police had found in Brian Lucietta's office and how Ken told him that his resources had a good idea where to find Straus.

He told her about Stanley Mix and Michelle and how he had spoken with Michelle. He told her that he helped them remain hidden from her husband and how he would continue to keep them away from her husband for as long as he could.

He told her everything he knew as she listened in absolute silence.

Finally she spoke. "Ken was furious when that Michelle Mix told him what the doctors in Chicago had done. I was too, but I was more heartbroken than angry. Imagine, all these years I've been grieving for a son that was still alive. I should have known."

"Janet, what those doctors did was horrible. There's no excuse for their actions. But now, Alexander Black is out in the world somewhere, and there are six people dead because of it. I need you to help me."

Janet paused before speaking. "What do you need me to do?"

Chapter 34

"Really, Doctor Straus, I thought it would be much harder to see you face to face again. I have only been waiting for you here in your luxurious automobile for less than two hours. I was expecting a much, much longer wait."

"Alexander," Straus said, "Whatever it is that you want or need, I can help you. What those doctors did to you by lying about your death and smuggling you to me all those years ago was wrong. Completely and utterly wrong. But I did my best to keep you safe, didn't I?"

"Indeed you did, Doctor Straus. Indeed you did. You kept me safe from having a family. You provided me the safety of never having a friend or, dare I say, a love interest. You kept me safe by reminding me that the world would never accept me. You locked me away, fed me, instructed me, and saved me from any resemblance of a normal life. And now, Doctor Straus, I am here to repay your kind acts. It's you who needs safety now."

"Is your father telling you what to do?" Straus asked, his hand finding the door handle. "If your father is behind all those murders and this whole scheme, I will defend you to the authorities."

"My father reached out to you in good faith just a few days ago, but you rejected his offer of negotiation."

"I saw what happened at my lodge. I saw you walk outside covered in blood, and I saw what you did to that man walking up the street. Your father didn't want to negotiate, he wanted to kill me."

"No, no, no, Doctor Straus. I was the one with the desire to kill you. It was I who killed Jacob Curtis and that pathetic Peter Adams. Though I cannot claim Mark Rinaldo's and Henry Zudak's demise, as you certainly should know, I can proudly say that I've dispensed of your entire team. Poor Brian Lucietta. He was so innocent, wasn't he? Just a simple doctor, wishing to be left alone as he experimented with my body. So immune from guilt. Beyond reproach, I believe his journal stated.

"Oh yes, yes, yes, Doctor Straus. I read his journal. Each page, including those that referenced your Plan B should I ever become a public figure. How brave of you, Doctor Straus, to say that Doctor Lucietta was nothing but gallant in his quest to learn the secrets of my life. And what a martyr you were willing to be by proudly saying that you would defend his honor and ensure that he would suffer no repercussions as long as he followed your prescription. Tell me, Doctor Straus, did you extend that same, noble promise to Jacob Curtis? How about to Michelle? And speaking of her, I do miss her. Have you kept in touch with nurse Michelle?"

"Alexander, please. I'd like to speak with your father."

"My father was more than willing to negotiate with you. You never showed up to your lodge to listen to his offer. But now, having learned that you saw the proceedings at the lodge that day, I am led to believe that you did arrive. Hide in the bushes, did you Doctor

Straus?"

"Where is your father now, Alexander?" Straus asked loudly, hoping to catch the attention of any remaining police officers outside of the hospital. "I am willing to negotiate in good faith," he spoke even more loudly.

"Detained. My father is detained. Shall we visit my old stomping grounds together Doctor Straus? If my memory serves, Ward C is but two floors above us. Shall we?"

Straus pulled hard on the door handle and launched himself out of the car. He yelled, hoping his voice would capture someone's attention as he fell out into the darkness. He hit the cool, damp concrete floor hard, then quickly scrambled to his feet. Then, though he thought it impossible, the darkness around him turned even darker.

Chapter 35

Ken O'Connell could always sense when things were getting out of hand. He could spot ideas taking on a life of their own from miles away. In business, he knew when to pull the plug well before his partners, investors, and employees could even sense that a change was needed. In his life, he loved to follow possibilities and trends out to their expected ends. If the end looked positive, he would go forward, always being sure to design a way out should things begin turning in the wrong direction.

Arranging a meeting with Straus in order to extort money was, in Ken's mind, a sound idea. He did all his due diligence before putting the plan into action. He verified the story that Michelle Mix told him. He got visual confirmation that Alexander Black was actually alive and was being held exactly where his sources suggested he would be. Ken made certain that Straus had enough savings and investments to make it worth his efforts. He then confirmed that Rinaldo, Zudak, Mix, Curtis, and Lucietta also had attractive portfolios, making them ripe for picking.

Once Ken was able to arrange a means of contacting and connecting with Alexander, his first test was to see if Alexander would make a willing and an appropriate associate. Ken was quickly impressed by his unknown son's intellect as well as his personal desire to exact his own unique flavor of vengeance.

It took months of surveillance before one of Ken's resources came up with a plan.

"Straus leaves the lodge every Tuesday morning and doesn't return until late Thursday evening. During that time, the only people in the lodge are any guests, of whom there are very few, and Alexander. He has a security system in place, complete with cameras and sensors on every door and window. However, the main door to the lodge is not monitored or alarmed. Straus probably didn't want to make his guests feel like they are being watched.

"Alexander is held off of the main entrance way, down a short hallway which is accessible only by a pass code and key locking system. The code was easily stolen since his system uses a WiFi to control and monitor the entire system. I hacked the network and stole all access codes in less than fifteen minutes.

"Picking the lock should take no more than five minutes, during which time Alexander will most likely be able to hear us in the hallway. He will be secured in his suite of rooms, which are, thankfully, very secure. However, should he want to alert someone, he does have access to a panic button that will set off a silent alarm which I believe will be sent directly to Straus.

"Assuming the panic button is not pressed by Alexander, you will be able to speak to him behind the safety of the hallway door that leads into his suite.

"Straus does have a hired gun within an hour of the lodge. Worst case scenario is that Alexander presses the panic button,

Straus dispatches his hired gun, and Alexander blows your whole plan out of the water."

"And best case scenario is?" Ken asked.

"Alexander does not press the button, you are able to speak to him for as long as you like, and I will make modifications to the underside of Alexander's bedroom. Once the trap door is completed, you will be able to deliver whatever necessary supplies to Alexander for his use and concealment. I will also leave behind a non-activated Smartphone that I've already connected to the lodge's WiFi, using a masked IP address. I doubt that Straus would ever notice the device on his network, but, as a precaution, it won't be registered as an active device."

"Will it receive and send text messages?" Ken asked, pleased with how well the final steps of the plan were falling together.

"No. No text messages and no phone calls. Only email and only when it's connected to WiFi. I've created a Gmail account for Alexander and have already pushed that email address to your contact list. He is listed as 'AB Lodge.'"

"Assuming Alexander is willing to cooperate, how long do you suggest we wait until execution?" Ken said.

"No less than five weeks. I need that long to set up dummy bank accounts and off-shore accounts to quietly transfer whatever money you are able to secure from Straus and the others."

"Five weeks will give me enough time to get to know my heartless son as well as giving you enough time to calculate the net worth of all the players."

"Initial investigations estimate the total money in play to be over ten million."

"Half of that sounds like a fair amount for my silence."

"As long as Alexander plays nicely, and the doctors agree to pay you off rather than face public exposure, I think five million is a very fair amount."

"What have you found out about Straus and his access to, how should I say, 'nefarious people?'"

"Straus is not an idiot. Seems like he's been planning something similar to our plan for the last few years. He has access to some muscle in Chicago through his contact here in Upstate New York. Not sure what his plans are exactly, but the files I pulled from his computer show an interest in extortion. I should also tell you, Mr. O'Connell, that part of Straus's notes did include how to dispose of Alexander's body."

"And we need to have the same idea in place. What was Straus's plan?"

"Sketchy at best. Seems Alexander is highly sensitive to electricity. Straus wrote about subduing Alexander with a stun gun, then dropping his body into Piseco Lake with enough weight so that he never floats to the surface."

"Good enough of a plan for me," Ken said. "I always believed that the best business plans are either stolen or borrowed from someone else. Make sure we have whatever we need when the time comes to dispose of Alexander."

"Can I assume that you have decided that killing him is really your best option?"

"If you are thinking that killing my son is a horrible idea," Ken replied, "then either I made a poor choice in hiring you or you have underestimated my resolve."

The following Tuesday, Ken and his team of two hired "specialists" made easy entry into the lodge. As planned, the locking mechanism securing the door leading to a hallway was picked open, and the code stolen from the network breach released the latch. Once in the hallway, Ken turned to one member of his team and instructed them to "standby."

"I want to have this conversation alone. You stay here just outside this door. If I need help, I'll call for you. If Alexander is agreeable, I'll give you a sign to proceed. Understood?"

"Understood."

Ken, usually confident in his approaches to all things, found his steps measured and deliberate as he approached to heavy steel door on the right hand side of the hallway. The hallway was dimly lit and ran the thirty-foot length of Alexander's suite of rooms.

When he reached the door, Ken saw a winch and pulley system next to the door. He then noticed a small, thick glass windowpane was cut into the steel door. A filtered light radiated through the windowpane.

Ken paused before positioning himself where he could see through the window and into the suite. He drew a deep breath, checked over his shoulder to be certain his per diem employee was where he was instructed to be, then took two steps and faced the steel door.

"An unexpected and unknown visitor," Alexander said. "How very unusual."

"Alexander," Ken said, his voice shaky with nerves, "my name is Kenneth O'Connell. I believe that I am your father."

Alexander was standing in his reading room, as if he fully expected someone to grace his doorstep. Though the room was dimly lit, his pale, gray skin and pale blue eyes were easy for Ken to see.

Ken could see a change in Alexander's eyes. A longing mixed with anger and fear. Alexander stepped closer to the door, his smooth, unblemished skin now no more than six inches from the windowpane.

"I don't see the resemblance," he said, his body held perfectly still, and then he smiled.

It was the smile that charged Ken's soul with terror. Toothless and vacant of any color. There was no laugh to accompany Alexander's smile, but somehow, Ken felt that the smile was genuine.

"A joke," Alexander said, sensing his father's discomfort. "I am well aware of my appearance and how unsettling I make others. I must say, however, that I do see that we share a common hairline."

Ken breathed deeply and ran his hand over his balding head.

"Looks like I haven't given you any good genes," he said.

"But I have to believe," Alexander said, moving even closer to the window pane, "that your visit is a gift and that I am to expect additional benefits."

"Alexander," Ken continued, "I know what they've done to you, and I am going to make them pay. I came here to see if you would be willing to participate in a little plan I've been working on for the last several weeks."

"Does this plan of yours involve me remaining in this comfortable prison?"

"No. It includes you being free and, hopefully, becoming part of my family."

"You plan on making me a part of a family that I was born into?"

"Alexander, you have to understand that my wife and I had no idea what those doctors in Chicago did."

"I do understand. And I know that you and Mom had absolutely no involvement or knowledge. My question was more geared to the fact that despite you wanting to include me in your family, you've yet to unlock this door."

"I've read plenty of Straus's reports about you, Alexander. They suggest that you may be very dangerous. I'm taking precautions which, if the roles were reversed, I'm certain you would take as well."

"You read the reports of the man who has kept me as his lab rat for twenty-two years, who subjected me to countless tests all in the name of science, and you wonder why he may feel that I am dangerous?"

"If I unlock this door, Alexander, and you attempt to harm me or to escape, my men will put you down. Understood?"

"Why would I want to harm or escape from my own father?" Alexander said, again through his empty smile.

"I need time to get the key."

"I have one," Alexander said, holding a brass key up to the windowpane. "Straus keeps his key somewhere and gave me this one in case of emergency."

Alexander bent down slowly and slid the key under the small gap of the door. The key sat inches from Ken O'Connell's feet. He reached down, picked up the key, turned, and nodded to his armed assistant who was dutifully at his post.

"I am trusting you, Alexander and hope that you trust me as well."

"You will not be disappointed... Dad."

As Ken lifted his hand holding the key closer to the lock, Alexander moved a few steps away from the door.

"In case you change your mind and choose to close the door, my increased distance should afford you more time to do so," Alexander whispered.

Ken slid the key into the lock, turned it quickly and heard the bolt slide into its home. Ken O'Connell was not a man who approached anything from a place of fear, but as he pushed the door open, he felt his legs grow weak.

"I will sit if that makes you more comfortable, Dad."

"No need," Ken said, stepping into the room. "I think we understand each other just fine."

Ken could easily remember how willing a partner Alexander agreed to be. How quickly he was to offer suggestions and make corrections when the information that Ken had regarding Straus was incorrect. He recalled how quickly Alexander learned how to use and to understand the Smartphone that he gave him. And how patient Alexander was when he told him the plan needed to be executed only when the timing was perfect.

When Alexander acted without thinking and killed two of the doctors whom Ken was relying on for a fair amount of his payment for silence, Ken worried about his partner. His rage was more powerful than Ken had expected. And when Straus never showed for their scheduled meeting, Ken began to realize that choosing Alexander to be a part of the plan was a critical mistake.

He had, at first, wondered if Alexander could have become an addition to his family. He was, after all, his son, and as his son, Alexander was entitled to a life well beyond the reach of most. Even when he first saw the photographs of Alexander and read the reports his team had delivered, Ken still wondered. It was when he first saw him, through the thick glass of hallway window that he knew. Alexander would never become part of his family or any other family for that matter. He was too different. Too unique. Ken needed to maintain his position in the business community and the expected media frenzy over a human being living without a heart would cause unwanted exposure.

He had a gift; it was an ability to ignore emotions. Pushing them down deep to the place his father used to call "the garbage pit of your soul."

He took Alexander to a "safe house" he had rented in Manhattan where Alexander agreed to focus his time on learning the fine art of applying make-up and learning how to "control his temper."

When Ken learned that Rinaldo and Zudak had been murdered, he instructed his men to "eliminate Alexander and to hide the body in the ocean." He needed to find Straus and Mix and salvage what was left of his plan. When he killed Curtis and Adams, Alexander and his rage cost Ken millions of dollars. The thought of Alexander getting to Straus before he had a chance to apply the intelligently crafted threat of extortion he had in mind, was a possibility that Ken could not accept.

"Worst case scenario," he said to his hired assistants, "is that we eliminate everyone who knows anything, and we walk away with lessons learned."

"And best case?" he was asked.

"We squeeze Straus, Mix, and Lucietta for three million and walk away richer with lessons learned."

The next day, when Ken learned that Lucietta was murdered in his office, he sent a resource over to make sure Alexander was still in the apartment.

"No sign of Alexander," the report came back. "He must have taken care of Lucietta and is probably looking for Straus right now."

Ken still had Mix and Straus to count on to prevent his plan from being a total disaster, but when Derek Cole reported that Mix had left the resort and that Mix didn't look like he was going to last much longer, everything was down to finding Straus.

That's when the entire plan fell apart. What angered Ken the most as he sat, tied to the cold metal chair in the rat-infested warehouse, is that he never saw it coming to this. He never fully trusted Alexander, but never thought he would actually resort to this.

The fire that Alexander lit before telling Ken how much he appreciated his assistance and that he "so wished that things had been different and that they would've had memories together of picnics in the park and playing catch in the road" was beginning to spread. As designed.

The rags were damp with an oil and gas mixture that was designed to slowly ignite but, without doubt, burn completely. One by one, Alexander placed them in a long, straight line that ended against a heaping pile of discarded pallets stacked in the corner of the abandoned warehouse. Ken's screams of anger and of pleading were largely wasted on Alexander. He went about the business of arranging the rags and pallets to ensure that the wick of rags would ignite into a raging fire.

"Alexander," Ken said as Alexander had finished arranging the rags, "I have resources that are instructed to find me if I don't check in every hour. I haven't spoken to them in over three hours, meaning that they will be here any second. And when they arrive, I will have to beg them to spare your life."

"Daddy," Alexander said softly. "Your only resource left in this world was assumed dead on arrival twenty-two years ago."

With that, Alexander lit the long stretch of rags, which accepted the offered match and slowly turned to low flame. "This fire will certainly capture the attention of the local fire department, but I am afraid to tell you that the department is a volunteer one. Their response will be tardy. And, given the assumption that there is nothing worth risking a life over in this warehouse, they will risk nothing. What I am telling you, dear Daddy, is that no one will know you are in this warehouse, screaming and pleading for your life until you can no longer scream or plead.

"Your imagined plan of vengeance was, in fact, nothing more than a way to line your pockets. Mine, however, has nothing to do with revenue. Didn't you wonder why I suggested that your name and your other son's name should be included on our 'lists?' You assumed having your family listed as targeted victims would provide you cover. I included your names not as a clue but as a thorough list. You were so quick to agree to add your own family's names to the list of targets, yet you never questioned why I wanted to add them."

As the flame slowly worked its devouring way from one rag to the next, Alexander walked to the door. As he reached it and pushed it open, he turned, faced Ken and said, "It is nice, isn't it?"

"What are you talking about, you sick, twisted freak?"

"Your twin boys, together again. It's nice, in its own sick, twisted way."

The door slammed shut.

Chapter 36

Derek understood that his presence anywhere near the vicinity of Hilburn would not be welcomed by the state police or by the NYPD who were certain to have been informed of his "freelancing" involvement. Captain Smith was probably too busy to be tracking his cell phone but not too busy to pass along his name and picture to the NYPD detectives.

When his Google Maps indicated that he was within a mile of Hilburn, Derek pulled in the nearest strip mall, parked his car, grabbed his backpack and started off towards Hilburn on foot. A quick glance at the time suggested that he find a way to kill some time so he could use the cover of darkness to conceal his entrance into Hilburn, which he was certain was being watched by at least several pairs of eyes.

As he spotted a Thai restaurant in the strip mall, he decided that consuming some spicy duck would be as good a way as any to spend a few hours. As he walked in the door, his cell phone rang.

"Derek Cole," he said.

"It's Janet O'Connell. I can't get in touch with either my husband or my son. I need you to find them and make sure they are alright."

"Janet," Derek said, "if I'm right about my suspicions, I'm

within a mile of them right now."

"I'm getting on a plane in thirty minutes to fly home. Please, call me the second you see them and let me know everything."

"I will."

"And Derek?" Janet added. "Please don't hurt Alexander. He's my son, too."

Janet paused after ending her call with Derek. As she glanced at the boarding pass she had printed out and was holding her hands, she wondered if what she was planning would cause problems. She was told, after all, to stay put, to not talk with anyone, and to wait. Her husband was always very good at giving clear directions.

Janet and Ken met shortly after she had graduated from college. She, the daughter of a self-made millionaire, and he, a struggling entrepreneur with a drive and passion that both attracted and concerned her. She never doubted that Ken would be wildly successful. He wouldn't have accepted anything less. And with Janet's father providing a generous amount of startup capital, she knew it would only be a matter of time before her husband would be even more successful than her father.

It took only three years for Ken's business ideas, hard work, and determination to pay off. He started with a used car lot and then expanded to own seven lots spread across the Chicago area. Within 18 months, she was standing next to her husband, cutting the ribbon to open the first O'Connell Jeep Chrysler Dodge dealership. Within two years, there were two more ribbon-cutting ceremonies, a move out of an apartment that had grown too middle class and into a palatial home and the decision to start a family.

"I'm not interested in a big family," her husband told her. "One son should be enough. If you produce a daughter first, we keep going but, no matter what, we stop at three kids."

She agreed once she realized that having four or five kids like she had wished for didn't make sense.

"A family of five or more creates problems," Ken insisted. "We stop at no more than three kids, two if I get my son."

Ken always had solid reasons behind his ideas. She learned to trust him, and after their third year of marriage, her belly expanded with twins, she decided that questioning his directions served no purpose. Her mother did the same in her marriage, and things worked out well for her. She began to understand that her decision to marry Ken assumed a willing acceptance of the role she needed to play.

Over the 26 years of their marriage, Janet learned to keep her ideas to herself. While there were times when she questioned her husband's decisions, she knew that he was much smarter than she was and had an ability to make things work out for the best. An ability she didn't see in herself.

She certainly didn't like many things about her relationship. The nights her husband wouldn't come home and offered no excuse as to why. The private conversations he would have with business associates, lawyers, accountants and people that Janet felt a particular unease about having in her home. She hated when he told her to "mind her business and mind her place" when she began to offer a suggestion.

In the back of her mind, she knew he was unfaithful and was leading a life very distant from the life she and he were living. Distant and different. But saying anything would risk so much. And who was she to tell him, a man who had given her so much, that she didn't like how she was being treated? She had a beautiful home, wanted for nothing, and had an enviable position in her community of friends and acquaintances.

But the uneasy stirring in her soul never became silent. At night, as she slept alone, she forced herself to ignore her feelings and to push down her anger. Despite her efforts, the feelings returned each morning and stayed with her through each of her days. She expected that one-day, some day, Ken would go too far and then, only then would she make her voice heard.

But was this the day to make herself heard? Ken and Thomas were nowhere to be found. He had told her the day he dropped her off at the airport in Chicago that he'd probably be difficult to get a hold of and that Thomas would be out of cell range most of the time. The fact that Derek Cole, a complete stranger, suggested that her husband may be involved in something criminal didn't surprise her. She couldn't accept, however, that her son, Thomas, would have involved himself in any of his father's activities.

She sat down on the edge of her bed in the resort, looking out over the resort's grounds. She shook her head, trying to clear her mind of the racing and conflicting thoughts.

"I'm being such a fool," she said. "Ken always has a plan, and his plans always work out in the end."

She glanced at the boarding pass in her hand and began to chuckle.

"What exactly could I do anyway?" she said as she crumpled the boarding pass and tossed it on the ground. "It's simply too nice of a day to spend on a plane."

She stood and walked over to the room's door. She paused for a brief moment as she turned and looked at the crumpled boarding pass lying on the floor.

"Ken will make sure Thomas is fine. I just know it."

Janet made her way to the poolside bar. She ordered a double vodka martini, and then found her place in a lounge chair overlooking the vast expanse of the ocean.

* * *

Spending two hours in a Thai restaurant turned out to be significantly more difficult than Derek expected. He dragged out ordering his meal for as long as he felt would be tolerated, ordered several glasses of iced tea, and ate as slowly as he could. An hour after he walked into the restaurant, his waitress dropped off his bill and asked if he needed anything else.

"Not right yet," he responded. "I just want to let my food digest before heading back out."

At the ninety-minute mark, the owner of the restaurant stopped by Derek's table to see if everything was okay and asked if Derek needed directions to wherever he was going to.

By the time the second hour drew to a close, the waitress and owner both suggested that Derek find a more comfortable place to finish his digestion.

"I'm actually thinking about getting another order," he said.

"Kitchen closed now. Come back in three hour," the owner said in an accent more similar to someone from China than from Thailand.

It was close to four o'clock when Derek started walking down the road that led to Hilburn. He veered off the road and followed an overgrown path that seemed to lead behind the largest of the Hilburn campus's buildings and up a small, tree covered hill. When he reached the highest point of the hill, Derek sat down and surveyed the area. He could see a marked patrol car parked near the side of the obviously abandoned hospital, several cars parked near other smaller buildings, and a few people walking around the campus. He trained his eyes on the darkened windows of the hospital, hoping to catch some movement.

With the combination of the afternoon sun, the patrol car, and the people walking around the campus all as factors, Derek decided that waiting another few hours for the sun to set would be his best course of action.

He lay down on the path, being sure to conceal his body from anyone looking up towards the hill. After setting his iPhone alarm to vibrate in three hours and using his backpack for a pillow, Derek fell asleep. After only forty minutes, his iPhone began to vibrate.

"Derek, it's Ralph Fox. Where the hell are ya?"

Still drowsy, Derek told Ralph where he was and what his

plans were.

"Well you better be damned careful. Just got word that your prime suspect Ken O'Connell was found dead in an old warehouse down your way."

"What?" Derek said, too loudly for someone trying hard not to make his position known.

"Fire department got a call of a structure fire. Got there quick enough to put the fire out but not quick enough to save your boss from dying of smoke inhalation."

"Anyone else in the warehouse?"

"Nope, and before ya ask, ain't got no leads about who the arsonist was."

"Think Alexander turned on his dear old dad?"

"Hell of a turn, if you ask," Ralph said. "Not sure exactly what you expect to gain by getting yourself into that old hospital, but it don't seem like there's much reason for you to risk your own neck."

"I'm kind of invested in this whole thing at this point. Plus, I feel like I owe Stanley and Michelle some peace of mind."

"You don't owe them nothing, in my opinion."

"Maybe not," Derek said, "but I feel for Michelle. Kind of have a connection."

"You just gotta make me one promise," Ralph said.

"What's that?"

"If things start to get ugly, you get your butt the hell out of the area and let the police handle things."

"I still need to find out about Thomas O'Connell. If he's at risk, I am obligated to keep him safe. But if things do turn, I'll get out."

Chapter 37

William Straus was awake. Thanks to his usually sharp but currently cloudy mind, he knew that he had to keep perfectly still with his eyes closed. He needed to think, to determine his next move. To do so, he needed to know exactly where he was, who was around him, and what was near him that could be used as a weapon. The gun that he had packed as part of his Plan B was in his duffle bag that he placed on the desk in the hub room of ward C. If he were anywhere close to the hub, his first move would be towards the duffle bag.

He thought back to his last memory. He remembered that Alexander had suggested that they should visit Ward C. He recalled throwing himself out of his car, screaming to get someone's attention, then everything turning black.

His logical conclusion was that he was in Ward C, probably on Alexander's old bed, based on the familiarity and the lack of pillows. He listened but could hear nothing. No movement, no breathing, and no sounds coming from outside of his immediate area. He lifted his right eye lid just enough to afford him a view and confirmed his thoughts. From what he could see through the dimly lit room, he was alone.

He opened his eyes fully and slowly let his sight roam as far as he could without turning his head. When he was confident that he was alone, he lifted his head. The pain he felt was immediate. Sharp, stabbing, shooting pain. It started from the back of his head and traveled down his entire spine, sending the muscles in his lower back into contractions. Despite the extreme pain, Straus lifted his head off the mattress, glanced around the room identifying familiar objects and shapes, then tried to sit upright. It was then that he realized that his left arm was tied securely to the bed's frame. So tight that his attempt at testing the knot caused the thin rope to dig into his wrist.

But he was alone in the room. He wondered if the police had apprehended Alexander or if Alexander's father had shown up and was now speaking with him, discussing what terms for release they would present.

Straus rolled to the left side of the mattress, sat up, and began exploring the rope's knot with his right hand. The battery-powered lights that he had positioned in the room had either spent their battery's life or had been turned off, making his attempt to loosen the knot an entirely kinesthetic attempt. The pain in the rear of his head was throbbing, reminding Straus that something, perhaps something serious, was wrong. He tentatively reached his free hand to his head and felt examined his skull.

"No blood," he thought. *"Just a nasty lump. That's good."*

He continued exploring his body with this free hand and discovered nothing was out of place, bleeding, or twisted into any shape that would prevent him from running once he freed himself from the rope.

He was so attentive to listening for sounds that he almost didn't notice the wafting smells that suddenly caught his attention. He paused, straining his mind to place the scents.

"Smoke?" he thought. *"And something else."*

The smell of stale, distant smoke, was certain but it was mixed with another smell: a smell both blended and separated from the smoky aroma. A distinct and familiar scent that, perhaps due to the throbbing pain that demanded much of his mental energies, could not be labeled as he sat, bound, and still on the mattress. It drew him, called to him, offering a glimmer of comfort and of hope. As his faculties slowly became fully awake, he identified the smell. It was not a pleasant scent yet, to Straus, it was the greatest aroma he could have ever hoped for.

"Tell me, Doctor Straus," the wafer thin voice of Alexander sounded, cutting through the darkness and pushing the scent from Straus's mind, "how long had you been arranging your response?"

"Alexander?" Straus answered, quickly twisting his body on the bed towards the origination of the voice. "Let me free. Now!"

"Again, tell me how long you had been arranging your response?"

"What are you talking about? What response?" Straus barked.

"Your response to the recent events that have unfolded."

"I don't know what you are referring to, but if you untie me, I am certain that you and I can reach an agreement that will make you, your father, and me happy."

"My father only wanted money from you, Doctor Straus.

Money from you and the rest of the doctors involved. In the end, it was his greed that consumed him.

Burned him to the ground, I imagine. I myself have very little use for money, and I'm afraid that there is nothing else you can bring to any negotiating table, should you ever be present at one."

"Alexander," Straus said, then paused, "you need me. I can smell what's going on with your body. You need me. My expertise is what I have as my bargaining chip."

"You can smell me?" Alexander asked. "How bizarre."

"That day at the lodge. The day you murdered Jacob Curtis and Peter Adams."

"Please don't forget about the stranger I murdered as well. He deserves to be remembered as much as the others."

"Jacob Curtis was there to tell you news. Did he tell you what we had discovered?"

"I am afraid to say that the words got caught in his throat. But, please tell me, doctor. I am curious."

"Did he tell you that he had good news?"

"In fact, he did mention good news. He was almost giddy with excitement."

"Untie me, and I will tell you," Straus said, his authoritative voice discovered.

"I struggle to see the benefit of releasing your bonds, doctor. I struggle."

"Jacob Curtis did have good news, but that's not all the news he had."

"A mystery. How wonderful! Do tell, Doctor Straus."

"Untie me," he commanded.

"My struggle for a reason continues," Alexander said.

Alexander moved from the hub into the bedroom where Straus was sitting. With him he carried a small, battery-powered lantern. The fading glow offering its dying light in a small, irregular shape around Alexander. His face and hand were all that Straus could see, seemingly floating into the bedroom. The grayness of his complexion accentuated by the cool light.

As Alexander entered the room, the smell became more potent. Straus drew a deep breath through his nose, smiled, then craned his neck to better see Alexander.

"You don't smell it, do you?"

"You need first to identify what 'it' is that I should be smelling."

"Untie me."

"Tell me what it is that is giving you the confidence to utter commands."

"The good news," Straus continued without hesitation, "was that the last test we subjected you to proved, at last, to be successful. We injected your cells with a virus, the cure for which has avoided thousands of doctors around the world."

"And that virus was?" Alexander said, then moved closer to Straus.

The smell began to overcome Straus. He covered his mouth and nose with his free hand as his eyes began to reflexively water.

"The HIV virus, Alexander. It was the virus that causes AIDS. I'm sure you've read about it during your studies."

"I have. And the results of the test?"

"Your cells seem to provide an effective defense against the virus. In fact, the virus was killed so quickly when introduced to your cells that we had to run the test over several times to be certain. You, Alexander, are the cure to a worldwide epidemic."

"How exciting," Alexander said, his sarcasm practically spewing from his mouth. "And what of the other news?"

Straus sensed concern in Alexander's voice and tone, though his facial expressions remained unchanged.

"Untie me, and I will tell you not only the other news, but I will also tell you how you can prevent your quickly approaching death."

"Come come, Doctor. Your arrogance surprises even me."

"Have you noticed that your senses are diminishing? The fact that you can't even smell the odor your body is releasing should be a sign."

"And how can you prove that a smell exists? Perhaps your clever mind is latching on to some imagined way to earn your release."

"I can't prove it," Straus admitted. "But I don't need to prove to you what will soon be evident. If, of course, my estimations are accurate. Tell me, have you noticed that you can't smell things as easily as you were once able to?"

"And if I have noticed?"

"Jacob wasn't going to tell you himself. He was waiting for me to arrive to deliver the rest of the news, but then you and your father interrupted things. Do you want to know the rest of the story, Alexander?"

"If only to satisfy my curiosity, yes."

"The virus, though destroyed by your cells, has also made your cells dependent on it. Without the virus, your cells are decomposing at an alarming rate. Thus, the smell of decay that you carry around with you. The fact that you can't smell it tells me that, as expected, your brain is rotting away. Slowly but surely, I promise you. However, when I discovered the rapidity at which the virus was breaking down your cells, I also discovered a simple cure."

"And that would be?"

"Unknown to you and will remain so if you kill me. And based on just how horrible you smell, it will remain forever unknown unless you release me, now."

The power of the blow Alexander delivered directly to Straus's face sent Straus's head snapping back. His nose was crushed and several of Straus's teeth were reduced to shards of bone. The blood and broken teeth poured into Straus's throat, making him cough up a terrible mixture of red and white. He slumped to his side, twisting his left arm beneath him into a position that it was not designed for.

Before he could welcome unconsciousness, Straus felt the iron grip of Alexander's hand grab his hair and pull his head straight. His body fell limp to his side, and only his head was held upright.

"I've grown tired of your games, Doctor Straus," he heard

Alexander say. "Tell me the rest of the news or, I assure you, you will die a very painful and very slow death."

Straus struggled to speak, but his thoughts were scrambled. Words that needed to be said were locked behind the veil of semi-unconsciousness and crushing pain.

"Tell me, Straus," he heard again. His head was being shaken much too forcefully for his already damaged neck and brain.

Then, the darkness returned.

Chapter 38

It was only a few minutes after he had ended his call with Ralph that Derek heard the unmistakable sounds of twigs breaking and footfalls scurrying on the path to his right. He crouched down behind a bush and held his breath as a figure came into view. His obstructed view only revealed that it was a man, tall and slender, who was heading his way. He thought at first about opening his backpack, removing his gun, and to ready himself for an attack, but then remembered that, though his backpack was in reach, it contained no firearm.

He sat, motionless and as quietly as he could, as the man moved closer. Then he saw the man stop. Derek could see that whoever it was, he too was surveying the hospital, looking for any signs of movement. After what Derek considered to be much too short of a delay, Derek watched the man disappear down the steep hill and towards the rear of the hospital. A minute later, he saw the young man dart towards the hospital, his path leading him straight towards a set of iron stairs leading to a door.

The young man climbed the stairs quickly and pulled hard on the metal door. It opened in surprising silence. As the man turned over his shoulder, perhaps making sure that no one had seen him; Derek saw the man's face clearly.

"Thomas," Derek thought. *"Son of a bitch."*

After again surveying the area, Derek made his way down the hill. When he reached the parking lot, he bolted across the lot, up the stairs, and to the door. He paused and listened for any noise on the other side of the door before pulling it open. He stepped inside to near absolute darkness.

Chapter 39

It was the sound of the knocking that brought Straus back to consciousness. Gentle, rhythmic knocking. His mind was too cloudy to accurately assign the direction of the knocking, but he was sure it was coming from the hallway door.

"Let me in!" He heard the knocker's voice say in an urgent tone.

Straus then felt the grip that he was unaware was still holding his head release. His body crumbled onto itself, sending a newly discovered stream of pain through his left shoulder.

Straus heard the bolt and latches of the door being pulled back, the door being opened then shut and secured again.

"Where's my father?" the voice sounded. "What did you do with my father?"

"He has, I'm sure, found peace at last," the familiar voice of Alexander whispered.

The next sound Straus heard was a scream followed by what he imagined a barroom brawl should sound like. The brawl lasted but seconds before a large and pronounced thud filled the room. Then a groan and the sound a body makes when it is being dragged across a floor.

Though unable to move without pain waiting for him, Straus

lifted his head off the mattress just in time to see Alexander dropping a body onto the mattress beside Straus. The impact of the body falling onto the bed uncovered an entirely new set of discovered pain in Straus's rib cage. He tried to scream in agony, but his cry was cut short by Alexander's hand covering his mouth.

"You were about to tell me the rest of the story, I believe," Alexander said. He replaced his grip on Straus's hair and lifted Straus back into a semi upright position. "The rest of the story now, if you please, Doctor Straus."

The battery-powered lantern's light was growing dimmer and began to flicker.

Alexander again released his hold of Straus's hair, stood and walked out of the room. Straus heard him fumbling through bags in the other room before returning with a package of fresh "D" sized batteries.

"I honestly didn't expect to have so many visitors," Alexander said as he replaced the dying batteries in the lantern. When he spoke again, the lantern jumped back to life and filled the room with a warm, yellowish light. "Recognize him?" he said, pointing to the person lying beside Straus on the mattress. Straus looked at the bloodied face of the young man lying unconscious beside him. "No. I don't recognize him."

"That," Alexander said before moving towards a chair positioned at the foot of the bed, "is my long-lost brother. You two actually met a while back. That day you were so generous to allow me time at the lake, we passed a stranger who seemed to appear out of thin air. That stranger was my brother. We had arranged that seemingly coincidental meeting. You see, Doctor, I grew bored and restless of reading the stream of books you provided me. Make no mistake, they were all appreciated, but when I happened to come into the possession of a device that allowed unfettered access to the Internet, books seem too antiquated for my attention.

"Facebook is absolutely amazing, don't you agree? Couple it with email, and the world and all of its citizens are practically within reach."

"How did you get a device that was connected to the net? Who gave it to you?" Straus demanded.

"You had left me alone when my father paid a visit. During that visit, he spelled out his plan of action. While I only pretended to share an interest in seeing his plan through to its profitable ending, my father was resolute in blackmailing you and the rest of the doctors involved in my life. So resolute that, I am afraid to say, he lost his perspective along with a healthy amount of suspicion.

"My father, Doctor Straus, gave me a Smartphone. And with that amazing piece of technology, I gained access to a world well beyond the control of anyone. Millions upon millions of names, articles, books, news items, images, instructions, and vehicles to contact long-lost friends and relatives rested in my hands. Your fear of entering my bedroom made concealment a very simple matter. A few times, I actually left the device connected to its charger on my nightstand while having conversations with you through the glass and steel bedroom door.

"My brother was, understandably skeptical of my request to keep our engagement a secret at first. But, bless him, he never approached our father or mother for confirmation. Instead, he conducted his own bit of research and discovered that our father was keeping something secret. That something, of course, was his knowledge of me.

"I contacted my twin brother through Facebook and filled him in on my life. It took a while but Thomas sent me an email, stating that he was going to make contact with me, face to face. I suggested that doing so would involve too much risk. I then suggested that he gain access to my room using the hidden trap door that was recently installed beneath my bed. Yes, Doctor Straus, I've had access to the outside world for quite a while. That was yet another revelation that you would have discovered if you hadn't been paralyzed with fear and had actually entered my bedroom. That day we encountered him on the street outside of your lodge, Doctor Straus, was just the very first of several meetings.

"True to his word, Thomas never told a soul, not even our parents, that he knew about me and that he and I were devising a plan of our own. While my father's plan was focused solely on financial gain, the plan my twin brother and I concocted was entirely about exposing the truth. My plan, however, differed from his.

"If I may pat myself on my back, the genius on my part was the successful blending of the two plans into the only plan that mattered. That plan, of course, being mine. I'm sure you've guessed that my plan had nothing to do with financial reward or exposure but was singularly focused on the list of names that, one by one, were crossed off.

"One of my most challenging obstacles to overcome, and the one that I am most pleased with, was figuring out how to time the executions of my father's and my brother's plan. It did take some convincing and more than a bit of deception to have my brother follow a late addition to the plan. But I needed him to delay. He had planned for me to escape several days before my father told me that his plan would have you all but offer yourself up to me in the quiet solitude of your lodge. I convinced Thomas that we needed a contingency plan if his plan failed. Poor brother. I had him marking trails I knew I would never tread on and leaving supplies hidden on those trails that I would never be in need of.

"I learned about how you and your hit men contributed to my list's exhaustion from my father. How he learned that it was you behind the murders of Rinaldo and Zudak, I'm afraid will forever remain a mystery. But, I do thank you for your contribution, though I wish you hadn't gone to so much trouble."

The look that shot across the distorted face of William Straus was evident. Alexander knew that look needed further exploration.

"I expected surprise but not the look of shock and despair that I see in your bloody and bruised face. It is too bad you didn't pack any instant ice packs. Your face is in dire need of something to reduce the swelling."

Straus said nothing.

"I hope I didn't damage your tongue, doctor. It would be a

shame if you find yourself unable to finish your delightful story. My curiosity remains piqued."

"Untie me and I will tell you the rest," he mumbled, each movement of his jaw sending streaks of pain.

"Considering the disabled position you are in, coupled with the fact that I know you are unarmed, I am willing to comply with your request. Yes, I did find your weapon tucked neatly inside of your bag. You shouldn't have left it so far away. A better place would have been in what they call an 'inner waistband holster.'"

Alexander moved slowly towards the side of the bed, the smell of his decomposing body preceding him. As he bent over and began to untie the knot, he leaned in close to Straus.

"Any attempt to leave the comfort of this bed will result in something awful, Doctor Straus."

Seconds later, Straus felt blood rushing back into his left hand, creating a deep, burning sensation. He lifted his hand and rubbed it with his right hand, hoping to massage away the pain.

"Now," Alexander said after returning to his chair, "you were about to say?"

"Your body is decomposing," Straus offered, the pain in his left hand slowly dissipating.

"I will grant you that one time delay. You probably don't recall, but you've already told me that part of the story. I'm much more interested in the rest."

"If I tell you, do you promise to let me leave?"

"No," Alexander replied. "I make no such promise. I do

promise that if you don't tell me, I will crush every bone left unbroken in your face, however."

"If you kill me, you will die within hours. Let me leave, and I promise to tell you how to prevent your death."

"You are suggesting that I let you walk free from this place that you love so, walk down to your car where you will certainly drive as fast as your car will go, and wait with baited breath for you to tell me the rest of the story? Honestly, Doctor Straus. What do you take me for, a fool?"

"Not a fool, just someone who has no other options. You let me leave, and I will leave a note where my car is parked, telling you everything you need to know and to do to save your life. And, I will tell you that you actually now have everything you need to save your life right in this very room."

Alexander glanced at Thomas O'Connell, who was slowly coming back to reality.

"That explains the look on your face when I told you that it was my brother sharing the bed with you. I must assume that he holds the key to my survival."

"Let me leave, and I'll tell you what you need to know," Straus said, his voice hiding the excruciating pain radiating throughout his body.

"I find myself with no assurances," Alexander said as Thomas opened his eyes.

"The only assurance I will give you is that you will die if you don't let me leave."

"I require more."

"Isn't the fact that I've always kept my promises to you enough?"

"You have been a man of your word," Alexander said. "But your promises were what positioned you, my brother, and me in this dilapidated suite of rooms. Your promises, though always held, are the reasons my life was and is nothing more than a series of experiments. Of isolation. Of misery. Your promises, Doctor Straus, are the precise reasons why I may rather kill you and with your death, assure my own potential demise, rather than to see you walk free.

"You are asking me to trust you, Dr. Straus? Trust? You never entertained even the possibility that I wanted to have at least a chance at a real life. You presented yourself to me as my protector, my savior, when all along you were nothing but my captor. I was nothing more than your chance at fame. I know it wasn't you who stole me from my family, but it was you who kept me from them. You could have said something. You could have kept the promise you made when you swore your oath to become a doctor. What of that promise, Doctor Straus?"

Thomas O'Connell had sat up and was quietly listening to the conversation between his brother and Doctor Straus. Neither noticed that Thomas held a gun in his hand, but both heard the loud knocking at the door.

Chapter 40

Derek turned on his Maglite once he heard Thomas's footsteps pounding up the stairway. He took no time to inspect the near vacant loading docks as he made his way across the area and into the stairway. He paused only at the bottom of the flight to listen to Thomas's steps. He heard a door creak open two floors above him then he heard nothing.

The stairway was littered with discarded papers, broken glass, and pieces of insulation. As Derek made his way up the stairs, he turned off his flashlight, not wanting to give Thomas any visual signs of his approach. He paused after each step, straining his ears to hear. When he reached the second floor landing, he heard Thomas knocking on a door and demanding to be let in.

Silently, he craned his neck into the hallway, just in time to see Thomas walk through an open doorway and just in time to hear the door's lock screech back into position.

He paused, catching his breath before moving towards the door. In his hands he held his small flashlight and a seven-inch, serrated, fixed-blade Gerber knife.

"Hope I'm not bringing a knife to a gun fight," he thought to himself as he reached the door. *"I wonder if this is a situation that Ralph would consider me leaving a better option than me staying."*

He pressed his ear against the cool, steel door. Though muffled, he could hear Thomas arguing with someone. He heard a voice return Thomas's demands. A voice so weak, so thin that Derek questioned if the person Thomas was speaking with was preparing to make the great leap into the unknown.

He then heard a yell, followed by a quick scuffle. The thud sent vibrations into Derek's legs.

He backed away from the door and stood in the pitch-black silence. His army and police academy training screamed at him to call for backup. He knew his life might very well depend on his next decision. And as he weighed the decision to either get help or to get into the room, Derek thought of Lucy and the look she would give him whenever he told her about his day at work. She never liked the risks he and the other members of the police force were expected to take on a daily basis.

"Risks are part of the job," he would tell her. "And, we never go into a situation without backup."

Now, standing in a dark hallway, the only glimpse of light coming from a setting sun and filtered through a dusty and smudged window at the hallway's end, he knew he had no backup. Only Ralph knew where he was, but no one knew the option he was considering. He had no set plan if he were able to gain access to the room. No strategy. No emergency plan. But Derek was driven by his sense of responsibility. He was paid to keep Thomas O'Connell safe, and while Derek thought the O'Connells may have set him up, he didn't know for certain. What he did know was that the person he was charged to keep safe was behind the locked door in front of him.

Derek Cole walked up to the door and knocked loudly several times.

Chapter 41

"Popular place, this Ward C is," Alexander said. As he turned away from the door and towards Straus and Thomas, he shuddered when he saw that Thomas was pointing a revolver directly at his head.

"If you so much as move towards me, I will blow your brains out."

"You have my full attention," Alexander said.

The knocking at the door resumed.

"Tell me," Thomas said, "what did you do to my father?"

"You mean 'our father?'"

The person knocking at the door switched from using his knuckles to pounding on the door with this fist.

"What did you do to him?" Thomas demanded.

"He was on the list."

"You son of a bitch."

"You also are on the list, dear brother."

Despite Straus's prognosis, Alexander's reflexes remained insanely sharp. He leaped towards Thomas, driving his shoulder into Thomas's chest. The shot fired came a half of a second too late, the bullet found no flesh, only concrete.

With little resistance, Alexander wrenched the revolver from

Thomas's hands. Straus, sensing an opportunity, bolted towards the door. He reached the door, slid the bolt free, and lifted the steel bar bracing and pulled open the door. A man he'd never seen blocked his way. Then the bullet entering his lower back, ripping through his muscles and sending him to the floor, halted his movement. He lay half in the hallway and half still in the hub room of Ward C.

"Kindly step into the room," Alexander said as he continued moving closer to the door, pointing the revolver directly into Derek's chest. "And, if it isn't too much to ask, kindly drag the good doctor inside as well."

Derek, having learned to obey the commands of anyone pointing a gun at his chest, stepped into the room with his arms raised. He then grabbed William Straus's legs and dragged him out of the hallway.

"I hope to learn your name," Alexander said.

"My name is Derek Cole. I've been hired by your father and your brother to protect them from you."

"I honestly never expected to cross paths with you, Mr. Cole. But I do know about you. You have been played a fool, I'm sorry to inform you. Have you yet deduced that you were not hired as a protector but as nothing more than one of my dearly departed father's minions?"

"I kind of figured that out, but, here I stand in the same room with you and a person I was charged to protect," Derek said.

"You have not done a good job, Derek Cole," Alexander said. "My father's intense greed caused him to have a very fiery death. As for my brother here," he said, gesturing behind him and towards Thomas, "he seems to have lost his will."

"Alexander," Derek said, "I am not claiming to know everything that happened to you, but I do know enough to understand how you must feel."

"Feel about what, exactly?"

"About feeling the need for revenge. I met with Mark Rinaldo and Michelle Mix. They told me what they did to you. I know that you've killed Rinaldo and Zudak, along with the others, but ..."

"Oh no, no, no, Derek Cole," Alexander said, inviting Derek to follow him out of the hub room and into the bedroom by waving the revolver towards the bedroom. "You've not done a good job with your understanding of your charged responsibilities at all. I didn't kill Mark Rinaldo or Henry Zudak. The man at your feet was the cause of their deaths. I can claim others as my trophies, but I cannot in good faith claim the fine doctors of Saint Stevens."

Derek glanced down at Straus. He was still breathing, moaning in both pain and astonishment.

Things began to fall in place. Though he had no idea how Straus had killed Rinaldo and Zudak, it made more sense that someone else had murdered the doctors in Chicago rather than Alexander.

"Please," Alexander said, "you appear to be quite confused. I think you deserve to know the truth. And it just so happens that my brother, Doctor Straus, and I can answer your questions. Please, continue dragging the good doctor into my old bedroom."

Straus squealed in pain when Derek grabbed his legs and began dragging him into the bedroom. The bullet hit no major organs but lodged itself deep inside of William Straus's ass.

When all four were in the bedroom, Alexander positioned himself in the doorway, preventing any escape.

"Doctor Straus," Alexander whispered, his voice becoming weaker with each word spoken, "would you be more comfortable if Derek Cole were to prop you up in a chair?"

"You're gonna die, you bastard," Straus said.

"Not before you do," Alexander replied. "Tell us about how you killed Mark Rinaldo and Henry Zudak. And please inform us as to why you did not send Stanley Mix to the same fate as his partners?"

"I don't know what you're talking about," Straus said through grimaces of pain.

"Now Doctor, remember that I told you that I read Doctor Lucietta's journal while I was waiting for him in his office before the meeting I had scheduled with him? What you may not have been aware of was that he took copious notes of your and his conversations. Complete with the details of your plans to avoid any ramifications of your actions. So, please, do tell Mr. Cole here about how you nearly pulled off the perfect murders."

Thomas had recovered his clear thinking. He moved closer to Alexander, who responded only by raising the revolver and pointing it directly at Thomas's head.

"Need I remind you that your name appears on my lists?"

Alexander said as Thomas backed away. "Doctor Straus? Please do not keep Derek Cole waiting. Proceed with your recounting."

Straus began to detail how, when he received the call from Ken O'Connell, he contacted an associate of his who was known to have "connections." He explained how he planned to counter Ken's scheme of blackmail by eliminating everyone who had knowledge of Alexander Black. He said that when he realized that Alexander had killed Jacob Curtis and Peter Adams, he set his focus on convincing Brian Lucietta to deny everything and to eliminate Rinaldo, Zudak, and the Mixes. Both Michelle and Stanley.

"I didn't want to have to hurt Michelle, but she knew too much. Problem was that they couldn't be found. Rinaldo was easy. My friend told me that they found him sitting at home in his living room, drunk as a skunk. My friend told me that finding Zudak took some time, but that he had made the mistake of staying at a hotel that is often used by people running from something.

"They never found Mix. Have no idea where he and his hot little wife ran off to. No matter. I hear that he is on his deathbed anyway. As for Michelle, I doubt that she really cares about what happens and probably won't say a word to anyone."

Alexander smiled at Derek.

"And now, should you wish for full disclosure, I invite my twin brother to explain his role in the deceptive plot."

Thomas was quick to begin his explanation, giving details about his plan to free Alexander and then to expose the doctors and their illegal and immoral activities.

"I only wanted justice. I never wanted anyone to get hurt." Thomas turned toward Derek and continued. "I needed to convince you that I was truly concerned for my life. I had no idea that my father's plan was to extort money from the doctors. Honestly, I had no idea."

The stench of death and decay was growing too powerful for the windowless rooms. Derek needed to cover his mouth and nose in an attempt to keep out the stench and to keep in the vomit that was threatening to escape.

"You are probably wondering what the horrible smell is, aren't you Derek?" Straus asked.

"Now that you mention it," Derek said.

"Our heartless captor here is dying a very smelly and soon-to-be-painful death. See, I injected a virus into his cells a few weeks back and discovered that the virus was having quite an unexpected and drastic effect on poor Alexander Black. I did, however, offer to provide a solution in exchange for my release. But I must assume that his brain is in a state of rapid decay because instead of allowing my release, he shot me in the ass."

"Your death will be much more painful if you do not tell me the cure," Alexander said.

As he spoke, Alexander began to shake and drift from side to side.

"It won't be long now," Straus said.

The next bullet that entered the body of William Straus hit his right knee dead center, shattering his kneecap and spilling a disturbing volume of blood.

"The next shot will award you with matching knees," Alexander whispered. "The cure, Straus. Now."

"In . . .my. . .bag," Straus said, struggling to apply pressure to his femoral artery.

Alexander, keeping the revolver trained on Straus, backed out of the bedroom and into the hub. On the shelving that ran the length of the two-way mirrors, Alexander spotted a black leather bag. He grabbed the bag and returned to the bedroom.

When he was back in the room, Thomas was standing over Derek, who had removed his shirt and was using it as a tourniquet on Straus's leg. The flow of blood diminished to a trickle, but Straus was slipping in and out of consciousness and had all the signs of someone preparing to stop slipping and of staying on the unconscious end of the slide.

Alexander pulled the leather bag open and saw a small, black box sitting beside three syringes still in their sterile wrappings. He stood straight, pointed the gun at Straus's left knee.

"Tell me now. My patience is at an end."

"Open the black box," Straus mumbled, his eyes rolling back. "Three vials inside. Your old blood. Inject the vial labeled 'Plan C' into your neck."

Alexander broke open the black box, found the vial marked 'Plan C' written on it with a grease pen. He tore open one of the syringes, used it to draw from the vial. Once the vial was filled, he turned to Straus.

"And this is all that I will need?"

"Not all," Straus said.

"Then what else?"

"Your brother has a fresh supply of blood. You'll need to consume at least two pints."

Alexander turned towards Thomas and pointed the gun towards his gut.

"It seems that I am still in need of our heart, dear brother."

Thomas backed away, tipping over the chair and falling onto the ground. As Alexander moved closer to improve his aim, Derek grabbed the seven-inch knife he had concealed in the small of his back and in one quick and trained moved, plunged the entire knife into Alexander's neck.

Alexander fell forward onto the bed, holding the back of his neck with his left hand. Derek leaped towards Alexander, hoping to secure the gun. As he landed on top of Alexander, Derek discovered that, despite having a deep and what would be a fatal stab wound in any other person, Alexander's strength was still much greater than his. With a single thrust of his arm, Derek was thrown off the bed and landed hard on the floor a few feet away from where Straus had slipped into unconsciousness.

Alexander stood, aimed the gun at Derek, and pulled the trigger.

Chapter 42

The .45 caliber bullet hit Derek two inches to the right of his navel. At first, it felt like he had been kicked hard in the gut. But seconds later, the burning and intense pain emerged. He reached his hand down to cover the wound. When Derek raised them to his line of sight, they were covered in bright, red blood.

"Too bad your blood won't suffice," Alexander said to Derek before turning back towards Thomas. Without changing the direction of his gaze, Alexander turned the gun towards Straus and pulled the trigger. Straus's body, already battered and near death, offered only a quick jolt of movement before becoming too still.

Derek reached around to his back, hoping to find an exit wound and praying that any exit wound found was not spilling blood. As his hand returned from its exploration, Derek saw that fresh blood covered his hand. Too much blood for a clean exit wound.

"Son of a bitch," he cried.

He knew that he didn't have long before the internal bleeding would stop. His heart, though undamaged from the shot, would soon run out of blood to pump and would, hopefully painlessly, stop beating. Derek rested his head on the floor and watched as his vision began to darken at the edges. Slowly, his pain began to numb as he felt his skin grown cool and damp.

Derek tried to remain as still as he could, knowing that any struggle would only serve to speed up the bleeding. He closed his eyes and concentrated on slowing his heart rate. He remembered reading about Tibetan monks that were able to get their heart rates down into the teens. He would be satisfied with any rate under seventy-two.

He heard voices in the background of his mind yelling at each other, but it seemed as if they were miles away. Then, clearly and loudly, he heard a high-pitched snap, echoing for what seemed like to Derek for several seconds before fading slowly into a distant hum. Another pop, followed by a series of crackles and ripping screams. And then he saw her.

Her face, flowing with the smile he had sought for so long, filled the side of his vision. It evaporated the cloudy darkness that had crept in slowly when the pain began to fade. He smiled back, remembering so much about that face, about her smile. He remembered so vividly the times he overlooked the simple and elegant beauty of that smile and still, the smile was offered.

The vision began to drift further into an expected distance when he remembered. That was what he saw that day. This was the smile that caused him to turn his head away at the last possible moment the day he tried to end his searching forever. It was always there, waiting for him. She had always beside him yet he had focused his sights behind him. He smiled in the knowing, then everything went still.

Chapter 43

Alexander stood over Straus for several seconds before confirming his suspicions.

"I am afraid that I lack the motivation to write out another list so that I can cross off another name," he said. "Good night, Doctor Straus."

Thomas had found his feet and stood, his back pressed hard against the wall. Alexander motioned for Thomas to sit on the floor. The pain in his neck was severe, and Alexander could feel that his left side was growing weaker and was charged with a disturbing sensation. The fingers of his left hand burned with the sensation, and he felt his left leg shaking under the weight of his body.

"Move an inch, and you'll join these two," he said to Thomas.

"I'm your brother. I helped you," Thomas protested. "That day I saw you at the lake, when you were walking with Straus and the other doctor, I knew that what I found out was true. I knew that I had to help you. And now you stand over me with a gun and threaten to kill me?"

"You stole my heart," Alexander said. "You stole my father, my mother, my life. Why were you chosen over me? What was special about you?"

"I didn't steal anything. Our heart was in *my* chest. I didn't make the decision to cut you off from it."

"You've been selfish with it too long. I need it now."

Alexander carefully plunged the syringe into the side of his neck, and depressed the plunger, emptying the syringe's contents into his body. He paused, hoping that the injection would provide an immediate report of effectiveness. Instead, he felt a terrible burning being pulled by gravity through his body. He cringed in pain as the fire reached his chest and abdomen. He dropped to his knees as the substance was pulled through his pelvis and into his thighs before finally collecting itself together in his feet.

Thomas stood, raced to his brother's side and removed the revolver from Alexander's limp hand. He backed away from Alexander, training the gun's barrel on Alex's head. When he reached Derek, Thomas reached down and was relieved when he felt Derek's chest rising under the pressure of breaths. He glanced at Straus and knew without the aid of feeling for a pulse or visual confirmation of a rising chest that Straus was dead. He was slumped against the wall; his eyes were cloudy and partially closed, staring at nothing. Seeing a dead body this close disturbed Thomas. Besides attending a few wakes of family members, Straus was the first dead body Thomas had ever seen.

"What have I done?" he asked himself. "What have you done?" he asked Alexander who had fallen to his knees in pain. "I told you that I would help you. I didn't mean to help you kill people."

"The help you offered," Alexander said, "did not include

specific forms."

"You're a animal. No, you're evil. I should kill you now," Thomas said.

Alexander seemed to collect himself, pushing the pain away from his thoughts.

"I still need to fill my prescription," he whispered towards Thomas. "And to continue working on my list."

When he stood as quickly and as authoritatively as he did, Thomas wondered if what Straus had put into the vial labeled "Plan C" really was the cure for whatever was killing Alexander. Thomas pointed the gun at Alexander's head and though his hands were trembling, squeezed the trigger, and released the hammer.

"Out of bullets," Alexander said, smiling his vacant smile. "I highly doubt that even if you brought additional ammo for your gun, that you can load the bullets and fire off a round before I tear open your chest and take back what is rightfully mine."

Sensing no reason to hurry, Alexander walked towards Thomas, who was still standing still, repeatedly squeezing the trigger of the revolver. Alexander was just beyond an arm's length away when he felt the barbs dig into his back.

"Now y'all had best move back a few steps."

Alexander was all too familiar with the Taser gun's barbs to wonder what would happen next.

"My name is Ralph Fox, Chief of Police in the town where you started all this ruckus. That man lying on the ground next to you is someone I consider to be a good friend. Now, I will admit to being tempted to just depress this trigger and see just how sensitive you are to electricity, but, being a man of the law, I'm gonna give you a couple of options. Option one is that you lay flat on your face with your hands in such a position that placing handcuffs on them would be a simple matter."

"And option two?" Alexander asked.

"Well now, Alexander, seems I don't really have another option," Ralph said. "Kinda just hoping you'd take the first one offered."

He could feel the acidic-like substance fading yet still burning in his feet. His vision was becoming disturbingly blurry, and he felt the sudden need for sleep wash over him.

"That option I gave you does have an expiration attached to it," Ralph said.

Alexander, sensing that Straus was truthful in his prognosis, felt he needed another option. An option that he needed to grant to himself. Thomas stood just out of his reach, his heart, pounding away in his chest. Alexander could almost feel the heart's rhythmic pattern. Could almost feel blood surging through his body.

"I do have another option," Alexander whispered then lunged towards Thomas.

The charge raced through the lines and the barbs and into his body. Immediately, his muscles constricted, then went utterly limp, though the current was still charging into him. There was no pain. No moment of regret or of remorse. Just a horribly familiar feeling, then nothing.

Chapter 44

When he again opened his eyes, it was the face of Ralph Fox staring back at him.

"Had me scared there for a minute. Thought we'd lost you" Ralph said, his voice sounding faded.

"Black. . .Thomas. . ." Derek struggled to say.

The area around him was brilliantly bright and sterile. Ralph's face was certainly familiar, but the others around him, those ushering orders, were wholly foreign.

"Don't worry about them. Old Ralph took care of things for you. You just need to hold on there for a bit longer. These fellas will get you fixed up and running like a horny colt in no time flat."

Derek drifted, thankfully to a place where his pain wasn't allowed.

Again his eyes captured light and his ears, sound. Ralph was absent as others, unfamiliar but comforting, darted in then out of his field of vision. Each offered something, some to him and some to others. His pain reemerged, and then was muted.

"I saw her," he said through a voice that sounded much too distorted for his own comfort. "She saved me."

"Relax and take a deep breath," a comforter said to him.

"She saved me."

Derek awoke to the sounds of dinner plates being placed onto a cart and wheeled away. There were sounds coming from a television hidden somewhere in the room that he found himself in. It wasn't the appearance of the room, the sounds he heard, or even the fact that a nurse was taking his blood pressure that let him know he was in a hospital. It was the person sitting beside his bed that made him fully aware of where he was.

"That was quite a nap you took there, son."

Ralph Fox sat in a rather uncomfortable-looking blue chair beside Derek's hospital bed. He has holding a Styrofoam take-out box, overly stuffed with French fries, potato salad, and the remains of three pieces of fried chicken.

"How long have I been out?" Derek asked.

"Two and half days," Ralph said. "Kind of lost track. Been busy cleaning things up."

"What happened?"

"You mean after you got your gut all busted up? Hell son, you missed the best part of your whole damn case."

"You feel like filling me in, or do I have to read about it in the paper?"

"Ain't never trusted no journalist to tell things accurately. You tell me when you feel up to it, and I'll tell you the truth. Gotta say, you ain't gonna be happy about being in la la land during what transpired in that room you were dying in. Ain't gonna be happy at all, I imagine."

"Thomas? Is he okay?"

"Okay is very subjective term, Derek Cole. If you're asking if Thomas O'Connell is alive, he is. Straus weren't so lucky, though. As for Alexander, now that is the best part of the story. Truth is, I don't know if he's dead or alive, but I suspect he ain't living."

"Tell me what happened. I'm okay to listen," Derek said.

"You sure you're up to it?" Ralph teased.

"I'm sure."

As Derek continued to reach full consciousness, Ralph detailed what had happened when he walked into Ward C.

"I suppose that after you walked yourself in, that old Alexander Black forgot to close the door. Hell son, once you told me you were heading down to Hilburn, I jumped in my car and headed down myself. Captain Smith weren't too happy when he found out that I was the one who stopped Black, but hell, this was my murder investigation from the start."

"What did you mean when you said you weren't sure if Alexander was dead or alive?" Derek asked.

"When I left that room, there were a whole mess of NYPD people milling about. Coroner confirmed that Straus was dead and declared Alexander to be dead as well. I told him what I knew about Alexander, but I don't think anyone in that room believed me.

"I was taken outside and was giving my deposition when I saw them wheeling out two gurneys with filled body bags lying atop them. I told them officers again, but I gave up trying to convince them of something that I ain't sure I fully believe yet. I imagine that Straus and Alexander are together again in some city morgue."

"If he isn't really dead, they're going to have quite a surprise," Derek said.

"Thomas was telling me, right before they cuffed him and brought him downtown for questioning, that Straus was telling Alexander that he was pretty close to dying as it was. Said that Straus injected Alexander with a virus that was causing his body to start decomposing. Sure did smell like a dog twelve days dead in that room."

"Straus told Alexander that he brought a cure with him. I didn't see him for sure but I half remember Alexander injecting a vial of something into his own neck."

"Yup, that he did. Thing is, Straus had a couple of plans himself. Found out about them once I was allowed to take a few glances at Brian Lucietta's journal. Seems Straus devised a Plan B and a Plan C. Plan B was to kill off all the other doctors so that he could blame them for everything. He was planning on holing up in Hilburn until he heard that the other doctors were all dead and that Alexander was apprehended.

"His Plan C was devised in case Alexander found his hiding spot. Hell, he even labeled that vial 'Plan C.'"

"What was in the vial?" Derek asked.

"Pure acid. Ain't sure which type. Didn't matter, I guess, but it sure weren't no cure."

Ralph and Derek talked about the case, how all the clues were there, and about what would happen to Thomas O'Connell. They talked about Straus and how, in the end, he got what he probably deserved: To die in agony in the same room that he held Alexander captive for so many years.

"What about the message I got when I landed in Albany," Derek asked.

"Thomas assured us that he had nothing to do with that message. Using deductive reasoning, I determined that it was Ken O'Connell. See, as you know, his plan was all about extortion. Thomas's plan was all about getting his brother out of the lodge and making everything public. Alexander's plan was all about killing all the doctors. That Ken O'Connell sure was a smart man, but he also sure did make a lot of mistakes. The way I see it, he called and left that message for you to get you to thinking that Straus was behind Alexander's release. That way, you'd be more inclined to focus your looking towards finding Straus."

"I still don't understand everything," Derek said. "Like, how did Thomas get away from the guys his father had watching him?"

"According to Thomas, those guys protecting him only did so during the night. During the day, they'd pull that boat up to shore and take off doing whatever it was that O'Connell paid them to do. Thomas received an email from Alexander, telling him that it was time to implement their plan. He just walked off the boat, jumped on a plane, and was going to meet Alexander at the lodge. Thing was, by the time he got there, the lodge was a crime scene. He told us that he and Alexander had a backup plan. Two of 'em actually. One was the path marked with the hearts that I showed you, the other was to meet up in Manhattan."

"How did Alexander find Ken O'Connell when he killed him?"

"O'Connell set Alexander up in an apartment in Manhattan. When he found out that Lucietta had been killed, he sent one of his goons over to find Alexander and probably to kill him. Alexander wasn't in that apartment, but he left a note that was addressed to Ken O'Connell. We found the note tucked into O'Connell's back pocket. Good thing he wasn't burned up, or we never would have solved that part of the mystery.

"Note just told Ken where Alexander was expecting to meet him. O'Connell showed up with one of his goons. NYPD found his goon dead outside the old warehouse, and they found Ken dead inside the warehouse."

"That means Alexander killed seven people, and Straus killed two. That's a lot of activity for a small town chief of police," Derek teased. "Good thing my old buddy Jared Smith was there to lend his hand."

"Yup," Ralph said, "this old Texas boy sure was in need of some help with this whole case."

By the time the nurse came into Derek's room and suggested that Derek be allowed to get some rest, Derek understood everything about the Alexander Black mystery. As Ralph stood to leave, he extended his hand to Derek.

"That glossy card you carry in your wallet? You think you got enough room to add another name to it?"

"I bet I can squeeze in a few more letters," Derek said

"Put my name down on that card. And Derek?"

"Yeah, Ralph?"

"If you ever get called for another case in my neck of the woods, just give me a call instead of sneaking round. Deal?"

"Thanks Ralph. And yes, we have a deal."

Chapter 45

He was cold. Frigid. He struggled to open his eyes, to move, but none of his muscles responded. His mind swayed from reason to confusion, never remaining in reason long enough for him to string together consecutive thoughts.

The voices he heard, muffled and distorted as they bounced inside what seemed to be a narrow space could not be understood. He knew that the voices were speaking words, but the meaning of them failed to register.

He slipped again. Somewhere deeper and much darker. His realization returned but offered no solution. No identifiable signs indicating a way to escape the deepness. He felt like he was in a hole, long, narrow, and too smooth for a hand to steal a pulling grip.

He then felt movement, the cause of which was not from his own choice but from some outside force. The movement was brief and halted with a shuttering shake. Instantly, he felt warmth, flooding over his still unreachable body. It offered a hope. A chance to come to some understanding and knowing. He thought the movement would offer an exit.

He imagined himself swimming in the cool waters of Piseco Lake, feeling the soft current wash over him. He knew that he still harbored the wish that he had taken the chance to swim that one day, so as to know what immersion would feel like. This feeling, now seen not as a dream but something foreboding, turned sour. It was cold, too cold, and was followed by pain; enhanced by his inability to prevent it's directed march.

"Son of a bitch!" the medical examiner said. "We have a serious issue over here!"

The medical examiner stopped once the body's chest cavity was fully opened, skin pulled back, and muscle tissue removed.

"Get someone down here, now!" she said to her assistant. "Now."

About the Author

Connect with T Patrick Phelps

Sign up

for my newsletter and receive a free ebook!

www.tpatrickphelps.com

[Image: firepic.JPG]

I find the questions and comments I've receive about this fictional book both amazing and curious. Several readers have connected with me on my Facebook author page, https://www.facebook.com/authortpp with questions that, for reasons known only to them, they felt more comfortable asking me in private. While I honestly enjoy hearing comments and constructive criticism, I have received a disturbing number of questions regarding the same topic. So I'd like to answer the most frequently asked questions here at the end of Heartless. I hope that you enjoy some of the questions as much as I did!

"I don't think it's realistic that someone could live without a heart or lungs. How can Alexander Black continue to live without these important organs?" Heartless is a work of

FICTION, meaning that it is not based on reality. I agree that living without a heart would present significant challenges.

"You wrote about the role genetics may have played in Alexander. Was his father also heartless?" No, Alexander's father was born with a heart. I created his character to be more allegorically heartless.

"Is Derek Cole a real private investigator?" I'm sure that there is someone out in the world with the same name that may be a private investigator, but, again, this is a work of FICTION and any and all similarities with anyone, living or dead, is 100% coincidental.

"At the end, it seems that Alexander is still alive. Will he make a return in another Derek Cole book?" Alexander Black is a huge mystery. From his birth to his time on the medical examiner's table. Will he survive and live to continue his evil ways? Only Derek Cole knows for sure, and he isn't talking to me since I had him take a shot in the stomach. (Sorry Derek).

"When is the next Derek Cole book coming out?" Heartless is the first in the Derek Cole Series, and has been downloaded over 20,000 times by readers all over the world. Those of the Margin and The Observer are the second and third (respectively) in the series. The newest Derek Cole book, The Devil's Snare, will be released

February 2016.

The follow up to Heartless will also be released in 2016. "Still Heartless" will put all the questions about Alexander Black to rest. But that doesn't necessarily mean that Alexander will be put to rest!

AUTHOR UPDATE: The newest (and best) novel in the Derek Cole Series, Deathly Reminders, will be available through Amazon beginning November 25, 2016.

Thank you for reading!

T Patrick Phelps

* * *

Other Books by T Patrick Phelps

The Derek Cole Series

Heartless

Those of the Margin

The Observer

The Devil's Snare

Still, Heartless (the thrilling conclusion to Heartless)

Deathly Reminders (November, 2016)

Stand Alones

The Demon Senders

The Girl in the Red Dress (December, 2016/January, 2017)

Connect with T Patrick Phelps

Sign up for my newsletter and receive a free ebook!

www.tpatrickphelps.com

Made in the USA
Las Vegas, NV
03 January 2021